All Pure Souls

All Pure Souls

AN ALIETTE NOUVELLE MYSTERY

JOHN BROOKE

Joe Brooke

Signature
EDITIONS

Cover design by Terry Gallagher/Doowah Design.
Photograph of John Brooke by René De Carufel.
Printed and bound in Canada by AGMV Marquis.

Acknowledgements

A Vindication of the Rights of Woman, Mary Wollstonecraft, Modern Library, Great Britain, 2001; *The White Goddess: A Historical Grammar of Poetic Myth*, Robert Graves, Creative Age Press, New York, 1948; "Le Pommier enchanté," *Chansons de chez nous*, Théodore Botrel, Editions Slatkine, Geneva–Paris, 1981.

Raoul Pelleau, Serge Reboul, Cécile Granger, Bernadette Granger, Annie Granger…for words, books, corrections and directions. Merci.

We acknowledge the support of The Canada Council for the Arts and the Manitoba Arts Council for our publishing program.

Canadian Cataloguing in Publication Data

Brooke, John, 1951–
    All pure souls

ISBN 0-921833-80-6

    I. Title.

PS8553.R6542A74 2001   C813'.54   C2001-903654-X
PR9199.3.B697A64 2001

Signature Editions, P.O. Box 206, RPO Corydon
Winnipeg, Manitoba, R3M 3S7

for Libby & JWB
and Mike L.
…pure souls par excellence

PROLOGUE

"I wish to see women neither heroines nor brutes, but reasonable creatures."

—Mary Wollstonecraft,
A Vindication of the Rights of Woman

H*ello, Aliette. How's your life, ma belle?*
Not so great, thank you.
What's the matter?
Can't sleep.
Well, no one can. Sit tight—your holiday will soon be here…
Sure. Thanks…

Inspector Aliette Nouvelle of the *Police Judiciaire*, lying there, enervated, bitched out in the middle of another impossible August night on the eastern edge of France. Thirty-two ugly degrees centigrade at one in the morning. A monstrous humidity has descended from the Vosges Mountains and settled in across Alsace. The oppressive system has killed the wind and dulled the local sparkle. Vines along the panoramic Wine Road hang punk and lonely. It's peak season but the tourist boats are empty, the Rhine reduced to a congealed swath of industrial murk. Disgusting. Dispiriting. Ten days and counting… This city smells stale. Her worries fester.

You're still pissed that Claude got the nod for Commissaire?
Interim Adjunct—they're still watching him.
It's his, Aliette. Just accept it and keep going.
Why should I accept it? It was me who broke the case.
True…Jacques Normand. Huge.
And where am I going? If I can go through all that and still get nowhere, what's the point?
You could have filed a grievance with the Divisionnaire. With Paris, too.

No…no, I hate that way of moving through.

Well then?

Why should I have to file a grievance? Why wasn't it obvious?

Do you really want to be obvious?

I want what's right!

Claude Néon got more paper work. You got more freedom and you know it.

He got the recognition! It should have been mine! I'm a professional!

Aliette…please. Is that really the core of you? I recognize you. I know exactly who you are. There has to be something you need more than professional approbation.

Sure there is. Sex. I need sex. Right now. I need to be screwed a deep and ragged blue. Licked into oblivion. I want to hold the biggest goddamn *zizi* in these fine fingers and—

Enough!

Not enough! I want sex.

It's the weather.

Do I feel better for knowing that?

Go then! Rutty sex in the dog days? Woof, woof. Put on something nice and go downtown to the clubs. You can make it happen in five minutes. Sex is the easiest thing in the world.

I will!

No you won't…

And that's true. She won't. It's this voice that lives inside her. It's always there to question everything, saying *yes* to this and *no* to that, and especially when everything is bad. Sets a balance to her impulse, puts a damper on her fun. The inspector rolls fitfully in twisted sheets and stares out her wide-open balcony door. No air anywhere… She hears traffic on the *rond-point,* a horn blast, tires screeching, then a chorus of horns blasting back in cranky reply. The city's wide awake, going in neurotic circles, in desperate search of respite.

Oh, come on! Why do I need permission from myself? Why not just do it? Go. Go out and get laid.

Propriety? Her mother's warnings…her mother's values? Surely these things have nothing to do with the life of a thirty-five-year-old professional woman living alone in a place that's about as far as you can get from Nantes, the west coast city where Maman lives happily with Papa. This is not their world; what a burden, having to double-think your way through the codes they've planted in your soul. She thinks of her sister Anne, also back in Nantes. Two years younger, no real job, no serious man, and no qualms either. Say what you like, for all her wrong choices, Anne had freed herself in that one essential thing. A night like this, Anne would be out dancing, sweating, reeling in a guy who looked just fine for a night. Aliette could almost feel her sister feeling it: a stranger's body, no questions asked.

Or is it simply a dislike of strangers? Not fear. Beyond fear. It's a woman's natural sense of privacy (as opposed to propriety), overlaid with a cop's inclination to be wary. With so many unknown people flowing by, how can you just latch onto one so arbitrarily, so closely? Aliette can't do it.

A professional hazard, then? Because tonight she wishes she could.

And could I ever stop you from something you really need to do?

More shrieks and groans from the traffic circle. She kicks her sheets away, swings her feet to the floor, pulls on her discarded pyjama. Piaf follows her out onto the balcony, brushing her ankles, pushing his luck. "*Va-t-en!*" She kicks, gently, but firmly, enough to let him know she's in no mood. The sixteen-year-old white cat knows her well enough to back away.

It's Myriam, out of her mind, out loose in the city, swaying through the night-time traffic, thumb out, oblivious to the alarmed horns and swerving cars, only looking for the next 300-franc trick. The inspector knows her as soon as she sees her. She had adopted Myriam as a "cousin," a source of information, someone who could have been arrested and saved from herself at any time but was more valuable left to fend for herself on the street. Myriam's another professional hazard for a cop whose instinct is to care, because she's a professional necessity when it comes to landing bigger, more dangerous fish. *Poor Myriam…* Mmm, sad: one of the ones without make-up, in jeans and ratty running shoes, bottom-of-the-line sex for sale. Even from a distance Aliette can see she's not doing so well. She's in pain, in need of more of the drug she lives on, and it's making her jumpy.

The inspector forgets her own itching, her own internal bitching as she stands in the dark watching Myriam do her pathetic and precarious dance.

Myriam moves toward each passing car, compulsive, purely physical, practically punches her thumb through the window of every car that dares slow down for a look. One guy slows, passes… Myriam whirls, waving the thumb high in aid of any rear-view second thoughts. Guy doesn't go for it… Two more gear down, take a look, pass by. And Myriam repeats her movements exactly: thumb out, shake it in his face, then spin. Yes: As if it were all a dance. But it's not working. Myriam gets off the circle and stands under the street lamp at the bus-stop. One more passes, she whirls around again—and watches another one go by. Fuck it! Standing there, Myriam raises her arms in a gesture of exaggerated incredulity, hopeless face saying, God I can't win! What is it—my breath?

It's exquisite acting. Tonight it's for no one except Aliette Nouvelle.

Now the haggard *pute* sits on the bench beside the bus-stop and bends double, clutching her belly, rotating her neck slowly back and forth, trying to relax. "Myriam!" Aliette calls down through the night, quietly, not wanting to disturb her fellow tenants. "Myriam!… Up here!…it's Aliette."

Fifty paces away, Myriam's vague eyes finally find her.

"Stay there. I'll be right down."

She slips on jeans and sandals and goes lightly down the stairs. She comes out the door just in time to see Myriam getting into a top-of-the-line Peugeot, the Peugeot pulling away. Myriam does not look at her as they pass. No, she's grinning at the guy, coy, sussing him out, already angling for the best possible price.

Merde!…climbing back up the stairs, returning to her humid room. Suddenly empty. Fatigued. The restless thing has gone with Myriam.

She lies there. Now she would sleep.

The voice says, *Take heart, Aliette: Myriam's a professional, too—and doing what she can.*

1ST PART
GARDE À VUE

A suspect may be held for twenty-four hours without legal representation pending the formal charge; the Procureur may extend.

"Other women, other goddesses, are kinder seeming. They sell their love at a reasonable rate—sometimes a man may even have it for the asking."
—Robert Graves,
The White Goddess

1

THE PERSISTING HEAT

The day is Thursday, August 6th, the first day of Quert, an ancient Celtic apple festival. Hidden away now, out of time. For most, the 6th is the Transfiguration; but on the old calendar the 6th coincided with the celebration of the Assumption of the Virgin into Paradise. The apple is beauty, innocence, the ideal of youthfulness and freshness as set against eternity. A lot like the Virgin, no? It also stands for wisdom and choices. Now Assumption Day is not till the 15th... But hardly anyone knows this. Certainly not Inspector Nouvelle. And if she did, would she care? Not likely. Not today. It's just past 8:00 a.m. and she's already sticky from the persisting heat. She sits completely still, barely breathing, comparing two photos. One, clipped from a glossy magazine, shows the universally recognized face of the American movie queen, Marilyn Monroe. Too many people had loved this woman for the wrong reasons so she had died—by her own hand. The other photo is a Polaroid of the murdered woman lying in a drawer four floors below. A prostitute; her obvious gimmick the physical impersonation of the American star: wavy platinum hair, an air of glittery surprise conveyed in the laughing smile, the slightly out-of-focus lusty eyes, and of course the bountiful proportioning inside the lamé gown. The likeness is serviceable, but only that.

"It's not perfect," opines interim Adjunct Commissaire Claude Néon. He's looking worse than usual this morning, skin pale and porous, eyes bloody, as if he's been up all night. Maybe he was. The humid heat is getting to everyone.

Aliette agrees. "It's not perfect at all. Who would buy it?"

"Lots, apparently. Personally, I'll never understand those Americans and the things they like, but their bad taste seems to be catching on here. She always seemed too much like a cow to me. That thick body. Those stupid eyes…"

Aliette has learned to tune out the more offensive aspects of Claude's observations. In any case, she's more interested in the more recent victim. "Poor girl. Who was she?"

"They called her Manon…Manon Larivière…no girl: forty-four last May. There's a bit of a past. A village in the Vosges. But no family has come forward, if that's what you mean."

Families of her kind rarely did.

"Forty-four?" She did not look forty-four. Then again, with the false face carefully made like that, age had nothing to do with it. Or age was all that mattered. Aliette Nouvelle knows that feeling: standing in front of a mirror putting yourself together for the world's approval, always aware that the world is strongly biased in favour of the young and the firm and the fresh. To the face in the photo she offers a quiet declaration. "Well, Manon Larivière, American fantasies or not, we'll see if we can't find a good reason for why you had to die like this." The woman had been stabbed, once, in the heart.

Claude, ever skeptical of her reactions, swings in his chair to face the hazy morning sky. "Looks pretty simple to me. That pimp…he's the one with the reasons. Sprawled on top of her when it was discovered. Took them ten minutes to pry the knife out of his hand."

She glances again at the information. "Herménégilde Dupras."

With a light push of his toe, Claude swivels his creaky chair back round to face her. "There's a record. Beat one of them up…" leafing through the file; "a Francine Léotard…well, twenty-three years ago." Well before the time of Aliette and Claude.

"Nothing after that?"

"Nothing here. From what I gather, the longer he stayed in business the better connected he managed to get himself. If there was anything else, it got swept under the carpet… No pals to the rescue this time, though…Proc has to charge him. Just a question of whether 221-3 or *passionnel*."

Article 221-3: premeditated murder—termed *assassinat*, a conviction gets life imprisonment. A *crime passionnel* is less categorical and the plea is often effectively used to mitigate. The Proc is the *Procureur*, like a Crown Attorney, the state's representative to the court. But barring *flagrant délit* (caught in the act), the initial information can only ever be *prima facie*. "You know the knife doesn't mean much, Claude. He was out of his mind when our people got there...couldn't put three words together." This too is down in writing and could mitigate against a 221-3.

"So was she. Loaded up with hallucinogens."

"Could a man so drugged manage a knife—and her? Looking at this, I wouldn't call her petite."

"He's a pretty large guy, Inspector. And there's this rage factor."

"That was twenty-three years ago."

Claude shrugs; it's too hot for a big debate. "Who else could it be? Everyone knows the gangs aren't in that place. It's a clear case of mixing too much pleasure with business."

That place is Mari Morgan's. Elegant and expensive, the brothel is tolerated because it would have been a large political mistake for anyone who might have had the power to make a fuss to do so. If you had made it that far in the local hierarchy and had not yet been to Mari Morgan's, the chances were too high you were in tight with someone who had. As for members of the Police Judiciaire such as herself and Claude, they're paid by the Minister of the Interior; as such, they've nothing to gain from the local meisters and too much to lose if they go poking their noses into pleasure pots where there's no real call. But it's true: never a hint of a gang or gang-type activity around Mari Morgan's. That *is* Aliette's business and she knows. "What about the guests?"

"The guests..." Claude yawns, fighting lethargy as he goes back to his notes; "a dentist, an accountant from Hôtel de Ville, a couple of lawyers you might have run into, two managers from Peugeot with one of their parts suppliers in from Lille, and a Herr Von Schorrker from across the river. Five of them were otherwise engaged at the time she was found, three were sitting in the bar. No one's above suspicion, of course…let's just say the guests all cancel themselves out of the picture. No need to ruin any careers, Inspector. Not with this heat…our public would hold it against us. Mmm?"

"Wouldn't dream of it."

"A big bother getting the Germans to comply."

True enough. "How many girls?"

"Ten… Rather: make that nine plus a cook."

"So, nine girls—five in bed, at least one working the bar; leaves three with time on their hands."

"Two actually—she was with him, remember."

"Right." With him? Often the mystery starts right there: A woman could be "with" so many different men, each of them in a different way; all the more so if work's involved. Why am I admired? Why am I wanted? Why am I privy? Between the personal and the professional, the reasons are seldom clear. Like most women, she has learned to live with it. But most women do not have their hearts pierced in the boss's office. Studying the information: "Says here she was very much in demand. Which means she was bringing in money. Why would a pimp be angry?"

"We'll see," mutters her Commissaire. He shrugs, "It's there if you want it, but…well…not really up your alley, is it?"

She watches Claude staring down at the collected information, shaking the head that is too small for the gangly body in that slow, morose way. Is he pondering the fact of the corrupting influences that always swirl around a man's carefully constructed life? He has, after all, been the beneficiary of such influence. The friendship of Louis Moreau, their former boss, with Jacques Normand, one of the country's most wanted criminals, had played itself out to a tragic end, leaving Inspector Claude Néon in charge. Whether justly so is a question not enough people have sought to consider. She knows he knows it; she hopes the lesson has not been lost: forget hard work; forget risk and results; pray for luck…maybe a penis to go with it? Mmm—bitter, bitter. *Stop it, Aliette!*

Yes, well, this heat will make you edgy. And he's just being lazy. Just another pute come to a bad finish at the hands of another man who thinks he owns her. Who cares?

She also knows Claude's not trying to steer her away from the murder in the brothel. Since taking over, that's one thing he hasn't tried. She has waited for it, but it's as if Claude hasn't the energy for that kind of confrontation. Inspector Nouvelle lost out on the big promotion but has won, tacitly, the right to pick and choose her cases, a new level of freedom as her consolation prize. While here, three months later, Claude Néon is still testing the waters of power. Tentative. Still very much the "interim" man. No way he'll tell her to leave it be. What he is saying is simply true: the thing might not be her concern at all.

One of professional life's paradoxes: Eight years prior, Commissaire Moreau had placed his new Inspector Nouvelle in charge of those *Mondaine* (Morals) cases deemed serious enough to find their way into the third-floor offices of the Police Judiciaire, situated above *Sécurité Urbaine* headquarters in the Rue Bons Enfants. Not an exciting posting, but one is eager and one dives right in… But specialization evolves in a different way in a small force in a minor city on the edge of the Republic. Displaying a style and instinct unique amongst the eleven inspectors comprising *la brigade*, Inspector Nouvelle had soon outgrown Morals, so to speak. She now deals mainly with a certain kind of potentially international crime involving the three-sided border adjacent to this region of the upper Rhine. Drugs mostly, but it could be anything from stolen cars to the illegal import of labour. Morals cases, per se, are usually handled by someone in Anti-gangs, Claude's old group. As are the ones they call Violent Crimes.

No, her boss merely waits, another gaunt victim of the unholy humidity as Aliette reconsiders the two faces: Manon Larivière…and sad old Marilyn Monroe. Not the starlet's real name, was it; and in quite the same way that this Manon's face is a borrowed one; i.e., a business decision. And she's thinking she should take the case. Yes, something endemic there. Something that speaks of people posing…or hiding—which was it?…then paying for it, too dearly. Too horribly.

But (but, but, but, but!): The inspector's holiday is coming up in ten days. She has a plane ticket for the 15th that will take her home to Nantes. From there she'll join Papa, Maman and Anne at Belle Ile. Start on something new today and she could be risking those prized four weeks bridging August and September—with the tourist hordes heading home, it's the best time for the beach at Belle Ile. She has no desire to go to Morocco or Côte d'Ivoire in November, the only slot that would remain. Claude Néon won't dare fight her over selected investigations, but holidays are an eleven-cop free-for-all... *Careful, Aliette! You need a break. You deserve it...* Still, the inspector finds herself touching the photo of Manon Larivière in the way one does when one is compelled to wonder why a life and a death like that occur. "It's not perfect at all, is it?"

"No," says Claude; "but under the shadow of dim lights, a head full of wine, hashish..." he concludes their meeting with another indifferent shrug: Anything was possible.

"Mmm," nodding yes to that. Not a bad place to start, *mon Commissaire.*

2.

From the man at the top to the men in the basement:

A young (younger than herself at any rate) pathologist by the name of Raphaele Petrucci presides over the small morgue. Smelly—those horrid chemicals; but a cool place on a stultifying morning. And after Claude's perpetually worried mope, a small pleasure to gaze upon that beautiful Tuscan face. He pulls Manon out and lifts the sheet. Her make-up has been washed away during the autopsy; now, once you look below the dyed blonde hair there's no trace of an American film queen. The wound under her breast is dried and sore, growing up out of marble white, freshly dead flesh. There is also Raphaele's long Y-shaped incision, from pubis to breast bone, then out toward each shoulder. "So? Our boss tells me she was primed and ready to roll."

"Did he say that?"

"Words to that effect...full of hallucinogens?" Apart from the way he looks—and looks at her, make no mistake—she enjoys Dr. Raphaele Petrucci because he is the lighthearted kind who knows how to take or leave the Claudes of the world. She guesses she has about five years on him. Oh yes, lots of articles in *Marie Claire* and elsewhere now, saying this is no longer an issue. Still, she wishes he were a bit older.

Raphaele admits to being puzzled. "It's a new one on me. At first pass I did actually have her down as an LSD freak. It looked like there was enough lysergic acid in her system to keep a rock 'n' roll band playing at full speed for at least a day."

"Find anything that might link that to her job?"

"You mean teeth marks or sperm?"

"Along those lines."

"No. She didn't have sex. Not last night."

"She took the night off, got high and got murdered. What about him? Maybe they were listening to the wrong song together… One of those stupid death-metal groups?"

Our pathologist is not a music critic. He shrugs politely and duly reports: "This morning the suspect peed into five different bottles. Last night they pumped his stomach and took blood. What a garbage can. He had everything in him from absinthe to Scotch and wine, lots of sugar, caffeine, a big supper, THC…and the morphine— opium, probably…no acetyls—that put him to sleep."

"Whew!"

"But there was nothing of what she had in her."

"This hallucinogen?"

"Yes. I mean no. The thing is, it was too much, the amount in her. Even by the standards of twenty-five years ago."

"I'm afraid I missed all that." Still happily playing with dolls and attending birthday parties.

"Apparently everyone was less inhibited." His urchin-like smile is clearly meant to tease.

"Except the police, Doctor…except the police." Does smile-plus-remark equal ask straight out if he's involved at the moment? *No idea…* She says, "So then: not LSD, but…"

"But almost. And natural. LSD is synthetic. She was taking some kind of ergot…a wheat fungus."

"Ergotamine? Like for migraines?"

"More or less, but homemade. Very homemade. A remedy, not a drug."

"OK…" weighing it, "a couple of drinks mixed with some of this almost-LSD."

"A lot of it. I'm thinking she either had a hell of a headache or was getting ready for one: dry out those blood vessels in the head before it gets a chance to knock you down. It's not a bad strategy."

"But with the booze…"

"Not a whole lot of booze, Inspector. I'd bet no more than an ounce or so."

"Wine?"

"Stronger than wine: grains, to go with the ergot. A Scotch or an eau-de-vie…although there is a fruity acid in there too: apple, pear…something. It's difficult to tell where one medicine stops and the other begins."

"A house cocktail?"

"No," polite but emphatic. "Our victim took something for a headache *and* she had a drink."

"You're telling me she wasn't really that…let's say high, after all."

"Maybe not."

"But she could have been sleepy, nodding off…"

"…or on pins and needles trying to hide from a migraine. For some women they come just as regularly as their periods." Then, almost an after-thought as he scratches behind his ear: "She was having her period. Just starting, I'd say."

"So?" Folding her arms, feeling less than enlightened.

"So I'm still working on it," replies the doctor.

Aliette draws near, examines Manon's forearms, then her thighs and pelvic area, places that are easily bruised, places where most women of her sort, particularly the ones who end up at Raphaele's, are a telling mess. This woman is white and clean. Aliette touches the rounded, hairless stomach, just to one side of the long gash which opens the way to Manon's insides. "In pretty good shape, considering the basic environment."

"Healthy, even. Did I mention there was also a lot of milk in there?"

"Well," notes Aliette, "milk coats the tummy, doesn't it? I have a couple of glasses myself if I'm going to be drinking. Or taking a pill."

"And it's good for the bones of women of a certain age," notes Raphaele.

Again she confronts that grin. And the extra thing she doesn't mind at all; it's there behind his honey-flecked brown eyes. You can tease away, monsieur, that's just fine. She's coming up thirty-six at summer's end, a long way still from that "certain age"—plenty young enough for the likes of him. And yet… Inspector Nouvelle feels herself instinctively withdrawing from the man's flirty comments, giving her attention back to Manon Larivière. "Pretty clean cut," she says.

"Not bad…but not totally." Raphaele believes the knife was twisted more than once before it was withdrawn.

"And no real signs of a struggle…"

"He's huge. He could hold her, immobilize her completely and slide it straight to sources."

"But he must have been completely befuddled…almost passed out. They found him collapsed on top of her."

Raphaele does not disagree. He only adds, "But anger or desperation or…you could call it a reserve of contingent adrenaline: this will guide a killing hand after the mind turns off."

The victim was wearing a nightgown, basically unsullied; and there's a plastic zip-lock bag, waiting by the victim's hand. The inspector opens it, unfolds a silk camisole, smeared and blotched with blood in the area of the wound, but, for the most part, still quite clean. Holding it up to the light, she recognizes an example of very fine couture. The needlework along the hem is exquisite. "Beautiful!" …passing a careful hand across the creamy opalescent silk. Nothing she owns comes near this quality. "*IJ* had a go at this yet?"

IJ is *Identité Judiciaire*. Front-line forensics. In a town of this rank, IJ consists of Charles Léger and Jean-Marc Pouliot; under-funded and too often over-loaded like everyone else, they have their own small lab directly across the hall. "This afternoon," says Raphaele.

Aliette holds the victim's garment close and sniffs it. Tobacco, perspiration, perfume. And something else. She sniffs the victim's wrists, her cleavage, around her ears and neck… It's not her perfume, which is almost gone in any case, overcome by the antiseptic odours of Raphaele's work. Ah: Her hair still holds the smell of tobacco smoke. And this same, almost sweet scent on top. No—another whiff of Manon's chemise, then the body: whatever it was, she had not been wearing it; but it, or someone carrying it, had been in the room. Aliette proffers the camisole under Raphaele's nose. "Do you smell what I smell?"

He sniffs it a couple of times. "I don't know. What do you smell?"

"I don't know."

"I smell cigarettes. Maybe a cigar."

"Lighter," murmurs Aliette, as if smell were a whispery medium; "like a candle wax…an incense, maybe. But lighter than that. Wood?"

He tries again. Shrugs, "No. Sorry."

She folds the camisole twice and replaces it under the lifeless hand. "Could you tell Charles to take it apart for me. And he should try at the scene." Charles' pug nose is always more in sync with hers than that huge beak the Lord had attached to Jean-Marc.

He promises, "I will… Do you want coffee, by the way? I have my steamer hooked to my sterilizer, some excellent biscotti from my mama."

"Thanks. Maybe tomorrow."

Raphaele Petrucci seems surprised as she leaves him—with her own kind of smile and something less than a promise. Well, everyone plays differently and everyone plays to win. No?

She proceeds twenty paces down the hall and into the cell block.

The suspect is sitting on his cot, bent over the morning paper, a large lump in a green velvet smoking jacket, swaying, yawning, shaking himself, then slumping forward; still in rough shape. Finally twigging to her presence, he attempts to pull himself into a standing position—and now she sees that the velvet jacket has been ruined with bloody smears. Very rough shape; but he is a gentleman nonetheless. His glazed eyes, bulbous and bloodshot, try their best to focus on the visitor and bestow the charm of welcome. Lurching forward, offering his hand, as if still unaware of both setting and circumstance, "Bonjour…Herméné Dupras."

She declines to put her own hand through the cell bars but does not mind being cordial. "Herméné…Aliette Nouvelle."

"Hot," he comments, swaying on tree-trunk legs.

"Hot," agrees the inspector.

"Horrible!"

"Horrible murder!" Prompting. Like talking to your deaf granny.

"Horrible…" Trying to think. Then, "…big mistake!"

"Yours?"

"My Manon…" He whispers, and takes another step forward and grabs the bars. His overfed face is wrinkle-free, moonishly round. It shines in varying shades of crimson and is everywhere lined with broken vessels like the surface of Mars. He has to be closing in on seventy. "Aliette, was it?"

"That's right."

"Mmm… Pretty." Then Herméné Dupras collapses against his cell door.

He slides like mud to the floor. She stands back and calls for the duty cop.

3.

Mari Morgan's is discreetly housed in a three-storey building in Rue Louis-Pasteur, between a three-story sixplex over the Boulangerie Erly at street level, and a clunky but grand six-storey Second Republic apartment building. Inside, the brothel is elegant in the style of a time gone by and the inspector is at first reminded of no place so much as her own late grandmère's home. The fine Aubusson carpet spreading to the borders of the dark oak flooring in the foyer reception area. The wine-coloured broadloomed path up the stairway bordered with shiny brass plating. The brocade on the drapery separating the entrance to the drawing room…where she spies a gleaming mahogany bar. The hand-carved chestnut backing and padded armature on the lounge chairs…and the tiny wheels under each elaborate leg. The dominating chandelier. Even the mock crystal handles on the doors. Although, c'est sûr, Aliette's Mémé would never have countenanced a full-sized bar.

The foyer and the bar make up the public area; the crime-scene lies beyond the double glass doors by the foot of the stairs, in that part of Mari Morgan's main floor where (as the small framed notice advises) clients are not supposed to go. An *SU* cop, trim and soldierly in shorts and polished black belt, ushers Aliette along a corridor to Herméné's office, where the victim and suspect had been discovered. She peeks in, then takes a quick tour of the rest of this back area, to orient herself as to access points. The office is directly across from a well-appointed dining room (more echoes of Mémé's house in Nantes). At the back, on the dining room side, is the kitchen, entered from either the dining room or a door at the end of the hall. In the kitchen there is a back-stairs up to the second and third floors. The back door opens onto a scruffy but serviceable alley. There are fire balconies and stairs leading down from the rear of the two upper floors. No basement.

Now ducking under the strands of yellow Police tape… In fact Herméné's office is a suite: an office with an inner door to a bedroom inaccessible from the hall. The inspector notes barred windows in both rooms, and that there is no door from the suite out to the back alley. These rooms show the same tasteful vestiges of a style almost a century old. The Louis XV *secrétaire*. The white satin divan. The well-oiled parquet floor… Manon Larivière's blood had leaked into the plushy Tabriz rug where she was found with the suspect sprawled on top of her in a stupor, a knife tight in his hand.

The bookcase displays framed photos of the "girls" of Mari Morgan's, present and past, usually with Herménégilde Dupras, in a variety of poses and scenes, giving the impression of one big happy family. The victim is featured prominently in several—always Marilyn Monroe, down to the smallest detail. From one image to the next, the inspector notes the faces of some of the other girls becoming older; but wherever her eye rests on Manon, time stops… There's a formal portrait of a large woman, clearly Herméné's mother, looking regal standing beside a baby-grand piano with a vase of violets placed upon it. There is also a blurry snap of a gangly, grinning man in dusty clothes standing on the front steps of a large provincial house; the bulbous eyes suggest the suspect's father. And here's a pewter bowl, sitting unobtrusively but certainly not hidden amongst these mementoes, containing a supply of the sticky black sap which Raphaele says made the suspect pass out.

Aliette puts her nose to work. There's leather, wood, paper, the wool and dust from the rug…the many smells of a dandified old man in the bedroom adjacent. She sniffs the dirty residue of opium. But there is no lingering hint of this other thing she detected around the hair and garment of the victim.

The girls occupy what could pass, if inspected, as bed-sitting apartments on the second and third floors. Manon's is on the second. Aliette holds still, closes her eyes and breathes.

Nothing… Well, soaps and oils in the bathroom. But nothing to connect the victim's chemise to the victim's boudoir where she took it off for a price, nor the victim's hair to the victim's pillow on this bed where men could pretend they were touching Marilyn Monroe. No smell at all in here. No air, in fact. Aliette goes to the window, opens it and breathes in the inviting scent of Erly's baking. Would it be so bad waking up to that after a night of being Marilyn Monroe? Manon Larivière hasn't left much of an answer. No stray papers or notes to herself, no family pictures. No books. Only a small pile of old movie magazines and a closet full of dresses copied from MM's films. The rest, from bidet to bras, is all generic. Standing there trying to fathom a deeper link, Aliette becomes aware of humming from the room across the hall.

The door to the room is slightly ajar. Unobserved, the inspector takes a moment to scan another whore's personal space.

Very mundane: She's hunched over her bidet, washing her lingerie. It's spread all over the room, bras slung over bedposts and drawer handles, stockings hanging from closed drawers, a slip suspended from a tower of magazines by her dresser, two more from hooks in the burnished ironwork supporting the chandelier, yet another from her closet door. Three pairs of panties hang in the window with the sun filtering through—violet, lime and rose: a colourful profusion of kinky silk. Aliette's wandering gaze comes back to find the woman looking calmly up from her labours.

She smiles. "We didn't have anything booked, I hope…we're not really open today."

It's a smile that brings a cop up short. "No…no, nothing booked. My name is Aliette Nouvelle. Police Judiciaire." Flashing her medal, looking to re-establish that sense of balance lost.

"Ah." Standing, offering her damp hand. "Bonjour. I'm Flossie. Flossie Orain." The same height as Aliette's five-seven; a gangly upper body and bowed legs in the jeans she wears for laundry day and mourning make her seem taller. Thinnish face; but the fleshy nose and ample lips lend a natural sensuousness. Her black hair, combed with a part on the side and hanging far enough to touch her seventh vertebra, is fine, silky—none of the lank druggy effect so usually apparent. And Flossie's umber eyes have an engaging twinkle that matches the luxurious smile as she leans forward, seeming to examine the inspector. "Nouvelle? …haven't I seen you somewhere? Wait." Smile tightening into a sort of librarian's pout, she turns and runs her finger up her stack of magazines. Stopping close to the top, she removes a copy of *Paris-Match* and flips it open. "Let's see… Yes, here it is: Inspector Aliette Nouvelle…"

The headline proclaims *The Killing of Jacques Normand!* The report features photos of a glaring, unshaven former Public Enemy (now dead), Louis Moreau, her former Commissaire, the enigmatic accomplice called Anne-Marie, scenes from that fatal morning, Claude Néon, and a picture of herself. "That's me all right."

Flossie points to a line in the story. "They say you have excellent instincts."

"Some people do say that… Were you working last evening, Flossie?"

"Oh yes. Christophe. Our car-parts man from Lille."

"But were you up here when—" A quick glance at her notes.

"Yes. We'd just come up and were getting comfortable."

"When Dorise Ménou found her? Found *them*, in point of fact."

"Poor Dorise."

"I haven't met Dorise yet… You were a friend of Manon?"

Flossie puts *Paris-Match* aside and goes to her window to see if her panties are dry. "They take ages with this humidity… Of course I was. We're like a family here. It's so tragic."

"What was she like?"

"Well," …her face, framed in the window and its morning sun is pensive, lovely; would a client ever see that aspect? "…like Marilyn Monroe."

"Yes. But underneath the act."

Now Flossie Orain grimaces, as if a mistake has been made in the gathered information. And then she sighs. Leaving her brilliant underwear to dry a little longer, she turns her attention back to the cop in her room. "That was what she was like, Inspector. That was her life… There wasn't much else, I'm afraid, if you really want to know. But she was still our friend. And very good at what she did."

"Why would he kill her?"

"I don't know… Any number of things could have been wrong. Herméné Dupras is one of those men who are very big on control."

"Is he violent?"

"He has a temper, sure—but I've never heard of any violence until last night."

"What would bring him to the edge?"

"Well… If things aren't working the way they're meant to. And his pride."

"How so? The pride."

"Some people take a certain view of us…of him. Herméné doesn't hold that view. None of us do. But some of us are more realistic than others…it depends on the circumstances. The wrong word, he'll erupt. But I really can't see poor Manon insulting him like that."

"And things were working as they're meant to?"

"Very much so—roaring right along. That's the mystery."

"Does Herménégilde Dupras treat his work as more than a business, then?"

"Don't we all, Inspector?"

The way Flossie poses it, she can only agree. "And Manon was Herméné's girl?"

"Well, yes. But we all are. That's the point. He goes from girl to girl, as he chooses."

"I see… How was her health?"

"Fine, as far as I know—apart from her migraines. But that was only once a month."

"Would he order her to work when she didn't want to?"

"Never…we don't work when we are having our menstruations. It's important in this business—a few days to ourselves. Money is not the issue here, Inspector—it's love." Flossie seems sure.

"All right. Love. But then how could this thing—?"

"Something to do with needing to have. To own us. Herménégilde Dupras believes we belong to him."

"Well…"

"Well, we don't!" Flossie follows this track into an impassioned description of the Mari Morgan's profit sharing scheme, not unique in the industry, but certainly amongst the more enlightened.

"Herméné's idea?"

"No. Louise—our redhead."

"Did he fight it?"

"No, he liked it. It was only those slimy City Hall accountants who wouldn't miss their weekly freebie if their lives depended on it. They advised against it."

Love then. Not money. A crime of passion?

"Perhaps," surmises Flossie, "but not your usual passion. It's this control thing. Too much mother, maybe?"

"That woman beside the piano?"

"Yes. She raised him in this business."

"That house…"

"*Les Violettes*. Small town to the south. Did a good business. Used him for it, too."

"In what way?"

"Lots of ways. From a *petit Jésus* to a prop for the theatrically minded to—"

"A petit Jésus?"

"A little boy, Inspector. Very profitable. He has lots of stories…" Here Flossie's eyes glaze and she laughs softly with a kind of affection. "He can be very entertaining when you get him going, our Herméné."

"And you know how, I'm sure."

Flossie's smile remains; but her demeanour, as she nods *oui*, is changed completely. "You see, Inspector, there is control, and then there is control. It's my business to make men lose it. Some women, too…" It's the suddenly chilly, non-committal eyes: "not that that has anything to do with the business of running a business."

Aliette has to blink. "I'm not sure I understand your point of view here."

Flossie is sympathetic and wanting to be clear. "I'm not saying I don't like him. As a matter of fact I love him, in my own little way. Thirteen years with Herméné Dupras and you come to love him. But no one should have any illusions about the kind of man he is."

"No… No illusions."

The rest of the Mari Morgan's girls are sequestered in their separate rooms and interviewed. Louise, Martine, Sophie, Julie, Lynda, Brigitte and Josiane… The gathered information is confirmed seven times without discrepancy: Sophie, a cutish, roundish cross between Edith Piaf and Betty Boop, had been working the bar, entertaining one of the Peugeot managers—"We don't actually drink, we pretend to drink. You could never drink with every client. Only Herméné does that…"—when Dorise had screamed from the back. She and Louise had been the first ones there. Beyond that, the same basic story: Herméné Dupras was a nice man with almost no self-control who had to be everyone's best friend and keeper. And: it couldn't have been money; something must have happened between them.

What were they doing in his office? None of my business. Would he force her to work? No…it wasn't about work; couldn't have been. Perhaps she was getting too old? Not at all; coming into her prime, sexually speaking… Yes, noticing the stack of *Marie Claires* by Brigitte's bed; Aliette has read the same article. But was Herméné worried about having to offer a forty-four-year-old "girl"? Marilyn Monroe doesn't get old. But was Manon growing tired of Marilyn Monroe? She never said a word to me about it. What was she like? Funny. Funny strange? Funny ha ha—MM, all the way. Was she happy? Seemed so; except when she had her headaches.

Is there a petit Jésus around here I should be talking to?

No, the market's much too fragmented now.

Oh yes, the market. Did they work hard? Three or four is a normal day, seven days a week. We work the same sort of schedule as *les pompiers* and *infirmières*, with time off every month… (Inspector Nouvelle sees rubber boots lined up in a row by a gleaming pole; hears white shoes squeaking through the dark.) We always make a profit. Clients can have us for as long as they want; the rate scale slides to meet the daily average. So very businesslike in every aspect.

Especially Louise Lebraz, the redhead with the civilized ideas about sharing the wealth. And a mean one, seemingly bitter by nature. Along with Flossie, she is senior. Older than Flossie—closing in on forty, reckons the inspector; Louise is formidable but you can see the signs. The rest, although pretty in their own way, are less than compelling women once you talked to them.

"We're professionals," says Louise. And Manon was not the only one; they can all do a "famous fuck" or two if you had the money.

She asks about the plausibility of the look-alike routine.

"The face is only a hook to hang a whim on," says Louise, whose own specialty (be-wigged) is Elvis Presley's ex-wife as seen on an imported American soap opera set in Texas, hugely popular throughout the Republic at the time. And Flossie's? ...Flossie's is the smart and elegant news anchor, married to the finance minister, who rips fearlessly into corrupt politicians (but not her hubby) and dishonest executives each evening on the national report. "The face is only there to get them started and keep it going until it doesn't matter. We're not here for our faces, Inspector."

She tests the air in each room, but the scent detected on the victim's chemise and hair is not to be traced to the upper parts of the house. Nor, apart from the boss's bowl of opium, is there evidence of any drugs. And in each of these women's rooms she senses that the tears shed for Manon Larivière are from the heart.

Except in the case of Louise Lebraz, who probably hasn't cried since she was three.

And Flossie Orain, who'd been humming whilst washing her things.

4.

Down to the kitchen. Dorise Ménou is slight and sinewy in her starched institutional whites. In her sixties, maybe seventy. Of all of them, her grief for Manon is plainly bitter, deeply sore; it shows all over her lined and haunted face. Aliette asks, "Why her?"

The pinched little shoulders rise and fall exactly once. "Probably because she was the only one not working. He would never interfere with anyone who was bringing in money. He called her to his room on her very worst day."

"He's a businessman. They say she was his star. Would he jeopardize that?"

The cook flashes a cockeyed smile. "They're *all* businessmen, Inspector, every one who has ever walked through that door. What else could they possibly be? Herméné Dupras's the kind of man who takes what he wants when he wants it. Not an ounce of self-control. He's grotesque."

She doubts it will help Dorise's anger much to know Manon and Herméné had not had sex the night before. Instead, she asks, "Why do you work for such a monster?"

Dorise glares at her. "I work for the others! I keep them healthy and help them make the best of what they have to do to earn a living. This place is not what you think it is. Not the part I run."

Just so. Dorise Ménou's kitchen is spotless and stocked with every sort of implement hanging from hooks over a central counter. There's a pot on said counter and some carrots, washed and set out beside it, waiting to be chopped. There's a cow on the far wall and Aliette is drawn toward it. "She's superb! ...Does she have a name?"

"We call her Céleste."

Standing proud on a metal panel about a metre square, Céleste adorns the front face of Mari Morgan's industrial-sized milk dispenser. She's intricately painted to capture every detail, her moulded proportioning perfect. Aliette runs her hand over it: not plastic; something older; a ceramic? "Where did you find her?"

"She's always been here." The haggard grey eyes of the lady who guards her immediately quash the inspector's delight in Céleste the cow. This woman is strung to the snapping point. How best to work with that?

Looking around with quiet admiration..."You take good care of them, I see."

Dorise says, "We have a rule: only milk in the mornings."

"Only milk? Is that one of Herméné's rules?"

"No, it's *our* rule."

"The women?"

Dorise nods in a proprietary way and begins to chop her carrots, rebuilding composure.

"So Manon had eaten nothing since morning."

"Nothing except milk…warm milk. When she has bad cramps, I give her warm milk."

"And what is it that you give her for her headaches?"

Dorise looks like a girl being tested for badges as she lays her knife down and goes to another cupboard where she fetches a large jar filled with a cloudy, amber-hued liquid. "I give her this."

Aliette sniffs a vague fruity, fermented vapour—but only on top. She lets it breathe a moment and tries again. The movement of air reveals something old, funky, distinctly grainy below the fruit perfume. "What is it?"

"A remedy…an ergot: rye fungus, with some barley. I soak apples in it when it's cooked so they can drink it."

"It's not just for Manon?"

"It's good if your bleeding's too strong. It's there for anyone who needs it."

"Can you give me small jar?"

Dorise finds a jam jar and pours expertly from the larger vessel. "It's the best thing for her headaches. She's very delicate." And still very much in the present tense for Dorise Ménou.

Aliette spies the oversized glass jug, the tubes, the line of empty champagne bottles arranged neatly in a shady corner waiting to be filled. "And you make cider too."

"Beer."

"Beer! Oh là là. I'd love to try some." *Oh yes!*

"It's not ready yet."

"Ah. But where did you get all these recipes?"

"They're my mother's."

"Was your mother a cook?"

"Not especially. She was a seamstress."

"Really… You're Bretonne, aren't you?" It's not her voice, but her face. The wide, flat mouth, often exotic in the young, yet so quick to inform a sullen sulk in the old; and the fine high cheekbones which kept the sullen cheeks from sagging. These traits are everywhere along the coast.

No reply. The cook chops a little more quickly.

"I was born and raised in Nantes," offers the inspector. "Where are you from?"

"North of there," mutters Dorise, "the boats come out from Douarnenez and Audierne."

An islander. A definite breed apart. "Lovely up there," she ventures. But how did she ever end up here? Dorise is not interested in elaborating. Chop, chop, chop… So, back to business. *But it's all business, Aliette, every word of it.* "What happened last night?"

"I went to check on her and found them…" Dorise chokes on the end of her statement. Tears are beginning to well again in eyes that look as though they've never been happy.

"You just walked in? Dorise, they might have been making love…"

"He had no business taking her in there when she was in that kind of condition!"

"And so you barged in and found them."

Dorise weeps as she chops and chops. Another interview appears to be over.

Dorise blurts, "I hope they cut that man in two!"

As a representative of the state, Aliette feels obliged to inform her: "I'm afraid they don't do that any more, Dorise. It was abolished in '81."

Dorise only frowns harder: doesn't matter, she still hopes it.

Merci, Dorise… Now let's go hear it from Herméné.

5.

But wait—there's a man in the bar. Drinking alone.

An old man. The *SU* officer has let him in, says he said he was part of the family. Despite the heat, he's dressed for death in the formal provincial manner of another time: dark wool suit, shirt and tie, stiff black Homburg on the table beside an ebony brass-tipped walking stick. A *very* old man, more than eighty, spindly, brittle, papery flesh mottling to absolute white from temples to cheekbones. He nods vaguely in greeting. His filmy eyes sparkle dully from the far end of life's road. He murmurs, "Did you know her well?"

"Never met her. Monsieur…?"

He sips his Scotch and water; stares into it, as if in wonder. Finally says, "I loved her."

She sits. Above the bar there's a motto of sorts, carved expertly into the wood: *I am the hostess of the irreproachable Ferry Tavern, a white-gowned moon welcoming any man who comes to me with silver.* Well, that's nice…looking around; Aliette could definitely enjoy a glass of beer at this point, but there's no one at the bar to offer.

The old man mutters, "I did… I loved her in my own particular way."

"Tell me about it."

He nods. He will. He wants to tell about Manon. But he's beyond hurrying. He scratches at his close-cropped snowy scalp; bits of him fall away. He's aware of it…brushes them from his cuff. "I suppose I've always been too much the doctor," he says. "For me, love was always like an investigation, to find the sense behind the sense, to see where the body and its love sprang from. That was my predilection. It became my addiction…mmm?" With a movement of his eyes, the elegant walking stick is suddenly part of his story. She shudders. Involuntary; not the cop, the woman. "And yet I always felt I was approaching the soul. I honestly looked for it. I did. In my own way, I searched. Manon was an excellent partner in these things. Could always make me laugh."

"I take it you're not really family, monsieur."

"From corruption, sweetness," intones the man, smiling softly, raising his glass in Aliette's direction. "To the next part of her journey."

He drinks. She takes pen and notebook from her case. "Could you tell me your name?"

"His name is Marcel." Flossie Orain is standing at her shoulder. "Dr. Marcel Cyr. As you can see, Inspector, the heat, plus the shock of this…it's been a difficult day."

"But he's…not really family?" she enquires—discreet, although Dr. Marcel Cyr is not the least concerned.

"We think he is," says Flossie, laying protective hands on the old man's stooped frame. "We'll eat together this evening and share some memories. Eh, Marcel?"

He repeats it: "From corruption, sweetness…" and drains his glass and dreams.

6.

The afternoon is well along by the time she gets back to the commissariat.

She goes to the basement and presents Raphaele with the sample of Dorise's remedy.

"Ah, this could shed some light. Good work, Inspector."

What was the difference between a flirtatious man and a mendacious woman? In high humidity, not a lot. "What's the verdict on the camisole?"

"Not in yet."

"Was the victim moved, Doctor? I don't recall you mentioning…"

"Moved?"

"Did she die where it was done?"

"Apart from bruising caused by an assailant twice her weight, I found nothing to indicate otherwise."

She goes across the hall to IJ. "Did you smell it?"

Charles Léger frowns. "As a matter of fact I did…I think. But this thing can't." His less than state-of-the-art system, the sort their kind of small operation is obliged to make do with; and when they get around to supplying him with the newest thing, it won't be any longer. "I'll go through the place again tomorrow."

"And nothing to indicate she was transferred to the scene afterward?"

Jean-Marc Pouliot signals negative. "Lots of extraneous feet and hands from everyone needing to have a look before we got there and sealed it. But, no—it appears she was stabbed where she stood and went straight to the floor."

She sniffs the silky thing one more time. "It's there."

Jean-Marc shrugs. "Have to send it north."

To the much better lab at Divisional headquarters in Strasbourg, ninety kilometres up the road.

"No time for that." They know. "Try, messieurs." They will. "Merci."

She peers through the cell-block door. Claude is smoking away as he interviews the suspect.

Thanks, Claude... In a cop's world, where a case can be your *raison d'être* and methodology lives close to the heart, this is tantamount to a slap in the face. This is her case—wasn't that settled this morning? She had the distinct impression that it was. Mmm, but it's also par for the course: the new Commissaire feels responsible for his inspectors' first thoughts and summary report as a case begins. Especially hers. Gets very worried about her ways of proceeding. Everything reflects on him, you see.

There's not much an inspector can do about it. Except petition for an extra day before submitting her report. It'll depend on how he's hearing it...

Claude and Herméné Dupras appear to be going at it quite intensely. Aliette leaves them to it and goes home.

A liette always walks—her apartment's not far. Today she stops at
Madame Chong's *épicerie* for cat food and beer. The rond-point
marks the boundary of the old quarter. The traffic cop is working the
sweaty, irritated home-bound flow; a blast on his whistle, the sea is
parted and she goes across. Her place, just there on the other side—
third (top) floor, overlooks the Parc de la République, a large green
space leading to the more prestigious neighbourhoods to the north
and west. Piaf is slumped on the porch, one hoary white paw dangling
through the balustrade. Always well ahead of the game, September's
Marie Claire is waiting in the mail. The cover girl lends credence to
the claim that breasts are getting bigger and women more realistically
shaped. Good news; she'll have an extra brownie. Her wiser side
knows next month's cover girl will be another toothpick, to keep
faithful readers slightly worried as they peruse the fashions and ponder
issues such as *Les 5 Secrets du Sexe de L'Homme* which…flipping to the
page as she climbs the stairs, well!…features a photo collage of penises;
or *L'Onde Qui Fait Maigrir*—the laser beam that will replace liposuction
with lipo*sculpture*; or, "look at this, Piaf…" coming in, putting her
case and groceries down on the kitchen table, still reading as she stoops
to give his head a scratch, "*Parfois Je Fais L'Amour Pour de L'Argent.*"
(Sometimes I Make Love for Money)… She gets out of her sticky
underwear, takes a quick shower and pulls on a loose shift. Far too hot
for a run—all those reports of people overheating and dropping
dead… Then she fills Piaf's bowl with two large spoonfuls of Cheese

Dinner Delight, opens a bottle of beer and prepares herself a salad of salmon and cold rice. By the time the inspector sits, the *Marie Claire* girl has bits of all these substances plus drops from wet hair splashed or smeared all over her chic smile.

Inside, *Marie Claire*'s journalist had premised her investigation with the basic question: "What woman has never asked herself, if only for five minutes at some point in her life, would I be capable of being a prostitute?" She went on to describe two case histories: "Lulu" was a down-and-out film industry artisan who did it out of desperation, only for enough money to eat. Lulu succeeded in eating but ended up considerably more miserable and alienated from herself than when she'd started. By contrast, "Nadine" held a good management position in a department store. Her problem was an ex-husband who chronically missed his alimony payments. Nadine felt she needed extra cash, not for her child, but for her own needs. Nadine said it was "so easy," and that most male fantasies were "so depressingly banal." Nadine got out of prostitution when she fell in love. *Marie Claire*'s reporter concluded that there were probably thousands of women like these two, "all of them ultimately the victims of economic crises, needing to live and consume in an urban society."

Aliette wonders if that isn't a sly bit of editorial self-service on the part of *Marie Claire*.

She sips her beer and turns to the piece on laser liposculpture. Cellulite is not one of her worries, not yet, but there's no harm in being prepared for "the battle," as it is commonly called in these glossy pages…

Eight o'clock sharp: the disappearing sun squints orange and bleary through the hazy dusk; three blasts of the horn as Georgette Duguay, the artist's model, pulls up in the old VW van. Aliette Nouvelle, apprentice artist's model, waves from the porch and hurries down to join her. Twenty minutes later the two women are standing naked in a room on the upper floor of the Institute, a fine albeit dusty old building in the business sector that had been abandoned by the business types and subsequently claimed by groups of artists, dancers, sculptors, cooks, AA adherents, practitioners of tai-chi, grass-roots politicos and the odd jazz or blues band working on its stuff.

Members of the drawing group are trooping in, their portfolio cases and materials under their arms, silent, anonymous, each with his or her own sense of the day just lived. They set up at easels spaced round the room. Georgette takes her position on the riser at the front and eases into her pose. Aliette ponders it, then attempts to ape it. Georgette's method is not to plan a pose but to arrive at it, bringing feelings and thoughts of the moment to inform. "Finding it" is what she calls this crucial part of the exercise. Aliette feels she is beginning to understand what that means. The hard part is forgetting yourself and focusing on Georgette, especially after a difficult day at work. The interesting part is that when she gets it, she always knows it; not because the form looks like Georgette's, but because the feeling it evokes feels as if it must be her own.

As the dust surrounding Jacques Normand settled, Aliette, in the spirit of new friendship, held true to her claim that she would be interested in trying to do what her new friend did; i.e., be a model. Here, four months later, her poses are still far less than subtle; yet she perseveres, showing up as regularly as her work permits. She finds she enjoys this role as a basic shape, a touchstone for the form and content of life. Now this amateur understands it's a vocation that takes a lifetime to perfect. And although they're as tricky to extract as an ingrown hair from a soft crevice, there have been some words of encouragement, if not compliment, on the part of her teacher.

Tonight it's going to be that flying pose again, a position they have tried on a fairly regular basis and the second time in as many nights: The arms are spread out, low—from the hips, like a jet. The face is fixed with purpose but the eyes are filled with a strange woe, a haunted look. All weight is forward, just short of falling... Now the model shifts, easing into the maximum lean, the point of inevitability, her chest forward, breasts suspended. There, holding, she strikes the pose.

Inevitability? The flying pose seems to coincide with the model's darker moods, and the bleak centre of this one is a mystery. One does not ask Georgette to explain. But allowing herself to relax into not-knowing, Aliette arrives at something, and holds it as best she can. Georgette, well into her seventh decade, yet still strong, straight and the consummate mannequin, is balanced and unstrained in all aspects of the position. If, in contrast, the neophyte appears gangly and contrived in her manner, her face is nothing if not dedicated as the drawing group begins to draw.

Just an hour, with a break to stretch and roam the room to see how they see her; and in complete silence, according to Georgette's unspoken law; such is the social aspect of an inspector's life at this particular time.

Afterward, the group packed up and silently dispersed, Aliette and Georgette stroll the plaza in front of the Institute. More comfortable now, but still too humid for a decent night's sleep. Their steps and conversation are desultory. Georgette has a problem; Aliette's problem is how to bring it out. She tries but it's not easy. They nibble tentatively at the edges of a subject, then, without cause or resolution, leave it for another as Georgette turns and heads the other way. Georgette curses, peremptory, "*putain!*" in response to Aliette's complaints about the weather. Doesn't care that the tailor's rendering of her flying pose has turned mawkish...or that the butcher has broken a barrier of sorts with the exquisite pain he has managed to bring to Georgette's eyes with a simple piece of charcoal. Isn't even much interested in the plight of her friend Anne-Marie, Jacques Normand's ex-partner/lover, still stuck in prison, refusing to utter a word: "*J'en ai marre!*" (I'm sick of it!) Mmm, ornery and almost not worth the effort...

But we need friends and friends have to try.

Yes. So what about the Tapie scandal?...what is it with all these rich and famous, best and brightest, who keep getting caught with their hands in the most blatant *merde?*

"*Je m'en fous.*" (Who cares.)

Fine. A trying friend gives up. Time for bed, Georgette. They head toward the van.

From four steps behind Georgette demands, "Did he really kill that woman?"

Aliette turns. "Herménégilde Dupras?"

A nod.

"I don't know. It looks like it. But—"

"But he wouldn't!"

"No? How do you know?"

"I know him."

"You do?"

"I used to."

Oh, Lord. Is she going to find out something about her new friend she might not want to know? If anyone needs a little extra cash from one week to the next it's an artist's model.

"...and he wouldn't kill anyone."

"Georgette, are you telling me you once—"

"That's none of your business, so don't you think it!"

She can be fierce, as if life itself were the enemy. "Sorry... Why wouldn't he do it?"

But Georgette is silent, angry at Aliette's presumption. Remains silent long enough for Aliette to believe she may be frozen there. Even in this heat. Oh well, forget it; besides, it's been Aliette's policy not to bring her work to the group. She continues down the steps. Georgette's voice comes through, low, heavy with contempt. "It's not in him to kill. What Herméné is, is pleasure-bound, pure and simple. There's no pleasure in killing unless one is crazy. Herméné is too much of this world to be crazy. He wouldn't do it."

Right or wrong, Georgette's theories always come with the force of conviction that can be daunting. Aliette floats a different one. "Flossie—one of the women there—she said it has to do with love and that he's one of those men who craves control."

"Flossie has been trained to say anything."

"You know her too?"

"I don't know any of them! But if she works there, that's her job."

"Sex is her job."

"Deception is the job...the sex is just sex."

"How well did you know him?" asks Aliette—gently, sensing fragile territory.

"Well enough, for a while."

Georgette looks away. Still angry? Aliette discerns something more akin to shame. She gazes at the profile: the green eyes, slightly bloody with the humidity; the shoulder-length silver hair, pulled back and tied up like a dancer's; the long nose, reminiscent tonight of Holbein's *Ursula*, on a wall in the Swiss city just down the line…but the strong, horsy jaw is nothing like the saint's. "This Flossie said he had a horrible childhood. Did he ever tell you anything about a petit Jésus?"

"Jesus?" The name is framed in one of Georgette's cold half-laughs. "He told me angels were meant to provide laughter. I hated him for that."

Aliette, as per their pattern, must prod. "Yes?"

"It was his weak excuse for getting rid of one and going on to the next… Herméné Dupras is too weak to kill anyone. The man doesn't love strongly enough to kill."

The inspector has no reply. She has never thought of it in quite that way before.

The tension of her secret out, Georgette is now simply old womanish as she opens the door to the van. "I detest this heat…detest it!" muttering, fussing, she climbs in and starts it up.

Aliette will walk back, thank you. In parting, she demands, "Then why do you care?" Not so gentle; needing far more clarity on this one.

"Because it would make the insult of his life that much worse… Salut."

The van jerks away, jolting off in the direction of the model's tiny basement bed-sitting room.

Aliette wanders home through the heat, mulling over her day.

So Georgette Duguay knows—and hates—Herméné Dupras. Small world. But it is! In a small and typically provincial city? Never hard for outsiders to find each other. Artist's models are outsiders. Putes and pimps are too.

And cops. Don't forget cops, Aliette…

Mmm, a murdered pute equals a cop's full day. Because Aliette trusts her nose, she has serious doubts the murder occurred inside the brothel. The inspector's nose has given her to believe Manon Larivière was brought to the office of Herménégilde Dupras after the fact. Raphaele and IJ contend to the contary. The inspector contends that a clean killing such as that one can be staged. A knife in a barely conscious old man's hand is easy… And that one or some of the other girls would have to have known. Or Dorise Ménou. Claude's contention that the guests cancel themselves out of the picture makes sense. The territorial factor: They're tight-knit, these women. And they're prostitutes; that house is their patch. If it happened outside, there was inside help. Aliette has to start inside and her feeling is that anyone involved would have to be closer than a client. That leaves only the members of the Mari Morgan's family, so to speak.

Family? Mari Morgan's surprised her. At the very least, a well-coached team.

Georgette's right: deception is the job.

Poor Georgette. And what is her relation to that family?

She's a cranky angel if ever there was one.

Not poor Georgette! Stop it! Because sympathy could be one of the inspector's shortcomings. *Always feeling sorry for someone, aren't we, Aliette?* Yes, always some poor so-and-so to deal with. Poor Georgette. Poor Piaf… Now it's poor Manon Larivière. There are cops in her circles—Claude Néon is one—who cannot abide this sympathetic streak. Impulsive. Unprofessional. Dangerous. Ultimately it's dangerous, is what they say.

Maybe so; Aliette can't separate it.

Even poor Claude. Sometimes.

It's why I'm here, ma belle.

I know, I know. She listens…

Now lying on a sweat-stained pillow, porch door and windows wide open, senses attuned to just a touch of air, please! in lieu of the lover who isn't there.

- 3 -
DAY TWO

Friday August 7th; heat wave holding stubbornly. She's in Claude's office with her breakfast—plain croissant and coffee, comparing notes.

"Says it was business as usual. Says he slipped away to have some dessert with the victim up in her room…says she was ill and wasn't working. But they argued…says she said she was going to leave."

"Leave? Like quit?"

"Says she sprang it on him, right out of the blue. Says she had it in her head to go that night."

"Why?"

"He doesn't know. He thinks she was sort of crazy from the heat and her period and these headaches that she always had. Says her pain could do that."

"And so?"

"They argued, but he says it was impossible so he left her to it and went back down to his office. He sat at his desk…the murder weapon was a keepsake he used to open letters, but he can't remember if it was sitting there in front of him…can't remember much of anything till they found him on the floor. Swears he was drugged and set up. Can't imagine by who of course. All his girls love him, you see. It was getting to me, some of the things he was telling me. All he ever does is have sex with whichever one he wants. It was gross. Like some kind of happy pig. When I suggested that, he was on his feet and would've hit me if it weren't for the bars. A happy pig, prone to violence... Very ugly. He's finally where he belongs."

"Don't be jealous, Claude." And insulting a suspect never helps.

Claude snorts, sardonic; he's learned to roll with her comments just as she has learned to roll with his. "Worst part is how he insists he's got nothing but love for all of them."

She tells him, "It didn't happen in that room... I don't think it even happened in that house."

He responds with a dubious smile. "So where did it happen, Inspector?"

"Somewhere where someone was burning something I can't find any trace of at Mari Morgan's. You can't get rid of smoke, and the smoke I smelled on her top—"

"Her top?"

"Her chemise—a camisole, the thing she was wearing...it's just not there in that house. IJ will back me up." She hopes.

"They'll have to, won't they?" Meaning: if the victim was planted, forensics would know it by now.

The inspector isn't cowed. "I need to talk to him myself. I need another day."

Claude's lips purse momentarily. "Look, my budget is stretched to the limit. She's a whore, we've got a real low-crawler in jug. This kind of thing is only worth so much..." A gesture, palms gently flattening the air in front him: Let's just go with the flow here, can't we?

She responds. "It's only me, Claude... Sir. I don't cost much. It needs a second look."

"I'm not stopping you. But I've already talked to Gérard and he agrees completely..." Gérard Richand, Chief Judge of Instruction, will assess the police summary report, add his own thoughts and confer with Procureur Michel Souviron, who will lay the formal charge. Claude sips his coffee. "Besides, aren't you out of here next week?"

"I definitely plan to be on that plane. But a week is a week. Everything else is pretty quiet. Too hot for all my usual idiots, I guess... Claude, I need to know why anyone would ever want to kill

a Marilyn Monroe doll. And why anyone would want to be one. Don't
you?"

He blinks. "Yeah, sure." But he does need to know. "OK, I'll
ask Michel for the extra day before he files his charge. Anything else
is between you and Gérard. Oh yes," gloomy gaze shifting to a certain
slip of paper, "the body was released this morning."

"Who authorized that?"

"Gérard, obviously."

"Claude! …why?"

"They asked. Raphaele says they've taken everything that needs
to be taken. I told Gérard, Gérard said fine. If they're smart, they'll get
her in the ground straight away, with this heat."

Ah, *merde!*

2.

"The chemise is gone! …With her?"

Raphaele Petrucci stays calm. He tastes his cappuccino.
Pronounces it, "Numero uno!"

Calm? More like off-hand, far too casual. It's starting to make
her mad and he can see it.

"Don't worry, I kept a sample." His smile says, Please don't
think we're unprofessional, we who dwell in the basement. "But,"
back to his notes, "there's only her perfume, her sweat, his cigars,
secretions from his hands…and green velvet from his coat."

"Let's see it…the sample."

"More of a scraping, actually. Doesn't look like the thing,
just smells like it." The smile disappears. The pathologist looks
away, exasperated. "Inspector, we can only recover a smell if it's
there. There was nothing else. IJ has the machines, the chemicals.
They tried." Pleading slightly here? "…You know that."

"Charles says he smelled it, too!"

"But Charles couldn't find it. He's over there now, going
through the place." Honestly, it's not as if he's enjoying disappointing
her. "Maybe it's your nose," suggests Raphaele, pointing to it, trying
to apologise; "…smell is like colour. Everyone experiences it in their

own way. It has to be a cigar. Or someone else's perfume…maybe from the other side of the room?"

"She wasn't working!"

"Well he was! And they were together."

"Only found together, Doctor, that's all we know for sure!"

"I tell you, she wasn't moved."

"Then why did I smell that smell?"

"I don't know, Inspector."

"Oh, *quel bordel!* (What a mess.)… I need that top."

His eyes don't bounce around like Claude's. They ask: Why are you pushing the obvious here?

In answer, hers say, Thanks a lot.

The moment passes. He brightens up as he taps his notes. "Ergot sample lines up perfectly."

"Not a drug?"

"A large dose might induce something beyond the normal. Still, I can't tell you or any judge, with any professional certainty, that it affected her mind or body in such a way as to be connected with the murder."

"So?"

Aliette waits as he reads up and down again, trying too hard to reassure her that he really is a thorough cop. "So the knife entered below the rib cage, ripped the lung and the pericardium and part of the heart. Result: massive internal haemorrhaging; she drowned in her own blood. Death was not instantaneous, but certainly within a few minutes." Then, shameless, unrepentant—it could have been sometime last year that this very minor professional disagreement had clouded their mutual attraction, he wonders, "You want a cappuccino?"

"No, I want to see that chemise. And smell it—with my nose." Which she touches. For his benefit. "Where did they take her?"

He checks a slip of paper. "Back to Mari Morgan's. Funeral's at half-ten. You'd better run."

That smile. It's not easy: being older, being senior, and being attracted.

And he has just messed up on her… Maybe.

3.

She runs but does not get to sniff the victim's underwear again.

French people aren't so obsessed with funeral homes, embalming, the whole (rather wasteful) rigmarole. It's there if you want it but it's not the law. It's perfectly OK if the deceased is washed and dressed by the visiting nurse, family members helping, and laid out on her usual bed. You hang a black ribbon or wreath on the front door. The rep from the local *Pompes Funèbres* (or it could still be the local cabinet maker in a smaller town or village) arrives to measure and offer a choice of boxes, make burial or cremation arrangements, make sure all state-required paperwork is in order. All done from home until you proceed to the church, if you have one.

Manon Larivière has no church. Aliette, bearing flowers and feeling damp from a quick march across the quarter, meets them coming out the door. The helping hands carefully lifting Manon into the hearse are supplied by the women of the house. Apart from Erly the baker, and a priest who will not meet anyone's eyes as he stands by, there are no men mourning in front of Mari Morgan's. Charles Léger of IJ is standing, sheepish, unopened kit in hand, at the door to a café just up the street. He'll go in and test as soon as they leave.

Aliette shares a cab with Erly. They follow the small cortège out of the city, forty kilometres north to a pleasant little cemetery near a hamlet in some foresty flatland by the river. It's closing in on noon as they roll up. The sun hangs in a cloudless sky over the yellowing green of high summer, the swaying willow tree by the bank, the calming rush and cooling whiff of the dazzling waters…a factory in Germany on the other side. The inspector steps forward, makes her bow, tosses a handful of dirt. She moves to the outer ring of guests as the last words are said and the box is lowered.

She watches them, faces quiet behind black lace veils. They are the sisters. Manon's family.

Because there is no weeping mother or empty-eyed father. There is one older woman at the graveside: tall…Aliette can see a grim, hardened face of advancing years behind the veil. She does not look like anyone's mother. The rest are men, a smattering, who've materialized here in the privacy of a remote graveyard, far from the eyes of the city. Dr. Marcel Cyr has made it, frail and bent under that same overly formal, overly warm black Homburg, supporting himself on that burnished brass—or is it gold?—tipped walking stick.

The procession drifts away to cars parked in the shade. Aliette feels she needs another word with the old man, but Louise and Josiane are protective as they escort him toward a well-kept pearl grey 1949 Citroën TA. Better than well-kept; a show-piece!—Aliette knows because Papa used to take delight in grilling herself and her sister Anne as to year and model of France's finer automotive creations whenever they spotted one. She'll catch up with Marcel Cyr back in town.

She puts the cab ride on her expense account card, but, respectful of Claude's budget, pays for two of Erly's *tartes flambées* and a dozen *religieuses* out of her own pocket. She has decided against leaving her flowers at the gravesite; they'll do more good for the living. Holding baked goods in one arm, flowers in the other, she backs through the door to the brothel.

There's no one in the lobby. She lays her parcels on the counter, checks Herméné's office, the rooms upstairs, but it appears Charles Léger has been and gone. Coming back down, the phone on the front desk is ringing and she stands there waiting for someone to appear. The caller gives up. Aliette wanders into the bar. Lingering, her gaze falls again on the motto carved into a panel over the mirror: *"I am the hostess of the irreproachable Ferry Tavern, a white-gowned moon welcoming any man who comes to me with silver."* Poetic and apropos; but how?… But Dorise is standing there watching her. The cook has not gone with them to the cemetery; she wears the same white habit she had on the day before. "Dorise…I just… The door was open. Where are they?"

"They were going to have a picnic by the river."

"Oh… Well, that's a nice thing to do. But what about you?"

"I don't need to go out there. I said my goodbyes this morning. I don't like this heat."

"It can't last," predicts the inspector. She picks up her flowers and food. "I brought these along," patting the baker's boxes, "in case you weren't in the mood for working."

Dorise accepts her offerings with a nod that is not quite a thank you. "I'm always working."

"Staying busy is probably the best thing." Withdrawing, a consoling smile for the unhappy woman, it occurs to her: "Dorise, would you know if that was Mari Morgan at the funeral?"

"What do you mean?" snaps Dorise, almost vicious.

"I'm…" What *is* her problem? "I'm just asking. There was this one woman, tall…"

"No! It wasn't her!"

"But Dorise…you weren't even there."

The cook stares at her. Stares daggers.

"Well who is Mari Morgan? Is she around? Still alive?"

"I don't know!…how should I know! I've never seen her!" Insistent brittle fury…now dissolving in a flood of tears. Aliette instinctively steps forward, arms out. The cook fends her off. "I have to work," she whimpers and rushes away, back to her kitchen.

4.

"I won't be able to pay my respects," gesturing at the bars confining him; "there's money, I think, that they took from my pockets along with my belt and my keys before they put me here. Would you take some of it and offer flowers from me?"

"Can't do it, monsieur."

"Herméné, please."

"Herméné. I can't touch anything that was on your person."

"Ah. Regulations. Your colleague the Commissaire was telling me all about the regulations last evening. Well…" His moon face droops.

"But I can see about the flowers." It's a reasonable request.

He smiles his thanks. Now he's recovered from the night of the murder, Herméné's green velvet, immaculately groomed male presence has resurfaced, utterly confident it will be accepted no matter what. A successful pander. What about a murder charge? It seems inevitable, given Claude's mood this morning and the fact that Gérard Richand has yet to call the prisoner before him. Will the suspect's bonhomie hold up? "Who's your lawyer?" Who'll be allowed to come into it as the legal transition from *garde à vue* to *détention provisoire* comes into effect.

He laughs, with telling resignation. "Probably no one, given the circumstances. I have several, but none has come forward. I suppose I don't blame them—people have reputations."

"The state will supply one," assures Aliette.

"I'd prefer a caterer, frankly."

"And maybe a box of cigars, Herméné?"

"Oh yes!" Black button eyes brightening on reflex.

"Talk to your lawyer. Your lawyer can see to your personal concerns." Comfort first, murder second. Pleasure-bound. Georgette knew him, all right. "Do you take drugs with your girls?"

"On occasion…depends on the occasion."

"Opium?"

"Was it opium?"

"Seems so. From the pot on the shelf in your office?"

"I thought as much…badly constipated all day yesterday. No, not much for opium these days. Takes away the desire—especially at my age. Last thing I need. But yes, I keep a supply if anyone wants it. Yes, in the office…don't like to offer it in the bar. We walk a fine line."

"But you did smoke some?"

"Oh, a puff or two to be polite. It's part of the job. But not enough to plug me up like that."

"And you didn't have sex."

"Not with Manon…we were very quiet. In a highly delicate state. Had one of her wretched headaches, her period, the works—right out of commission. She went up for her bath, I went up a bit later with cake and wine to say goodnight, to try to make her feel better, then…" Sad shrug.

"You argued because she said she was going to leave Mari Morgan's."

"Highly delicate," mutters Herméné. "She can turn hysterical at the drop of a pin. It's so sad. You want to help her but there's nothing you can do or say… I went back down. All you can do is wait till morning and hope it's gone away."

"What is the last thing you can remember?"

"Sitting there at my desk feeling ill and sleepy…sad, mainly. For Manon. It's a sad sight."

"No one came in?"

"Not that I can remember…I suppose I was waiting to see if *she* would. To say goodbye. Very tragic and dramatic about it all… But I didn't really believe she would. Apparently I drifted off."

"And she was there, more or less in your arms when you woke up."

Herméné Dupras stares into space and slams one steel bar with the palm of one huge hand.

Aliette steps back from the force of it. "But she wasn't exactly dressed to go out. No packed bag…"

"No…" Deflating, bewildered, he returns to his cot and sits. "I did not do this thing, Inspector."

"The knife…"

"Yes, yes, it's from my mother's house. I use it every day to open mail. Anyone who knows me, knows this."

She asks, "Herméné, did Manon want to leave Mari Morgan's?"

"No. Of course not. Why would she?… More to the point: where would she go?"

"Did you have sex with anyone earlier? I mean someone more special than her?"

"All my girls are special. Very special. But no, I didn't. But I might've later. Every night's a new one, Inspector. That's my motto."

But not the motto over the bar.

And going over certain other points, certain other observations dovetail. Flossie Orain had touched on something germane:

"Only milk, you say? If that's all they're having then they should be having more. They have very busy schedules…" Expression grave, but it's just for show. He knows nothing of Dorise's remedy, nor, for that matter, a ceramic milker named Céleste—at least not by name. Doesn't know about the records the police have on six of his girls and when confronted, shrugs it away. "This is normal in our business." His grasp of Mari Morgan's financial situation is better, but is childlike when compared to Flossie Orain's. His sense of Flossie is jarring. "Like a daughter to me…knows every inch of the place. No way I could manage without her with the way things are these days." It becomes clear the man has little idea what goes on in the inner workings of his house.

Herméné's in sync with the rest of them on one thing, though: "No, no, no… You don't understand. She never took it off, as you say. She was *like* Marilyn Monroe."

"She thought she was Marilyn Monroe."

"She pretended she was Marilyn Monroe. But she was Manon, never any mistake there."

"But she was like Marilyn Monroe."

"Yes…more or less."

"That's a tricky one, Herméné."

"You have to love her to know her. We all loved her, we knew exactly who she was."

"And all your girls love you."

"Obviously. Everything depends on it. Place wouldn't last a week if it weren't for love."

"And laughter."

"As often as we can manage it."

Piggy, clued-out, vainglorious in that weird way presumption will grow on a man without his even knowing; and yes, presumption is first cousin to an obsession with control. And that large anger. Intentionally or not, did Manon push him too far on a night when hellish humidity plus this apparent need for pleasure—mixed with all the pleasure-producing devices at his disposal—would have brought him to the edge? A word, the weather, a milligram too much of this, an ounce too much of that; so many murders happen when two people go over that ever-shifting edge.

But he does not appear to possess the hard, mean, money-grubbing thing Dorise Ménou ascribes to him.

Her own diagnosis: a temper, yes, arising from a pride and loyalty of sorts—odd, hard to fathom, bred in the bone in the life of a useful but eternal outsider. Sure, you get whatever you want, my friend. The greater part of Herméné Dupras is needful…this need to please and be pleased. The social element is his heart's prop. A child of the business in more ways than one? This is to be explored, if not by herself, then by experts in the field. Michel Souviron, our Proc, will rip him apart in court. When he's finished ripping, Michel will see the essential hole in the soul of this pleasure-bound pander. Like Georgette says, no abiding passion there—no one, nothing to be passionate about. Nothing to drive the knife.

She believes Michel will also see the man's not lying, even if Claude cannot. Or doesn't want to. Green velvet and never-ending fun. The very best available. And yet he takes a break from it all for dessert, a quiet moment with the one who's "out of commission"— like he's running a bus service… It's words like that, that side of the man that give offence; but he truly seems to care.

That shifting edge: the fact of two people colliding at the wrong moment…the murderous impulse is as varied as the vagrant soul. Coming up nine years on the job, Aliette knows this.

But so is the impulse toward love.

One more thing: "Who is Mari Morgan?"

"Mari Morgan?…Mari Morgan is a song Ondine used to sing."

"Not a person?"

"If she is, I never met her."

"And this Ondine?"

"Ondine was… God, that's it! It was her. As sure as I'm sitting here…of course! Ondine. Who else?" The suspect sits there, nonplussed by this notion, eyes wide, shiny head bobbing slowly.

Aliette lets it settle…finally has to snap him out of it. "Well? Who is she?"

"Ondine Duguay. A seamstress. Used to be my partner. Ran the kitchen, kept them organized, made all their things. Left us in a big huff…mmm, about ten years ago. Maybe twelve. Still does their things, though. Very talented… She made this coat for me."

"Manon's chemise?"

"Of course."

"She does beautiful work… Ondine Duguay?"

"*C'est ça.*"

"Have a sister?"

"Georgette…prettier."

Aliette's heart turns over. *Steady, steady…* "What was Ondine's problem, then?"

"The ambience…the liaisons that are naturally formed amongst the staff in an establishment such as mine. Like I say, we all love each other. Her problem was she thought she was the centre of the universe."

"Where is she now?"

"She has a shop in the quarter somewhere. I haven't seen her for years. She refused to have anything more to do with me. But my girls continue to enjoy her things."

"Are you telling me you rejected Ondine?"

Of all her questions, this one leaves him taken aback. "I never reject anyone. Not my style."

No, perhaps you don't…"But how could she have drugged you…set you up without some help on the inside? You *were* inside the whole evening?"

"Where else would I be?…All my girls love me, Inspector."

No they don't, Herméné; but it's probably best for both of us if you continue to believe it. *Bon*; gathering her notes; "a shop in the quarter?"

"As far as I know."

5.

The sister of her friend the misanthropic artist's model and she made lingerie for putes! If you were their mother, which one would you love the better? The inspector will withhold her judgement till she finds the seamstress who thought she was the centre of the universe. From what she knows of the Duguays thus far, that does not surprise her at all. But the centre of the universe is hiding. Ondine Duguay is not in the phone book. It would be nice to have a car on a sticky afternoon, but a car comes with a partner (this one is very high on Claude's new list of budget-oriented rules) and Aliette does not want to work with a partner. Sticky or not, she'll walk it…

A shop in the quarter somewhere. She passes several every day on her way to and from the commissariat, and pops into the occasional one if she needs a new bra or pants for work. Nicer stuff she buys downtown; or from Marianne at Palais on Belle Ile, who's also known to supply the President's wife—good for conversation's sake (or might be), surmises a lonely cop… Who can't recall ever passing one called

Ondine. She asks at *Au Coin des Bas*…at *Chez Rose-Marie Lingerie* and *Deuxième Peau*…then at *Lili Lingerie*…and at *Maison des Rêves Doux.* It has never really hit her, the sheer number of enterprises in such proximity dedicated to the sale of women's underwear. At *Lingerie Piaf,* she allows herself to relax for a moment as she waits for the salesgirl to go and ask her boss. She imagines her own Piaf wandering out from the back with the next pair of silky pants hanging lightly between his jaws, then rolling over on the floor while the lady thought it over, or looking out the window at nothing while she went to try on a very special *soutien-gorge.* The report comes back, "No, never heard of any Ondine." The lines favoured at *Lingerie Piaf* are *Passionata* and *Chantelle.* Aliette leaves with a glossy brochure entitled *Des idées provocantes* and continues on through the homebound crowds.

She loves to walk but is going too fast, intent, determined to find this woman, on a personal level as well as the professional. The endorphins, which always seem to rise when an enquiring soul is in motion, are kicking in; but they're out of kilter on this broiling summer's day, wired, worried by impatience, ultimately leaving her own underwear a cause for concern. Aliette wants to get out her clothes and wash the sweat off… She wants more than that. She thinks of Martine and Josiane and Julie, all the girls at Mari Morgan's, taking off their clothes, reclining…

Shhh, Aliette, it's just a job… You sound like Claude.

It's not work, fucking people.

No? Well then it's not work looking for people either, is it?…All it is, is walking and thinking.

She's dripping sweat when she finally stops. *Ondine:* stencilled unobtrusively on the glass above the door handle. The inspector is not even sure she's still inside the quarter. This street is so rundown. She checks her hands for grease before wiping the salty layer from her brow. There are three oily mechanics conferring at the place across the street. Peaches and cherries in boxes outside the épicerie next door are turning. She can smell sugar being boiled somewhere near. Ugh! it seems like a crime to add sugar to the weight of the air… The *couturière's* window fits right into the gritty scene: a bald plaster mannequin standing in barren isolation in a plain white peignoir. Poor thing: no hair, a chipped finger, Aliette can't see how she'll ever find a place in anyone's fantasy. But the endorphins—great for a run, not so great when trying to stay cool—subside. Looking at it a second time, re-focused, the peignoir in the window is as elegant and finely made as any the sweetest bride might ever wish for. And as fine as Manon Larivière's chemise. A bell tinkles overhead as the inspector steps inside.

The front room contains a hardback chair and a threadbare rug. No displays. No mirrors. The woman comes out from the back. It's the woman behind the veils at the funeral: tall, thin to a worrisome degree, and much older than Aliette had first made out. Still, with that long medieval nose, that stubborn equine mouth—Georgette's sister, no question about it. "Ondine?" The woman nods like a mournful Boris Karloff. "I'd like to order a camisole, if I might."

Aliette endures her scrutiny. The vivid foresty green of Georgette's eyes is replaced by fading hazel; but the aspect—that faint, probing scorn—it's another shared family trait. Finally, making a gesture, Ondine Duguay says flatly, "Very well…come through."

Back of the shop's a different story. A busy workshop. An old stand-alone Singer sewing machine predominates. A centre table is cluttered with tools and cuttings, several items in the works. There are bobbins arranged on a smaller table, bundles of ribbon, jars of beads, bales of materials, and a rack hung with partially finished and repaired garments. Three more dressmaker's mannequins, each as old and chipped and bald as their sister in the front, stand in the corner by the window gazing out at the small yard littered with apples from one small tree, a dried-out clapboard fence, the drab alley, the backs of houses on the other side. "Would you take off your top, please?" The inspector obliges. Ondine measures with an experienced squint, stepping to her table to note each one, stone silent as she goes through this procedure. Until she asks, "What colour?"

"You make such lovely things. My friend had one in a pearly pink tone, with this exquisite trim, and a monogram down around here…" Touching her right hip bone. "What colour do you think?"

Ondine Duguay again peruses her with what once could have been the lovely eyes of a willowy girl as she considers Aliette's eyes and skin. "A steely blue that's almost grey will be perfect. How did you find me?"

"It wasn't easy."

"I'm very exclusive."

"Exclusive? Madame, it's as though you're hiding. I've never been on this street in almost nine years in this quarter and walking is one of my favourite activities… Does steely blue get the trim?"

"Yes, yes…" With a touch of crankiness that has a familiar ring as she measures from Aliette's shoulder to the mid-point of her buttock. "Who is your friend?"

"Her name is Manon. You were at her funeral this morning."

Ondine steps around to face Aliette. "Just who are you?"

"My name is Aliette Nouvelle. Police Judiciaire."

"Ahh…I was thinking you belonged to the baker. So it's you— our new champion."

This is cold and catty and from out of nowhere. Aliette blushes and bristles before she can find words. Bloody *Paris-Match*. "I have no control over what they write…I try to do my job."

Ondine's bleak gaze cuts through her excuses. "What do you want with me?"

"Some answers."

"I haven't set foot in that place in years."

"How many years?"

"Ten, at least…eleven, twelve. I've lost count. I've put that place behind me." But Ondine's tight face is getting more so by the second.

"And Herméné?"

"He's out of my life."

"But still in your mind, Ondine—it's quite plain to see."

Ondine goes back to her table and notes another measurement. "A sore spot, Inspector, to be sure. But life is like that, is it not? We have to carry on."

"We have to try… Did you know Manon?"

"Your *friend?* I knew someone who called herself Manon. Still a girl the last time I saw her."

"Forty-four when she died. Not a girl at all."

"Whoever she was, she was quite lost in someone else's supposed personality and I gather she stayed that way till he killed her."

"I'm sure she wasn't so different underneath it all. None of us are, not even the stars." Aliette picks a full-panted silk culotte from the rack, almost like a man's boxers, and holds it to her waist, testing its attraction. "But you accepted her? You liked her?"

"She was not an unkind person. I accepted lots of strange women when I lived there. No, you're right—none of them were that different underneath."

"But still," the inspector wonders aloud, "how do they arrange themselves? Who leads, who follows?"

"Some were harder than others…at the core. Some were very hard indeed. That was the difference."

"Flossie Orain?"

Ondine is not sure. She considers it. Her face is more transparent than her sister's. Older, younger? Aliette can't guess. "Flossie Orain is another generation," comes the answer, a shade sardonic. "In fact she's like you…something admirable, I could sense it whenever I saw her… Admirable, and something else I'll never understand at all. All I really know about Flossie is her sizes. And now yours as well."

"I'm only a woman."

"Time changes us, Inspector."

"And Louise?"

"Very strong."

"Happy?"

A cold shrug: What the hell does that mean?

"Why were you there, Ondine?"

"I was with him. They accepted me…a family of sorts."

"You still do their things."

"They still like my things. I have to survive, the same as anyone."

"Why don't you set up in a better place…downtown, where people can find you?"

"I'm not interested in business any more. I just want to do my work."

"You sound a lot like someone I know. Someone you know as well."

"Another friend?"

"Georgette Duguay."

Ondine looks up from her notes, only for a moment, then continues with her figuring. "Just a name from the past. There's nothing there at all… She lost a fight and walked away."

"But who did you lose to, Ondine? Manon, perhaps?" Or would that be Marilyn Monroe?

"Please…" as if the implication were absurd; "I left. It was my business. I ran it and I made it what it was. But I got sick of being associated with his sort."

"His sort? You were partners."

"We were lovers. I made a mistake."

"Getting involved in the business?"

"Getting involved with faceless people. All the so-called friends it took to make sure nothing ever changed. We were protected, we were enjoyed, we were despised, we didn't exist…all the while, Herméné slapped backs and shared bodies. I couldn't do much about it, so I left."

"What did you want to do about it?"

"I don't know… Give it some integrity. Give it some rights and some meaning. You can hate it, but it's there and it always will be. And I got tired of the gimmicks… That poor girl: who was she? That's the tragedy."

"Why would he kill her?"

"Maybe she wasn't giving him what he wanted."

"I'm told she was the best. Very popular. What more could he hope for?"

"Maybe she was getting tired of it. Maybe she wanted out. Forty-four, you say?"

"But the American…the image is eternal."

"Maybe that was the problem."

"Time changes us?"

"*Voilà…*"

The seamstress has what she needs. Aliette puts her blouse back on. "May I look upstairs?"

Ondine gestures blankly: suit yourself. Aliette climbs the stairs in the corner.

Just a kitchen overlooking the yard—with a bathroom attached, and a bed-sitting room over the street. No keepsakes by the bed. No photos of the young girl who had grown into this joyless woman. Nor of an ex-lover who is now in trouble. Nor of an estranged sister…

But in the closet Aliette finds treasures! It's packed to bursting with bustiers, camisoles, corsets and culottes, negligees and slips…all made of pure cottons, laces and silks and fashioned in all the finest conceptions of elegance and romance she has ever seen or read about, harking back to the turn of the century. Each item is a showpiece, perfect in every detail. Opening an ancient hatbox, her over-eager fingers cause a tiny rip in the felt-covered cardboard… Oh là là! A billowy boudoir bonnet, circa 1915, made of ninon silk, festooned with a bouquet of satin flowers. I need to try it on! *No. You're working…* But what she'd give for such a piece! Place it between her brown Derby from England and her Dodger-blue LA baseball hat from America… This stony Ondine's an artist.

The sad irony is that Aliette can't picture Ondine in any of her own creations.

Mmm…a joyless woman. But the centre of the universe? Of course she could have been; it's a perception that depends on the one you're "with," n'est-ce pas? Aliette senses a much more fragile sort. And all the more so when she places her beside someone with the force of Georgette.

Replacing the hat in its box, she shuts the closet gently and goes back down.

"Are those crab apples?" The tree is glittery and magical in the light of the late afternoon sun.

"Sorb apples. They're good, but you have to let them rot a bit… From corruption, sweetness, is what we say."

"Who is we?"

"We who believe it to be true."

Well… *Wait. Build some trust.* All right. All right…"Ondine, investigation or not, I really would like that top."

The woman actually smiles. "And you shall have it. Come by Monday and try it on."

She escorts Aliette to the front. Feeling pally…at least accepted, the inspector ventures, "If it weren't such a sad day I'd ask you to sing me the song about Mari Morgan."

"Oh, I don't sing any more…that's for a younger woman. One with a strong heart and an active spirit. Is that you, Inspector?"

"I do my best, Ondine… Tell me, is Mari Morgan real or not?"

"Oh yes. Quite real…quite alive."

"Where is she?"

"At the door to Paradise, welcoming all pure souls." With a vacant-eyed bow, she ushers Aliette out the door. "Please…I've had a tiring day. I will see you Monday. End of the day would be best."

The bell tinkles. The street is empty now, everyone home eating supper. Piaf will be waiting.

<h2 style="text-align:center">6.</h2>

A shower, a bite, and straight back out. No drawing group on a Friday night, but no time to relax either. See you later, my Piaf. Have to put some things down on paper for the Instructing Judge.

But one more visit first. The door to the sixth-floor apartment in a respectable building at the top of the park is answered by Léonie, a trim woman in her fifties with pencilled-in eyebrows. "The doctor's non-live-in…clean, cook, shop a bit, check to see he's still alive in the morning." The doctor has not yet returned from the funeral. Something about a picnic near the grave site. "No, not worried. He spends a lot of afternoons with them…usually makes it in for his supper. I feed him and then go home."

"He left by himself?"

"Oh yes, very independent."

"Still drives, then?"

"I wouldn't call it that…I gather his friend Herméné pulls strings to help him keep his permit. I refuse to go with him. But he always seems to arrive."

"They're close, Monsieur Dupras and the doctor?"

"I've only met him over the phone. But yes," allows the maid, "he's always calling to check on Marcel. At least once a day. Seems like a nice man. He's almost like family, really…I gather they've known each other since forever." She's already closing the door. Without a mandate, an inspector has no right to enter and this Léonie seems to know it. Musing, "But you never know about people, do you?"

Aliette Nouvelle agrees: you never do. Leaving her card, she asks Léonie to make sure the doctor gets in touch. *From corruption, sweetness.* A nice idea. Does that old man believe what Ondine believes? And a pute called Flossie Orain: what does she believe? What she needs is a mandate for an in-depth chat with Marcel Cyr. And Ondine Duguay. And *them*—all of them, but especially her. Flossie. And that chemise: I believe we should have that chemise back out of the ground and in to the best lab money can buy...

Working late as thunder rumbles in the distance. Trying to give it some form, legal integrity, a compelling shape a judge will have to notice. Unless the inspector's summary report can sway the Instructing Judge, they will likely be proceeding under a murder mandate aimed expressly at Herméné Dupras. If they go for him it means that, legally, her own first thoughts will be considered extraneous, and so all the more difficult to explore.

But there's something else here and the inspector works to etch it clearly.

There's lightning cracking over the city now, the wind whipping up, chill gusts whistle in the courtyard outside her office window. A storm coming down from the mountains.

Good. Rain. Rain like hell. Just do it!

She shuts the window, gets back to work.

It's summer, she's alone. She feels a need to explore.

2ND PART
DÉTENTION PROVISOIRE

Four months maximum; the charge is laid;
both sides build their case.

"Man is a demi-god: he always has either one foot or the other in the grave; woman is divine because she can keep both her feet always in the same place, whether in the sky, in the underworld, or on this earth. Man envies her and tells himself lies about his own completeness, and thereby makes himself miserable; because if he is divine, she is not even a demi-goddess—she is a mere nymph and his love for her turns to scorn and hate."

—Robert Graves,
The White Goddess

- 4 -
SPEAKING OF LOVE

It rains, the air clears, people decide not to kill themselves. Or their spouses or their neighbours or their neighbours' dogs. Residual drops falling from charming medieval eaves and the leaves of hovering plane trees are like blessings for the clean new morning, lightly touching people's heads as they venture out: it's OK, it's over now, let's all just get back to business. It's a Saturday but the city complies, buzzing, working twice as hard, as if secretly ashamed for anything untoward it may have said or done, the whole place acting as if it never happened.

But one person *has* been killed. It happened. And so Chief Judge of Instruction Gérard Richand has also come in today, in anticipation of clearing out next Friday for his own hard-earned month in the sun.

Because community pressures are too often liable to inform the decisions of a Procureur, and because more visceral pressures can weigh on the actions of a cop, the system has created the Judge of Instruction. Not a judge *per se*, the kind you meet in a courtroom, the J.of I.'s role is to more or less referee the investigation, keeping it fair and clean for all involved. He (or she; lots now) literally instructs the Police as to their rights and scope while in the process of investigating; he conducts his own interviews and has the means to order his own investigation if he feels the need. Then he reports back to the Procureur as to whether the facts, the suspect, and, indeed, the crime fit the charge, recommending: Yes, it looks like this one did it; or:

Maybe, but let's find out more; or: No case to answer here, the suspect should be released and we should look elsewhere. There are countless nuances, legal, political and systemic within this basic range.

Two gendarmes escort Herménégilde Dupras down to *le Palais de Justice* for an interview.

The eight Judges allotted to Aliette's sub-prefecture occupy a musty corner on the third floor of the Palais, a fortress fashioned in the blocky Second Empire style. Their offices overlook a quad whose geometric pathways are shaded by plane trees and coloured by beds of well-planned flowers. Gérard Richand is a man who appreciates the civilized atmosphere; to him, the landscaping motif reflects the fact that the law is rational but not devoid of personality and he always aims to conduct his affairs accordingly. His office windows are open wide. The new breeze allows both men to relax somewhat—a sense of clarity seems to have returned. Sipping tea with lemon, finishing a plate of biscuits, they've worked carefully through the things Herméné does and does not remember relating to the night of August 5th. Monsieur le Juge has offered a cigarette, the prisoner has accepted. They smoke at a measured pace and the discussion turns toward the philosophical.

"Well, why her?" asks Gérard. "Why would she choose that American?"

Herméné watches a ray of sun play on the toe of his shoe as he considers the judge's query. "I suppose it's not quite accurate to say she just picked her out of a hat… From what I gather, she found a photo and realized she could do a good job of her. More like a natural choice, if you look at the two women."

"I mean, why now? The face—why does it still work?"

"It's the times. When I was a boy, most clients were more than satisfied with the new body, the momentary change of attitude, a bit of unencumbered fun… Now, it's different. I think it's access to the special they're all looking for. I don't even think it's really the sex any more…not deep down."

"Not the sex?" Gérard Richand is dubious.

Herméné Dupras can read it. "…well, just look at poor Manon and her American movie queen."

"I have. But what's the attraction?"

"Exactly, monsieur: this pouty, slightly stupid-looking blonde from the American movie factory. Yet she charmed sports heroes, artists and the President of the United States… Better than that: some even say our own magnificent Montand, when he played opposite her. Why? God knows. Maybe it was just one big snowball effect. But she endures, doesn't she? A star, and people love her. They talk about her vulnerability. I suppose there's something in that. Personally, I think it's mostly on account of television—I mean, if you want my opinion." In fact, explains Herméné, chat-show hosts, journalists out covering wars, and fashion-smart cuties who foretell the weather are also now among the pantheon of goddesses that clients came looking to touch at Mari Morgan's.

Hearing this, the judge is moved to consider one particular woman who reports on local news stories. Every night she sends her magnetic smile from various points around the city straight into his bedroom. He has himself, maybe a dozen times now, spoken into her outstretched microphone. He can't say he knows her and probably doesn't want to; professionally, he resents her presence in the halls of the Palais. It's numbing, and dangerous, too, in that one can never remember the actual answering; one must watch later on to see what one has said. Once on the screen, however, she becomes something else again. She distracts him from his wife and this bothers him. But he never misses the news… Gérard sighs and puts it out of his mind. "When you were a boy, you say. What do you mean by that? How exactly does a man like you get involved in your kind of business?"

Herméné's answer to that one is straightforward enough. "I was born into it."

Incredulous, but still smiling, Gérard folds his arms across his belly. He's here to listen.

Herméné was born in a house similar to Mari Morgan's, in a small town to the south, "in 1922, on St.Valentine's Day, to be precise," returning the judge's smile—he has always been proud of his birthday. Most children born under such circumstances, and there were many, usually stayed until their fourth birthday at the very latest, then were sent to orphanages or relatives; or they went with their mothers to a new, and, everyone hoped, more stable life. But because his mother owned the place, along with Jean, his stepfather, he'd grown up in close and comfortable proximity to sin. "*Les Violettes*. The place had seen better days by the time I arrived…had been going strong in one form or another for sixty-odd years. Paggiole listed us in his original directory—a remarkable compendium, monsieur, covering almost any town or city one might happen to visit in France and north Africa, and all the major cities of Belgium, Holland, Italy, Spain and Switzerland; and people could always find us in *Le Gervais* or *Le guide rose* after Paggiole was banned from publication. My mother and Jean were doing a good trade on closing day, and, I guess there's no harm admitting it now, for a few more quiet years after that…"

On April 13, 1945, the *maisons closes* of Paris were ordered shut in compliance with the newly passed *Marthe-Richard* law. At the time it seemed like the ultimate victory for the moralizing *non* side in a political war that had been going on since the beginning of the nineteenth century. The houses in the regions around the country all followed suit, albeit in no great hurry.

"Your mother was a whore?" asks Gérard, not offensively—never offensively—but pointedly, hoping to hit a sore spot.

"I only knew her as *la patrone*, monsieur. And she was as bourgeois as…well—as you perhaps?" But yes, *Maman* had been a whore: a smart one, who allowed the right man to fall in love with her. Together they bought the house from another couple who had met and prospered in quite the same fashion a generation before. As was the custom, Madame acted as hostess while Monsieur worked in the background, on the plumbing, for example, or driving to the station to meet a new girl. "But he was a bookkeeper by profession, so he could help with other things…" Such as their taxes, which they paid without error as they cultivated their connections and served the community…or at least part of it. "My mother always went to mass with her head up, monsieur, make no mistake."

Herméné however, was the inevitable result of a momentary lapse. It occurred when his mother decided, against all good judgement, to try a "tryer." Tryers were an obscure class of itinerant men who entered houses such as *Les Violettes* with the express professional duty of testing and reporting on the skills of recently arrived girls. The tryer was wined and dined as if he were the most honoured guest, then sent along to sample the charms of the new Marie or Pierrette. When he was done and had reported, he was paid and then forgotten until his services were required again.

"Lucky bastards," mutters the judge.

Not so. Herméné shakes his head. Most men reacted that way when they learned of the tryer's trade because, on first hearing, it did sound like a great job—perhaps one of the best ever invented. In truth however, the lot of the tryer had more in common with that of the opium eater than the lolling pasha. Most were wandering flesh addicts, consumed by a never-to-be-filled need. This need may have made them useful to the industry, but it left them alone and highly distracted at the end of the work day. Most tryers died alone and empty, in every sense of the word, more often than not the raving victim of advanced venereal disease. Herméné's father, Gros Paul, as the ladies of the district came to know him, had been one such accursed fellow. "I could not kiss my dying father adieu, monsieur, for fear of catching something…"

But the man, when he'd been around, had taught his son everything there was to know about carnal pleasure; and, despite the ignominious ending, Herméné could always take professional pride in the fact that when Gros Paul had been at the peak of his career, the women with whom he was paired were known to reappear in the drawing room later that evening imbued with a new sense of inspiration (not to say craft) for their trade. Gros Paul's report, though duly heard and discussed, was always slightly redundant. Madame could tell at a glance she had a winner in the new (often just fifteen or sixteen) wide-eyed Suzette; or that jaded-looking Julianne just in from Brussels knew her business despite the red-rimmed pin-prick eyes born of too much belladonna. Gros Paul did not just test and approve quality, he instilled it.

Herméné's mother, Jeanne, to the everlasting contempt of her partner and husband Jean, had been curious. This large lady (about as large as Herméné), who'd left the sheets behind to become a diligent and dispassionate manager, had, since her move to management, learned to fend off the desire for the taste of something more exotic, and, let's be honest, more ultimate than her husband, by subsuming it in the sweet taste of a pastry or two whenever the urge came on. "…But she let all that self-control go by the boards after seeing one too many blissful smiles planted on the faces of her newest charges. She told me: Herménégilde, one afternoon I just said to hell with the *gateaux*—this Gros Paul is something I should know about."

"You were a business decision."

"You are very perceptive, monsieur… That's exactly what she told me whenever she was angry: Herméné, you were strictly business, and not very smart business at that!" And he leans toward the judge, confiding, "It took me a bit of time to sort that one out."

Gérard nods…go on, sensing he has tapped a weak spot in the pimp's thick armour.

Indeed, Madame Jeanne's recurring harsh words linking her son's conception with careless business practices, and her love of pastry which always seemed more dear than her love for him, brought on identity problems in early adolescence, the physical marks of which were his obesity and high blood pressure. The child had been wounded and remained so. However, the mother's boy was also the father's son. Herméné entered manhood and the trade, first as a *videur*—a bouncer, with an innate and completely accurate feeling for sexual enjoyment. And that was good for business. When Herméné gained controlling interest of the house that was to become Mari Morgan's—in 1952, when the tryer's trade was long since obsolete and the business of running a house could no longer be legally registered as such—one of his first moves was to re-institute his father's craft to a more or less official standing… "with myself, of course, as the tryer."

"Of course."

"I made it a house rule. But the trouble with regulations, monsieur, in my experience at least, is that people interpret them in different ways. They get too emotional. They don't know how to separate business from other things."

Gérard suggests, "This Manon Larivière broke the rules in deciding to leave, so you put a knife in her."

"*Mais non!* You misunderstand." Herméné's point is that, professionally speaking, it was simply prudent to carry on the tradition of Gros Paul. It meant that when he presented a girl who bore his personal stamp of approval the buyer would know she had to be special, worth every franc Herméné was going to charge. Knowing everything there was to know about his girls had played a major part in the success of Mari Morgan's. But it was by no means the easy way to go: women tended to get jealous. Some men, too. "She, Manon, must have displeased someone… Or maybe I did." Herméné pauses, holding his hands over his eyes, trying again to fathom it, "but I just don't know who or how or why."

"Maybe she didn't want to play her little role any longer."

"Of course she did. This notion of leaving us, I really believe it was just a sort of hysterical whim brought on by her condition. It would have passed by morning, poor thing…"

"And Marilyn Monroe?"

"She loved it."

"Why?"

"Because *they* loved it. The clients. Check my books." A disclaimer: "…of course they're not about the business as such. As far as taxes for services go, Mari Morgan's is an apartment-hotel."

"We know all about it."

"But we have a profit-sharing plan and it's all there. I can interpret it for you at your pleasure. My Manon was building a solid nest-egg, monsieur. She was at the peak of her career. Look-alikes make money, believe me."

Gérard has to laugh. "Profit sharing…I like that… Pimps are the original profit sharers."

"I resent that!" Herméné is on his feet. "I am not a pimp, monsieur! If that's what you think then you have no idea…" Holding firm till the judge backs away from this squalid assumption.

The two attending cops are waiting outside Monsieur le Juge's door; and there's a button fixed to the underside of his desktop he can push if necessary, if he perceives a threat…which will be included in the charge. But acquiescence is the better part of assessment. Gérard Richand rolls his eyes, puffs in a nervous way on his cigarette, and backs off.

Herméné sits and continues: Types, and the fetishes they tingled, were timeless: nuns, pubescent girls, school teachers, housemaids and ballerinas, the kindly nurse and the more violent modern dominatrices clad in steel and leather; or women who looked and acted like executive vice-presidents; all were available upon request. But look-alikes, at first just a hunch on Herméné's part, were fast becoming the most fun of all. It started quietly, with an Englishwoman, strangely enough, an alcoholic called Sue, who, when lucid, could affect a remarkable resemblance to the then young English queen. "Sue's Elizabeth… It was just a joke, good for a laugh in the bar sometimes, or, more usually, for the sleepy pleasure of the girls and myself over coffee in the morning. The foreign words didn't mean much, but we could hear the accent and see the royal mouth pointed so very correctly as she spoke. I overheard an English client wishing out loud one evening in the bar and I thought, why not? When the Englishman returned on his next business trip he was offered his wish—and it worked. The most pleasing thing was that poor Sue was actually happy for a year, with a new sense of purpose and the pet corgi we gave her for a prop. Soon Bardot became a standard…and still is, for men of a certain age. There's always one girl on staff who can do her with ten minutes notice. I mean, film stars…" A large gesture here, indicating the obvious: they were made to be loved. Schneider, Deneuve, Ardant, Adjani …or, looking in the opposite direction: Moreau, Signoret, Michèle Morgan and Arletty— because "older men can have powerful dreams too, monsieur, and they are very loyal customers"—they had all performed their magic for the exclusive pleasure of Herméné's clientele.

Monsieur le Juge lets the prisoner talk, thinking he would let him dig himself a deep hole where he could spend the rest of his life.

"All you need," says Herméné, now gazing out the window, remembering less complicated times, "if you have a good group, and by that I mean a happy group, a creative group!…all you need is a subscription to *Paris-Match*."

"*Paris-Match*?" Gérard's wife subscribes.

"…or *Life* magazine, monsieur. America! Not long after the Queen of England left the scene we created an exquisite copy of Elizabeth Taylor, about thirteen years old, with that lovely white skin.

Some of my more sentimental clients brought their sons in for their first experiences. Those were happy boys, if ever I saw any."

"What happened to the Queen?"

"Oh…well, she was killed, as a matter of fact. In the street, after she'd left us. Strangled… Girls are a lot safer when they have each other and a solid roof over their heads."

Life magazine: now it wasn't such a force in pricking the public's imagination. But Grace Kelly, or "…the wife of the American president! When she was in mourning? The sunglasses? The kerchief? Many men were touched. They wanted to hold her and make it better. We provided that opportunity. Oh yes, for a while there, we always kept a copy of *Life* magazine close at hand…" But Herméné is fretful. "It all seems like so long ago, especially after something so tragic as my poor Manon."

"Monsieur Dupras," advises Gérard after a respectful moment, "there are at least ten excellent motives for murder in your statement to me. It would make everything so much simpler, and less costly to the state, if you would specify the one which actually impelled you."

"Monsieur," replies Herméné, "I am not cynical, so please don't you be. Until you and your colleagues believe that I love those girls, that I loved Manon especially and that there is no reason on this earth why I would do such a thing as was done to her…that they are my bread and butter…that I was drugged and I have been framed in the most vicious way!…well, you and I will not make any progress at all."

"More's the pity for you." Gérard's fascination has come full circle and is now arriving back at a deep sense of revulsion. "How can you speak of love?" he demands. "It's disgusting!"

Herméné has to pause. Is love really such an incongruous element? He spreads his arms, shrugging as largely as he's able. "Monsieur, we live in the same house…are involved in the same business; we share many things. One becomes attached. I insist again: Manon was a wonderful girl! Full of joy… You know, she could make me come while laughing heartily at the same moment."

"What?" A lob shot; the judge is taken by surprise. No context he can apply in returning…

"I told you: she was a very talented woman. Why would I kill such a one as her?"

"Mon Dieu…" sighs Chief J.of I. Gérard Richand, turning to a fresh page (in much the same manner as Commissaire Néon had done). "Explain, monsieur…please explain that!"

Of course Herméné would explain. But why did they get so angry?

THE GODDESS

A liette sleeps late, awakes refreshed. Bearing flowers from Herménégilde Dupras, she jumps another puddle and lands at the brothel door. Lynda's at the front desk. They've set up a small memorial: flowers in a vase with Manon's room key attached to a black ribbon slung around its neck. Leaning against the vase is that same photo depicting their late colleague in her lamé dress, platinum hair swept up to the right, eyes merry, scarlet mouth stretched wide in laughter.

"Flossie?"

"Upstairs…"

In Manon's room a woman is sitting at the desk, hunched over a book, nursing a glass of milk. A woman? She's probably about seventeen. Her unpacked bag is open on the bed. Since Flossie Orain's door is shut this morning, Aliette taps on hers instead. "Bonjour…"

"Bonjour. I…I, uh, don't think we're open quite yet."

"It's all right…" presenting her medal as she enters; "my name is Inspector Nouvelle."

"Oh… My name is Vivienne." She stands and extends her hand. "…Vivi. I'm new."

"But you know why I'm here?"

She nods. Lush eyebrows and extravagant sienna eyes add gravity to a sallow and delicate heart-shaped face. "It's very sad… She was the best… It's an art, you know. And he just killed her."

"And you're her replacement?"

"Yes."

"But aren't you afraid?…I mean, isn't it a bit strange sitting here in her room?"

"No… They've got him. Why would I be afraid?"

Facing this Vivi's expression, the inspector has to suppress a blush; yes, it was a stupid thing to ask. But the next logical question is still more gauche. "How old are you, Vivi?"

"Old enough," is the easy reply.

Alors…another awkward pause. Aliette sighs. "I'm sorry, but I don't understand."

"Understand?"

"Why you would come here."

"Something to do. Nothing much happening in my life… I can make good money."

"So I'm told."

"And maybe I'll have some family."

"Family? Don't you have anyone?"

"Only my mother." This with a blasé shrug.

"Does your mother know you're here?"

"*Mais oui…* She sent me."

The girl's not lying. The inspector gapes as the weight of this settles, not sure whom she should hate. Vivi, clearly a veteran at meeting distraught stares, sips her milk and turns back to her book.

"What are you reading?"

"It's a verse."

"May I look?" Yes… Aliette bends and reads the lines.

> *Song of Amergin*:
> I am a roebuck displaying seven tines
> I am a floodwater covering the fields
> I am a wind over a deep lake
> I am the tears of the Sun.
> I am a falcon circling the ledge
> I am a bramble hooked in the skin
> I am the perfection in every garden
> I am an enchanter—who else
> will set the whispering voice to song?

I am a battle-waging spear
I am a fish turning 'neath the surface
I am a call beckoning from paradise
I am a path where poets wander.
I am a charging boar
I am a gathering wave
I am the current inside the tide
I am a child—who else
sees through the unshaped sacred stone?

I am the knot in every weave.
I am the glow on every ridge.
I am the queen of every hive.
I am armour for every heart.
I am the tomb of every hope.

Repeating the last line aloud. "I am the tomb of every hope…"

"I have to study it," says Vivi. "It's part of my apprenticeship."

"But what does it mean?"

"Flossie says it's about love."

"Flossie says that?"

But the apprentice pute is looking at her, telling her to please leave her alone. Same eyes Aliette uses when she too wants some privacy. "Sorry," Vivi adds, gently—a nice girl; "it's my first day, you see…"

2.

The bar is sombre on a quiet Saturday morning. Aliette Nouvelle faces Flossie Orain and Louise Lebraz, still in their nightgowns. "What is that girl doing here?"

"She's going to work," replies Louise with cool disdain, not happy at having been yanked from her bed by an agitated cop. Flossie gives Louise's arm a calming rub and speaks to the inspector's righteous implications. "Vivi came of her own free will and with her mother's blessing. She's free to leave whenever she wants."

"With a decent bank account and a hell of a lot more sense about the world than when she arrived," adds the prickly redhead.

"I'll show you the letters if you like," offers Flossie.

Like Tweedledum and Tweedledee, but harder to enjoy.

The inspector asks, "What letters?"

"From her mother, practically begging me to take her Vivi in with us."

"You know her mother?"

Flossie shrugs. "I used to. She's had a lousy life. Met the wrong people."

"Was she…did she work here?"

"No."

"Then how could she possibly want her daughter to—"

"Because," says Louise, "it will be better here than anything she could ever give her out there."

"Ah, *voyons madame!*" Are you serious?

Yes, Louise is. "Vivi gives her body. Vivi gets a life." Simple.

"I won't let you."

"It's her choice."

"And you know how impossible it is," adds Flossie, not without some apology in her voice.

She's right. Mari Morgan's is registered as an apartment-hotel, essentially a private dwelling. In accordance with the French obsession with privacy, the law forbids the authorities from bursting in anywhere private from between nine in the evening and six in the morning without due cause. Which makes it difficult, and usually more trouble than it's worth.

Louise Lebraz smiles—with no apology at all. "It's a business like any other."

"Yes? And what if she ends up like you?" Trying to hit something…somewhere.

Louise feels nothing. "…a business in an industry. The sex industry. What are you going to do about it?"

What am I going to do about it? Give it some integrity? Some rights and meaning? Ondine Duguay's bleak notions are echoing in this still room. But Aliette, who's a cop and not a politician, much less a stony old seamstress, has no ready answer. She can only move forward, into the case. She asks, "Is this some kind of cult?"

Flossie Orain's perpetually interested eyes register laughter. "Where did you get that idea?"

"Ondine Duguay."

"This is a house," states Louise. "We have some ideas we share that make it a home."

"What are you—witches?"

"We're prostitutes, Inspector. Whores. We don't make soup with toads and snakes. We fuck, and otherwise offer and perform a wide range of sexual services. Please try to keep that straight in your mind."

Yin to Louise's yang, Flossie remains conciliatory. "Ondine hasn't been in our house for several years now, and we'll do our best to protect her from this thing. She's not exactly young any more. We're not going to let her connection to Herménégilde Dupras mean the wrong thing."

Aliette sneers. "I'm sure she appreciates it." Flossie's niceness is wearing thin.

"What about Manon!" demands Louise, disengaging from Flossie's arm, sitting forward to meet the police head on. "You don't like what we do so you spend the taxpayer's money digging up an old woman who makes underwear, and getting on your moral high horse over another new girl in the business. Why don't you leave us alone and do your job?"

"Louise, two days ago everyone here including you was telling me this case was about love! Fine. I can go along with that—love is always a good reason for murder. Much better than money. But if it's about love, then it's a two-way street: the victim's love, and the suspect's. Ondine Duguay was in love with the suspect and she lived in this house. These things all relate... No?"

No answer. They only watch her. Two whores sitting in judgement. This is disconcerting.

"You say I'm being moralistic. Well, no offence to the sex industry—heaven forbid that we should offend the sex industry—but if it's about love, it's about self-respect and when I meet a girl like that one studying to be a prostitute, I have to wonder what kind of love you're talking about! Sorry—I wasn't raised to be in the sex industry. I don't know anyone who was!"

"Herméné," notes Flossie.

"Right," sighs Aliette.

"You don't know anything about us," sniffs Louise.

Aliette massages the slight pulsing in her temple. Her mouth is dry. "When does the bar open, by the way?" She chews on her thumbnail, looking from one pair of pute-eyes to the other. "It would be nice if we could work together on this."

"Only on the case, Inspector…not our lives." Louise again.

Flossie gets up and goes around behind the bar. "What would you like?"

"Beer."

Louise heckles: "It's not even noon…you have a problem?" Aliette just nods: Yes, Louise—guess who? Flossie brings a bottle and glass and places them on the table; makes a be-right-back sign as she walks out of the room, across the foyer and up the stairs. The inspector pours her beer slowly, watching it rise, hoping Louise will go away as well. She takes a sip…wipes the foam from her upper lip. It tastes good, it calms her down. She drinks. Louise continues to sit there.

Flossie returns bearing the old book Vivi was reading, and a bundle of stationary wrapped in an elastic band.

A red book—no title is inscribed in the faded morocco binding. Nor overleaf. And no author's name is ascribed. Only "Ondine Duguay," written in fountain pen, clearly many years before. Aliette turns a page. The yellowed paper is thick between her fingers. She reads aloud. "*Must all things swing round and round forever? Or how can man escape from the wheel?*" After another sip of her beer she comments, "That's a pretty big question for a little girl."

"A basic problem," corrects Flossie, leaning across the table and opening the book to a page in the middle. "It's Druidic…" There's Vivi's verse: *Song of Amergin.*

"Who is Amergin?"

"We don't know. It's a collection of Celtic poems and stories, but they could have come from anywhere. Amergin?…maybe he was Syrian or Greek or Welsh or Egyptian; it doesn't really matter. This is a calendar."

"A calendar? Vivi said it's about love."

"It *is* about love," says Flossie; "love between light and dark, weak and strong, masculine and feminine…love between the elements, the love of life that accepts death, and the aspects of death that give back again to life…and love. A year is a cycle, a wheel. The verse ties all these things together." Flossie smiles. "Vivi will have to know these things… We all have to. It's how you get off the wheel."

The inspector sits back, sips a little more beer, absorbing. Her eye finds the motto carved along the top of the mirror: *I am the hostess of the irreproachable Ferry Tavern, a white gowned moon welcoming any man who comes to me with silver.* Gesturing at it: "Is that Mari Morgan talking?"

"No, that's the goddess."

"And the goddess is not Mari Morgan?"

"Mari Morgan is fate…she's the one who takes us off the wheel and delivers us to the goddess. There's a difference."

"Will Vivi understand that?"

"I hope so. It's why we have to teach her."

"And Herméné Dupras knows nothing about it."

"If he does, he doesn't care… Never much for the spiritual side, our Herméné."

"Do you hide it?"

"Not at all. But we don't shove it down anyone's throat, either. It's only for us."

"Why?"

Louise rises from her chair. She looks down at Aliette with a kind of pity—just a hint. "Because everything we do here, from our milk in the morning till the last happy little businessman is put out the door, is for something better. That's why." With that, she leaves the room.

Flossie watches after Louise, wistful, maybe sympathetic too, then expands on the notion of improvement. "When men get jealous. When they get sentimental and weak. When all they care about is the shape of your ass. When they try to control what they worship and then worship what they control. There's the wheel, Aliette…Manon and that one who killed her were spinning around on it, full tilt! The goddess gives us strength to cope."

"Do you hate men?"

"No…although when you scrape the surface, most of them aren't worth much more than the money in their pockets. I like them…I like sex. But I thank my stars I'm not in thrall to any of them."

"In thrall?"

"Married to, in love with, working for, dependent on…I've had every man I've ever wanted." Flossie is blank for a moment. She asks, "Do you like men?"

"It doesn't matter what I like. What about Louise…does she like men…does she like anything?"

"There are men in this city who have given up sex forever after going up with Louise…I almost gave up sex after going up with Louise." Again that gauzy mix of sly and shy.

Aliette wrinkles her brow, not amused. What was worse: Louise's bite or Flossie's solicitude?

"Louise is right," continues Flossie. "You seem more worried about us and what we do than about the murder of our friend. Louise was expecting that you would be more—"

"More automatic in my response to Herméné and the murder?"

"More open minded about us… We read about you. We thought you would be a different kind of woman." Shaking her head, acknowledging an apparent mistake; and the inspector is shaking hers: sorry to be so normal… Flossie reaches over and pats the inspector's hand. "Only you know what you need. As long as you're happy. You seem happy. That's what's interesting about you."

"Stop it, Flossie."

"I'm attracted to you."

"Well, don't be. Please." A professional smile, totally neutral. Another sip of beer. "Who brought your goddess…and Mari Morgan?"

"Not our goddess…*the* goddess. Ondine."

"Before you?'

"Long before me."

"And Manon was here before you?"

"Yes."

"Could the goddess have stood in the way of Herméné's fun with Manon? Is that the love you're talking about?"

"No, I don't think she ever would. It's too personal."

"So is sex."

"Not when it's a job."

"And she never talked to you about leaving?"

"Well, we all have our little dream home in the country, if that's what you mean."

"I mean the night of the murder."

"No…but I didn't talk to her that night. Or that day… Her headaches always made her very quiet. She would keep to herself and try to ride it out."

Aliette swallows the last of her beer. "How did you get here, Flossie?"

"It's what all the men ask me… Luck? Fate? A friend brought me into the bar one night. I met Ondine. I asked about that…" The motto over the bar. "I was attracted."

"Enough to stay? I think a woman such as yourself is probably not as limited in her choices as some others. And from what I've read, the goddess is everywhere these days."

"Yes, but this is ground zero, Aliette. This is where the world will change."

"Is it a war?"

"Mmm…more of a transformation, I hope. Some people are bound to get hurt though."

"Appears so… Is that why you attacked the Pope?" In 1980: His Holiness' first visit to Paris this century. Florence Orain, history student at La Sorbonne, steps out of the throng and whips a chunk of mortar at the bullet-proof Popemobile, and gets arrested. The only other thing in the file are two minor drug charges, one in Paris, and one in Dijon the following year…

"It was a gesture. I paid the fine." Old news, inspector.

"We look for patterns, madame. What if you killed her?"

"Why would I?"

"For being a dumb blonde?—a traitor to the cause?"

"On the contrary, Manon was our hero. Power to burn, you might say. She was our sister and she believed what we believe."

"Solidarity," says Aliette, rising.

"It's the only way," replies Flossie, rising with her. "It's lovely out…"

Aliette turns and sees the sun in the street. She collects her coat and case. "You were with Marcel Cyr yesterday after the funeral?"

"Yes. He ate with us. We had a picnic."

"Where?"

"Right there. On the other side of the wall—by the river."

"And then?"

"We drove him back. We left him in his car at the top of the park and walked home."

"His maid hasn't seen him since yesterday morning."

"No? I have no idea. It's two blocks to his place from there. Did she look in the garage? Poor Marcel—with the heat, he was liable to drop at anytime."

"We'll find him."

Flossie picks up the bundle of letters and presses them into Aliette's hand. "Take these and read them. Self-respect is what it's all about, Inspector."

"Not the book?"

"The book stays here. Vivi's new Maman…"

"Of course." Until it becomes evidence, that is.

3.

The noon air is crystal clear, the breeze is perfect. *This* is summer in Alsace. She meets Michel Souviron the Procureur coming across the street, a young Substitute (Assistant Procureur) marching in step. He's looking good, he always does; whether in court, sitting in his red robes on the Prosecution Throne, or, as on this day, on his way to inspect the scene of a crime in a seersucker jacket and summer-weight flannels, Michel was made to be noticed and respected. He is, like Commissaire Claude Néon and Chief Judge of Instruction Gérard Richand, another of Aliette's generation who has recently made a major step. His appointment that spring had been a highly praised and popular choice. And with the suede brogues, skin a manly brown from cycling through the Vosges with his very *sportive* wife, finely shorn black locks combed back from a widow's peak in an aristocratic manner, Michel gives the status quo a chic credibility it's bound to value. Which is not to say he isn't an urbane and enjoyable man. "Salut…how's my friend Aliette?"

"Bonjour…getting along, merci. What brings you out on a Saturday?"

"Just want to make sure everything's in order before I disappear…" *Mmm, me too…* Monsieur le Proc looks past the inspector. "How is it in there? What are we going to do with old Herménégilde Dupras—call him a distraught lover or a deranged fiend?"

"I wish I had more time for this one, monsieur."

"More, Inspector?" Amused. "Gérard might extend for you."

"Has he got discretion?"

"If he asks he probably does… Inspector, I'd like to present Maître Cécile Botrel, just arrived…" and to his colleague: "…Inspector Nouvelle, PJ."

"Bonjour," shaking the new prosecutor's hand. Short raven hair, smart glasses, and, like her boss, suitably (elegantly) understated in a grey silk blouse and an unrumpled white linen suit. Aliette always wonders what those who take the Proc path are aiming for. So many of them end up walking a high-wire stretched between politics and law. She imagines they wonder the same about her, at least in passing, because so many of her own kind never go anywhere; or get shot… Making the most of the casual circumstances of their meeting, she tells the new woman, "I'll be interested to see if you advise your boss to order backgrounds on some of the inhabitants of this place."

Cécile Botrel blushes. But one of the *(don't you dare say it out loud!)* advantages of being a woman in this business is being able to read another woman where many otherwise competent men cannot.

"And I'll trust her completely," laughs Michel. Yes, casual. No point being confrontational at this early stage. And not on a Saturday morning.

…Gérard might extend? Gérard Richand could not have been through her report yet, but she's picking up the message that Gérard and Michel have spoken; and that Michel's blithe nod to "old

Herménégilde," found with the victim, a knife and all the rest of the damning circumstances that are his life and occupation, contains the message that the state does indeed believe the pimp's their man.

Damn. She must proceed accordingly. So much depends on the charge.

In the initial stage of a case, the Procureur directs the police and the Instructing Judge to work toward *décharge*: the charge. But it's the Proc who lays the charge and, if necessary, orders a background investigation into the circumstances of anyone else connected. If this is not ordered—if, after the prima facie facts and circumstances have been submitted, the Proc's focus remains on the primary suspect, the police have no business snooping elsewhere. The charge defines the scope of the investigation.

Well, Michel is reasonable; he knows how obvious the media can be and so far he has been unafraid to go against popular opinion if real facts are put forward suggesting the truth lies elsewhere. What about this Cécile Botrel? Is she disgusted by prostitutes? Does she have a goddess she invokes to help make things clear? It's always interesting to meet a new player. Aliette tells Cécile, "*Bon courage.*" Gesturing toward the sky, proclaiming, "Thank god for the rain!" she leaves them to their business at Mari Morgan's.

4.

Sun, and the newly fresh air bring her to a corner parkette, carrying a roast pork sandwich and a bottle of Evian water. She sits on a bench, opens her lunch and takes the bundle of letters from her case.

> Dear Flossie. Today I was raked across the coals for taking more than my allotted fifteen minutes away from the phones. In fact I left exactly when I'm supposed to leave—the girl who sits in during my break stopped for a chat on the way to take over and so the phones were untended for five minutes. God knows what big contract may have disappeared into thin air! That's my ex-boss talking. I was mad and bet my ex-boss God doesn't give two damns who's winning in the cellular phone market. He said he thought I was pretty when I was angry. He was reaching out to touch me as he said that and I slapped his hand away. So he changed his tune and said it was a pity I wasn't more flexible and

it looked like it wasn't working out. I didn't say anything. I just left. Again. That's three minimum wage dead-end jobs down the tubes since New Year's. Not bad, eh? Back to zero.

Why can't something happen? Remember you used to say that? What's the point of believing in something if nothing ever happens? I get so angry. And after that, hopeless. I truly identify with those people in the paper who murder their children out of pity, so they won't have to live in such a stupid world. Vivi just gets embarrassed when I burn a twig and try to read to her. When I try to tell her it's a way out, she just looks at me. She'll never explore the way you and I did. She'll cut off her hair and put nails through her nose instead, and watch while the boys she runs with go around screaming at North Africans and Turks and Blacks. She's already doing it. It makes me want to walk away from her as well.

She would be impressed by you. She would listen. She would have a chance to get off the wheel. Maybe my only purpose was to have her. Now I have no power at all. Excuse the wobbly hand. It's hard to concentrate after a day like today... I had to have a glass or two.

Please write back. Not for me—for Vivi.

Faithfully yours, Colette

There are several stains on the cheap bond: some pink, from her wine; and some clear...from Colette's tears, supposes a not overly sympathetic Aliette. The Ursulines who had tried to educate her had been less than perfect but they *had* tried. How could she feel sorry for someone whose first choice for her daughter's betterment was a brothel? It was medieval.

Dear Flossie. What are you supposed to do when you walk out of the house for a job interview and your stocking catches on a splintery door and runs straight to hell? And then when you rush upstairs to change you discover the stress has decided to start your period for you? Then what happens when you go to the bathroom and discover you're out of tampons? And then if you slam the bathroom door and break your nail and find yourself hyperventilating, listening to the sobs as if they were coming from next door? I don't know either. Vivi came home and said forget it, Colette, but it didn't sound like comfort. She won't even call me Maman, and the way I lose it sometimes, I don't blame her. Maybe I really should just go. I wish I could do something for her. Why don't you take her at MM's? She's a good strong girl. She needs someone who isn't a *nul.* (That's me—don't you love it?) to show her how to live in this world. And like my last social-worker used to say: some structure. Please

> consider it. If it's a question of money, sometimes my ex-asshole
> sends the cheque he's supposed to send—that can be her little
> dot. Please. She needs to be with you and the goddess, not with
> me. She needs a life. I wish you'd call me sometime.
>
>   Colette

…But she did; she wanted her Vivi to be married to Flossie's goddess. She was right out there, this Colette.

> Dear Flossie. Your friend Louise was not very pleasant on the
> phone the other day. I know it's a business and not a day-care.
> Nobody's asking for care. Vivi could do the job. I know she can
> do it. I've seen her. That sounds horrible but I let her do what she
> wants and I know she knows how to deal with men.
> (Boys?…what's the difference?) Actually, the truth is, I can't
> really stop her. Anyway, it's not the job, it's the place. Sex: who
> cares? Any one of us can walk down to the corner and have sex
> whenever we want to…and for money. Even me, when my
> cheque doesn't come. It may be a business for Louise, but I know
> *you* wouldn't be there if it was only a business. How old is Louise?
> Maybe she should retire and make room for some new blood—
> I mean, if it's a business. That would make sense to me. Won't
> you see us for an interview? I'm not very good at them, but I
> know my Vivi will impress you.
>
>   Thanks and love. Colette

It was the same story, over and over again: abuse and failure for Colette Namur; hope for her Vivi at Mari Morgan's. The woman was as persistent as she was pathetic. And apparently Flossie Orain was not so nice to some people as she was to others. Apparently some *were* bound to get hurt as the world changed. Aliette re-bundles Colette's correspondence, closes her eyes, lets her head drop back on the park bench. A pleasure to doze for five minutes. When a fly lands on her nose, she swats it away with the bundle of letters; then she scratches…

There's that smell again, in the paper: smoky—but not a cigarette.

She rouses herself and hails a cab which takes her to a development on the northernmost edge of the city, where factories and warehouses merge with grubby *HLMs—Habitations à Loyers Modiques*: low-rent housing, with tenants to match. The man lets her out at a circle lined with identical adobe-coloured two-storey sixteen-unit blocks. There's a playground in the middle—you couldn't call it a park, most of the untended grass has been worn to dirt. One tired mother is monitoring the jungle-gym while teenagers in black leather and ripped denim hog the swings. She walks clockwise looking for the number. Two ladies, too old to be running, come dashing out of one of the units and hurry off. A woman bursts out of the same door carrying a beer bottle, screeching at the two in flight, "You spend your whole lives being stupid! Look where it's got you! Fools! Idiots!"

It's summer; and yes, it is the HLMs; but this ranting woman is less than presentable, clad only in a T-shirt and canary-yellow panties, ripped on one side. "You'll never get a *sou* from me. Never, ever!" She heaves her bottle. It crashes and shatters well out of range of her targets, who continue quickly away. The woman, about Aliette's age, stands there. Now she stares at the ground, pensive, perhaps realizing what she's (not) wearing…

"Hey Colette," calls one of the boys on the swings, "…got any pills or anything?"

"Fuck off!" Screamed across the playground for the benefit of every mother and child.

She goes back inside. Aliette follows, up the concrete stairs to a landing with four battered yellow doors. She knows which one to try because there's an odour of smoke, not as strong as incense, but distinct and foresty…wafting out from behind it. She knocks.

The voice calls, "Leave me alone or I'll call the police!"

"It's not them," calls Aliette.

"Then who the hell is it?" she hisses, yanking the door open.

"It's the police." But with a smile as she flashes her medal; "…what are you doing?"

Colette protests. "It's not me, it's them! They come here looking for money for the damn parish. They invade my privacy and try to talk me into it. Do I look like I have any money, much less for the Church? Do you know how rich the Church is? Those stupid women. There should be a law!" She's completely disgusted by the whole thing. "Do they ask themselves how the Church treats women…and how it promotes economic and conjugal slavery? All they can do is have their babies and walk around asking people for money. But actually *thinking*? Do you think they ever try that? No way! Never even heard of it…" Shaking her head, incredulous.

Aliette's mother collects money for the parish. Every spring. Old clothes too. Spring *Kermesse* is always one of her main activities. And Aliette always tries to give them old jeans and socks, the sweater that's been left the longest at the bottom of her drawer. Did that mean she's a "believer"? Not really…not lately. At least not in the same way her mother is, nor, she suspects, the two ladies who've just been by to see Colette Namur. But the parish is not the issue. "What's that smoke?" …looking into the apartment.

Colette moves to block her view. Up close, the woman is a sorry sight: Vivi's mother, certainly—but with tired eyes, bad skin, hair lank and split. She had portrayed herself well in her letters to Flossie. "It's just smoke…from a twig. No drugs here. Who are you?"

"My name is Aliette Nouvelle. I'm investigating the murder of Manon Larivière."

"Manon Larivière?"

"The Marilyn Monroe girl at Mari Morgan's. You have a daughter who works there, I believe."

"She just started today!"

"But you've been trying to get her accepted there for months…" Pulling the letters out of her briefcase and waving them in Colette's face; "for more than a year you've been begging your old friend to give Vivi a job as a prostitute."

"It's not a job… You sound like that cunt Louise."

"What is it then? …Colette!" Aliette does not use force; she has some rudimentary training if she needs it, but almost never… And she has no legal right either, but she can't help grabbing this sullen woman by the shoulder as she starts to turn away.

"It's a place. A position…" mumbling, looking for some words. Then she flares again. "It's a home for her…a decent home—finally! and I'm glad she's there and I don't care what someone like you thinks!" She slaps Aliette's hand away. "You hear me? I don't care!" She walks back to her table, sits and stares at the blue china bowl from which the aromatic train of smoke is rising.

Aliette steps into the dingy room. "What's the matter with you?" she asks, not unkindly.

Colette Namur makes a face: how absurd… "Everything."

"What's all this?" Sitting opposite the woman.

"Twigs…twigs from an apple tree. For wisdom, and a little bit of eternity… Wouldn't it be nice?" A sad smile, apologetic and self-deprecating. "It's just something I believe in." Now she strikes a match and stokes the tiny fire.

"Is this always part of the ritual?"

"The way I learned it, yes."

"The goddess?'

Colette nods. "It's important to make a sacrifice. An offering. She needs it…it's energy."

"What are you offering?"

"Myself?" Smiling again, the smile of the hopeless. "Think she'll take me?"

Aliette doesn't know.

"I doubt it," sighs Colette. "But you have to try. Right?"

"Yes, you have to try. What about Vivi?"

"Vivi has a chance now. A chance to succeed where I've messed up at everything. She'll make her own offering in her own way, and it'll be a strong one…in a different time." This is a prophesy as she rises and goes to the refrigerator. "Do you want a beer or anything?"

"No thanks…I already had one."

Colette opens one for herself and lights a cigarette. "It wasn't easy writing those letters. Some of them are disgusting, I know that…I had to push myself to get them across the park and into the mailbox. A couple of nights I didn't make it back…just sat down and passed out on a bench. You can bet those little pricks out there were looking up my skirt while I was snoring." Another big sigh. "Poor Vivi, having a mother like me… Poor Flossie. But I won't bother her any more. I got it done…" Nodding into her beer with some hard-earned self satisfaction.

"How long have you known Flossie?"

"Since school."

"Here?"

"Up the road…Colmar."

"What's so great about her?"

"She's strong…she's smart…she knows what's right. I looked up to her. Like a sister."

"Smart? She got caught selling hashish in Saint Michel…and she threw a stone at the Pope. That's not so smart."

"I was there," says Colette, grimly triumphal. "If he hadn't had that stupid bubble she'd have dropped him like Goliath. You should have seen him freeze. I clapped and some old nun smacked me. God, I laughed!"

"But it wasn't a joke."

"Not at all. She hates him."

"Hates?"

"When she was ten…eleven, twelve—it went on for a while, she watched her mother have a breakdown trying to have a love affair with this priest who thought he loved her…but then he *just couldn't*…but then he *had* to…but then he was *so guilty*, and so was she. It tore her apart. And what could Flossie do?…I heard all about it, every day, piece by piece. She hates him."

"And so you hate him too?"

"She was my friend. I loved to hear her talk. She went off to Paris…I went off to Paris."

"School?"

"No, just jobs," shrugging away her life. "She was the leader. Flossie was always the leader. So serious. And needing to know. And the best of it, she was completely fearless when it came to finding out… One day, we were five or six—at the very beginning…she led a group of us off, away from school one morning, tracing the stream along the gutters, head down…marching, marching, marching…" Colette's fingers go marching across the table, her face mimicking the expression of a determined little girl; "…for hours, not the least bit worried about getting lost, just dead set on finding the source of all that water. She's always been like that, has Flossie. She was trouble, but she was the most exciting person to be around."

"Now she's a prostitute."

"Doesn't matter. If there's no love, it's just a machine—might as well put it to work. It's the way they live that's the important thing."

"Why aren't you there?"

"I met a man—what else? We always have to meet a man, don't we? …Had Vivi. Got in one mess after another. He walked out, we ended up here. After that…I guess she and Louise got together and…well, we've been losing touch. And they never had a place for me. It's always nine."

"Why always nine?"

"Because there were nine virgins on Sein, guardians of Mari Morgan's island… Flossie says you have to have imagination…a story—if you want to carve out a little space to live in."

"Sein…off the coast?" North of her parents' holiday home on Belle Ile.

Colette nods, her bottle stuck in her mouth. "Mmm, somewhere out there."

"They're hardly virgins," says Aliette, for want of commiseration. I feel pity for this woman but I can't like her. A halfway intelligent sheep. *Mmm, the worst kind…*

"Virgin has nothing to do with a bit of membrane. Originally it referred to a woman who was separate, self-contained, strong. It's more an adjective than a noun… It's about the soul. There's something else the Pope and his helpers have stolen from us and perverted: Couldn't control the integrity of the soul so they put it all on the body. How desperate can you get? Vivi would never listen to me about these things, but Flossie will get through… She'll be fine in this damn world."

Aliette seems to remember the nuns telling her something about the sanctity of the flesh and the holiness of matter. *We believe because God became Man…* Was that it? "Did you know Manon?"

"Nope…"—she burps; "but whoever she was, my Vivi's better."

Now she strikes another match…restokes the dish of twigs. Smoke curls up.

The inspector withdraws. Colette Namur closes her eyes and sits with her small offering.

- 6 -

SUNDAY

On Sunday Procureurs and Chief Judges of Instruction take their families to mass, have a nice pastis followed by a large lunch with the in-laws, snooze, poke around in their gardens... The wheels of justice rest. A solitary inspector will call her parents to check on the weather back home, go for a run, go to the market, do some laundry, wash the kitchen floor, have a beer and read a book. Or go back to the lock-up to find out more.

A guard has been cajoled into supplying a cigar. Watching its smoke curl through the pin-like mote afforded by his meagre window, the prisoner tells her, "They came from over near Nevers, but I never knew much about them at all. I only knew their father. Jean. It seems our mothers shared him."

"Shared?"

"In a manner of speaking. I mean, he was the one with the job with the railway, some kind of bookkeeper till he quit, travelling around on a certain route each month helping the station masters manage their costs and profits. And when he wasn't travelling he was always home, with Maman, helping her run the house. Always. I knew he wasn't my father—my father was Gros Paul, but as far back as I could remember, Jean would get off the train and he'd be home until he left again. Same story at the other end: Jean the bookkeeper went back and forth between the two. You wouldn't think it possible if you knew him... My mother was just as surprised as theirs was when it came to light."

"What happened?"

"She showed up in the drawing room one evening—I remember it was early, still light out—she just walked right in and made a scene. Somehow she finally found out about his life at the other end of the line and she came to confront him… It wasn't the first time we'd watched a wife come in looking for a husband. I was, what?…fourteen, fifteen, but I'd seen it often enough to take it in stride. I came down from my room, saw a woman screaming at Jean in front of everyone… Poor Jean was embarrassed, Maman seemed surprised, but it wasn't anything unusual and I went back up to my *devoirs*. Next morning, Jean was gone. Maman told me who she was and the sad thing that happened… She walked out of the house and straight down the tracks, as if she were going to walk all the way back to Nevers. But there was a trestle bridge just outside our town and she threw herself off it. Very sad…a long way down."

And the inspector's heart is beating like a bird's. Georgette: her obsession with her flying pose?

"Jean came back in due time. Maman needed him, in her way, and she forgave him because he'd forgiven her—for me. I gathered there were two daughters in the picture, but with the war and everything, well, soon he was full time with us. I'd no idea till Georgette came to find me, here, almost twenty years later, back from Paris—her life there with all the artists…

"Why me? Because Jean was dead by then and they'd had no contact. Nor with each other for that matter. Georgette and Ondine. They'd both left. Even before the war they were both gone from Nevers…wanted nothing more to do with him. She needed to find out about her mother. What had happened that night. And I was someone who knew."

"And Ondine?"

"Came back from the coast about five years later. Didn't really know Georgette by then and it seemed she didn't want to. She went to ask my mother the same questions. My mother answered as best she could and then sent her up here to me by way of helping her find some work and get established. *Voilà*… And then we had our time together. I wish I could help you, but she never talked about it much. Bits and pieces. She always said it was like another life… Yes, Sein. Some little

island. Where Dorise comes from… No, no, Ondine was mostly in
Quimper; worked in a shop… Dorise?—she showed up a few years
later, all wet and thin and miserable. Had a letter of introduction
Ondine had written all those years before. We took her in as our cook.
Ondine felt obliged. She'd obviously had a difficult life. I hope they're
not all like that out there… No, never been out there myself."

The inspector asks, "What do you mean—you hope they're not
all like that?"

"I mean, all like Dorise."

2.

Georgette is another who's pretty much at loose ends on a
summer Sunday. Aliette entices her out of her basement to share an
early supper at the Rembrandt Café. *Tarte flambée.* A local dish: take
a filling of bread-and-milk sop, eggs, heavy cream, lard, onions and
bacon…a pinch of nutmeg; bake as a bready pie; serve in large slices;
eat with fingers. A mix of pizza and quiche. The inspector's treat.

And some wine? "Please…"

Proprietor Willem van Hoogstraten presents and pours, then
in his gracious way withdraws…

Georgette approves of the wine; but, "Do I need to tell you these
things?"

"Yes, I think so." Sharing. It's what friends do.

"I never slept with him. And I never did that for my daily meal.
Never."

"Georgette, I never thought you did."

Don't lie, Aliette.

Sure enough: "Don't lie to me," mutters Georgette. "I know
what you think."

"But I wouldn't!…I mean I won't…"

How does she know what I think?

Everyone knows what you think, Aliette. It's the nature of your life…

"She allowed herself to be seduced. Into his bed. Into that
house, that business. I told her what I thought. She told me to leave
her alone, so I did… Alone with him and them and her useless beliefs."

"How do you know they're useless?"

"Look where they left her. It ruined her life… You think my sister was involved in the killing of that woman?"

"I think it's tied more to goddesses than to putes, and she's the one who invited the goddess into Mari Morgan's." Aliette pours more wine for both of them.

They eat, they drink. Maybe it's the wine. Georgette pats her lips clean and declares, "You don't choose your siblings. You don't have to like them…or love them."

"I disagree with that," says Aliette, and Lord knows she has a hard enough time with her own sister Anne. "At the end of it all, they're likely to be the only ones you really know."

"But I don't know my sister," counters the model. "She walked out of my life when I was eighteen…or maybe nineteen, and I didn't see or hear of her for almost twenty years, then—"

"But why would she even go out there in the first place?"

"Our mother was from out there, the Finistère… Our mother…" She gulps more wine, closes her eyes and sits back.

"I know, Georgette. He told me."

"Ondine thought she could find an answer. Our mother used to tell us about it when we were young. Read us stories and verses. A different way of seeing things. Beautiful. At least for children. And childish people…"

"That red book…"

"It used to be mine. I'm the eldest and she gave it to me… We took it when we left that empty house, that feeble man who was our father, who was supposed to be her husband. When we split up, Ondine took it with her, kept heading back there, hoping she could make sense of it. Of what happened."

"Why didn't you go too?"

"I didn't like her. My mother… If suicides go to hell, then that was what she deserved for giving up and flying away. I wanted to be away from both of them—my father, my mother, that whole shameful lie. I told Ondine she was wasting her time… I left my sister and went to Paris to find my own way of seeing things. When she came back into my life I didn't know her life at all. When she tried to tell me about it, I admired her even less. When she asked what I thought, I told her to get away from him… I have no idea what she found out there. I don't want to know."

Later, near the bottom of a second bottle, the last of the passion fruit sorbet, Aliette hears herself asking, "Is it something like being a falcon circling a ledge?…the flying pose? Georgette?"

Above it all, protected from it, seeing it all so clearly? That makes sense to me, Inspector…

But wine or not, Georgette can't answer. The creaky wheels in her old heart lock.

That's it for Sunday. Time to go home.

You Circle but Don't Touch

Procureur Souviron opts for the assassination charge against Herménégilde Dupras.

Inspector Nouvelle requests a meeting with the Judge of Instruction. "I'm still asking for three *interpellés* and one body." An *interpellation* order: a mandate for a background investigation; a citizen, not necessarily suspected or involved, can be legally compelled to speak to the police.

"Heading for?"

"Not sure…some kind of conspiracy."

"This cult." Gérard Richand smiles a here-we-go-again smile. Not snide; on the contrary, they used to sleep together, for about a year, boyfriend/girlfriend, when first arrived as lonely newcomers to their respective jobs in a faraway border city. Gérard has since married and produced two fine boys. But they still understand each other, more or less. Sitting a little straighter, focusing on the material; "…one body? There only is one body."

"It's been buried. I need it back… To smell the thing it's wearing."

"That would be…" shuffling his pages, "that would be a pearl-coloured camisole?"

"Yes."

"It was thoroughly analyzed." Flashing a page at her.

"One of the IJ people will attest to an unexplained odour. You've read my memo?"

"Oui, oui…" Shuffling deeper, pulling it out, adjusting his glasses. "We have a woman in an HLM burning twigs which produce the same alleged odour, who has been obsessed with and has now succeeded in placing her teenage daughter at Mari Morgan's…" He glances across at her: not quite clear here, Inspector… "To do what?"

"*B'eh*…to take the place of our victim. To be one of them."

Gérard shakes his head: he never ceases to be amazed. "It's the fathers who hit them and take them to bed, but I'm starting to believe it's the mothers who are crazier."

"Shh…" admonishing, "we can't have judges who categorize."

"Well it seems Herménégilde Dupras had a mother too."

"She loves her little girl, Gérard—believe me."

"Love!" The judge throws up his hands. "I don't want to hear that word again, Inspector. The man's totally amoral. Sociopath and then some, if ever I've seen it. Give me a good solid psycho any day. He's so charmingly bereft of any shred of basic decency—I felt I'd lost my bearings."

"I know, I know. But he's not the one… Gérard, I need that camisole out of the ground to confirm the smoke. It didn't happen in that room."

"All forensics say it did."

"And I need an order compelling Dupras's ex-partner to talk to me."

Back to his pages. "Ondine Duguay… Seamstress. Odd beliefs."

"We're dealing with a…well, a goddess. She brought it into the place."

"Mmm." Dubious.

"I'm afraid so."

"Not against the law, though. Let's stick to homicide," suggests the judge.

"Gladly. One of the ways they honour their…their goddess…" *Is it so difficult for you to say the word, Aliette?* "…is by burning apple wood."

"I see. Why?"

"Wisdom. Eternal life."

"Those sorb apples make good jelly… I have a service tree in my yard."

"So does Ondine Duguay."

"Was she burning her tree unsupervised? That's definitely in the books."

Ha, ha… Listen to me! "No, but this other woman was. Not a tree…twigs."

Gérard blinks. And with the slightest adjustment of his sightline, still at her, but now down a fraction, the judge acknowledges an inspector's professional need; and his own position as arbiter of such. He taps his forefinger on the polished walnut desktop, like an egg timer, as he considers her thoughts. Yes, it's why I'm here, but only as far as it goes. "…this Colette Namur."

"Who is an estranged friend of the one who's the boss—"

"Dupras is the boss."

"Dupras is the owner. Dupras is the doorman. Public relations. Beyond that…" shaking her head: you guys have missed it by a mile; "it's Flossie Orain, and for the last sixteen months this Colette Namur has been obsessed with having her daughter accepted into the house."

"To be a prostitute."

"No—to be a member of the cult."

"Is she a member of the cult…the mother?"

"No. But she believes in this goddess. *The* goddess, actually."
There!

"Is she a prostitute?"

"Strictly freelance and very low-end… It's this cult, Gérard. Herméné Dupras knows nothing about it."

"How could that be?"

"You were talking with the man. Didn't you find him a little preoccupied with the things of the flesh?"

"Love, too," mutters Gérard.

Poor man: law and order, family values, civility, the things upon which we build: Gérard is a true believer and the Mari Morgan's killing seems to have affected him. "You seem disturbed."

"Some of them can do that to me. He's quite something, he really is…" See the judge's fleshy brow crinkling with incomprehension. Now see some anger mixing, too. "I still don't see where your cult connects with a drugged-out pimp slicing one of his putes. My guess is she was sick and tired of playing movie star. I gather that's all she ever did."

"That could tie to it, definitely. But let me finish."

"Please…" But it better be good. Finger on desktop picking up the beat…

"There can only be nine of them, so someone had to go."

"Why only nine?"

"Space is the easy answer; there's only room for so many beds. But I understand from this woman with the daughter and the burning twigs that nine is another one of their structural things…like twelve apostles, in a way. Part of their ritual. A rule, basically. And—"

Gérard holds up a hand: stop!…staring hard at the information on his desk, wheels turning as he tries to get a grip on Aliette's idea. "And you're suggesting Manon Larivière was killed somewhere else, perhaps by this Colette Namur, but maybe she was helped by the group or some of the group; and that he was drugged and the killers brought her back and set it up?"

"Something like that, yes… The point is, with them moving around, upstairs, downstairs, and Dorise—"

"Dorise?"

"The cook, Gérard?" Frowning. Monsieur le Juge has not read as closely as he might've.

"…Ah yes."

"…and with Dorise in the back, there was a lot of movement that is not well accounted for by any means."

"Hmm."

"Plus easy access through an unsecured kitchen door on a hot night."

The judge mulls it over… "Why was she helped?"

"She's not the kind of woman who could do it alone. And she's an outsider."

"If she's an outsider—estranged, you say—why would they help her?"

"That's what I can't see—except to get rid of the old one and bring in the new."

"Marilyn Monroe being the old…"

"Flossie Orain, Gerard. Make her talk to me on my terms. She's the one in charge now. She's the one Michel Souviron was talking to before he called in with the 221-3 for Herméné Dupras. Flossie Orain is the one who arranged to take in Colette's child… She's the one who more or less took over from Ondine Duguay. She's in the middle of this thing, I can feel it. Herméné Dupras is like a toy to the likes of her."

"And Michel Souviron?" Eyeing her, askance —in defence of his colleague; we know our business, Inspector; we're not kids; we are wise and respected men…

Oops, careful, that fraternal/paternalistic thing pops up at a moment's notice—a double-barrelled impulse they just can't seem to contain. "It's just that to Flossie, men are things to be worked with. Go and meet her. And her friend, Louise."

"All this from a whiff of a burning twig?"

A shrug: *voilà*…Gérard Richand sighs and goes into his reading mode. The inspector gets up and goes to the window, stares down at the flowers and trees in the quad. The pattern below is logical and pretty. She knows the one just presented to the J.of I. is far less so. But she cannot work in a vacuum…

"Why this Doctor Cyr? Odd beliefs. I thought it was just for girls."

"He said something to me, something that connects. They were hovering around him like he's one of the family…and he never came back from the funeral. And he's known our suspect for years, since he was a boy."

"What'd he say?"

"From corruption, sweetness."

The judge shakes his head; returns to his deliberation. Finally, motioning her back to her chair, he tells her, "You circle, but you don't touch. There's a hole in the middle of all this, Inspector—and it leaves your threads quite circumstantial, I'm afraid."

"But not a very big one!" *Don't whine, Aliette!* "…Give me the body back, Gérard. And a decent lab. I'll swear the smoke I smelled on her top was the same as from those twigs!"

"How close is this Ondine Duguay's connection?"

"I don't know. But the goddess thing was her baby… They say they want to protect her."

"That's what I'm afraid of."

"No harm in talking."

"*All* the harm is in the talking… They could create such a mess. God knows who's been in and out of that place. Procureur won't risk it for a perverse old pimp. Says best to leave the rest of them as quiet as possible…implied someone made it clear pillars of our community could come tumbling down if they feel too threatened."

"Someone like Flossie Orain."

"Whoever it was, it's something he doesn't need."

"He'll still get paid."

"And so will you and I. Community standards are sometimes ineffable and quite relative to boot. Isn't it so, Inspector?"

"Absolutely… But the law isn't."

"But the balance is a miracle and we should feel privileged to play a part… Look, regardless of Michel's 221-3, I'm going to use my discretion and send in the shrinks full force. We need more information on what makes this kind of man. They'll quietly pronounce him insane in a couple of years, and the thing will be forgotten."

"But he's not insane. Just a slave to pleasure. Gérard…?"

Gérard folds his arms and looks out the window. "Did he tell you how this Manon Larivière could make him come and laugh at the same moment… Laugh out loud?"

Pardon…? "Come and laugh?"

"Climax? Ejaculation, Inspector?"

"Ah… Well, no. Not in so many words."

"This just doesn't happen… Does it?" Gérard can't smile. Gérard's embarrassed.

Yes, we used to sleep together and we actually had some fun. But never *that* much.

"The man has something seriously wrong with him. Plus a violent streak. I saw it."

When you insulted him because you didn't like to hear about his life? This is not a question you put to a judge, regardless of your shared history. But she can read him and she hears male spite… Yes, that righteous jealous thing she also sensed in Claude. Are Gérard and Claude really so angry at an old libertine's silly life? That can't be their guiding light here… She too folds her arms, affecting a certain look; it's a challenge, conveyed with a tinge of bitterness that a judge might not appreciate but which a serious cop cannot suppress, telling him in no uncertain terms: To hell with community values. They gave you the big job, now do it right. Be brave! Go to the heart of it!

Gérard can read her too; he knows her impulses…or remembers them (time does go by). He nods: all right. "We're heading off Friday…" to Collioure, his wife's hometown on the sea by the Spanish border. "You find something of those twigs in the house and we'll talk about the exhumation when I—"

"But I haven't and I won't… Of course I won't."

"Find the old man then. That shouldn't be too hard. I'd like to know more about the suspect's childhood. We'll go from there, slowly, when I get back from the south…" making a note, then standing and reaching to shake her hand. You always end formally when you meet with Gérard. "What about you, Inspector—aren't you about due for the coast?"

"Saturday…maybe. I don't know…I mean, this thing is starting to get to me."

"Which is an excellent reason to take a break. God knows I need one."

*Oui, oui, oui…*Gérard, you're starting to sound like my mother.

2.

Find the old man, *maybe* we'll go from there. The concierge calls back in fifteen minutes: The doctor's apartment is empty, Madame Inspector… No, haven't seen the maid since Saturday. Or was it Friday night? …And there's no classic car waiting in the garage.

A 1949 Citroën TA, pearl grey, plate number 8244PD68. She sends a memo downstairs to Commissaire Duque of the Urban Police: please have your people look as they make their rounds. She sends similar notes to the gendarmeries in outlying towns, and to her friends at the Swiss checkpoint fifty kilometres down the road. Bridges into

Germany are a different matter. No checkpoint; partners in the EU means free-flowing traffic, the major portion of it local and daily. For information on northbound traffic she'll have to ask… But wait; wait! slow down…give it another day or so. Dr. Cyr is eighty-seven; he can't get too far, not if he's travelling alone.

But what if he's not?

And where does a non-live-in live when she's not on the job?…looking through her notes: Léonie Brandeau. Nowhere to be found in the directory. She tries every agency in the city and comes up empty. She rather thought she would.

Commissaire Duque's SU (*Securité Urbaine*) occupies the main and second floors, your typical "police station," busy with officers behind counters listening to complaints, still more in little rooms ready to help find your stolen purse, stolen car, stolen children, stolen wife, members of the public, both innocent and guilty, coming and going at all hours of the day and night. Most of the community's crimes, misdemeanours and small mysteries are dealt with here, and they always have an artist on call for composite portraits of the furtive wanted, the sadly found. Aliette rings downstairs, "Might I requisition…?" After lunch, who should walk into her office but the lady who works at one of the window-side easels at Georgette's group. A Madame Jarnet. Handsome, with the kind of organized and cared-for bearing that suggests the privileged bourgeois life of some sort. But the people at Georgette's group keep their distance—it's not a social thing, and Aliette, who's never done more than nod *bonsoir*, would never have guessed. They're both charmed to see each other. "You do this for a living?"

"Pin money, change of scenery, something to do now that the kids are up and gone." But not really essential, left unsaid.

The inspector doesn't ask for details; like drawing groups, police work should involve a bit of distance too. She begins to describe her subject. Madame Jarnet, listening…thinking, begins to fashion a face. After a few tries, Aliette suggesting even heavier eyebrows… "Still too young," she muses, "but getting there. You know her perhaps? Save me a lot of running around." Ladies of Madame Jarnet's ilk are always on the look-out for good non-live-ins.

"Can't say I do. But she really does look for all the world like Arletty in *Les Visiteurs du Soir*... Ever seen it?"

France, 1942, b&w; an allegory (lots of allegories produced during the war) wherein two of Satan's minions show up at a castle in time for the wedding feast, Arletty being the one with the regal voice, the magnificent face loved throughout the Republic. And those eyebrows. "Oh for the love of... Come with me!"

Madame Jarnet, enjoying herself, collects her stuff and hustles down the stairs behind the inspector, who is cursing under her breath.

The prisoner is savouring another cigar as he passes the time.

"Do you know this person?" Sternly; showing the drawing.

"Could be Francine...or Arletty. Depends on the context." Copious chins folding over each other as he stares at the pencilled face.

"Is it Francine?"

"She could look like that. Act like it, too. Big aspirations for the theatre at one point, or so she said. But she missed it...had a habit. She could be a handful—horrible tantrums. Something very loose in there..." Tapping the top of his head.

Aliette hands the drawing back to her artist. "Give me some more years, madame." A few moments later, there's Léonie. To the prisoner: "Could that be her now?"

"Definitely where she was headed," confirms Herméné. To the artist, in his convivial way, he adds, "You're very good."

The lady is not sure how one receives a compliment from a man behind bars accused of a vicious murder. Aliette, without thinking, offers, "This is Madame Jarnet."

"Ah... Husband a banker?"

"Why, yes. You know him?"

Herméné, caught short, demurs.

The lady is thanked and dismissed, worried, perhaps with a whole new view of life...

"Francine's the one you hit."

"Because she hit me."

"Why?"

"Inspector, it was years ago. Who can remember these things?"

"You have to remember these things, monsieur. Some very important people have noted a tendency." The suspect shrugs: why bother if it's already noted? She glances at Claude's notes: *MM arrives 1966; a film; replace Francine.* "What does this mean: a film, replace Francine?"

Herméné relights his cigar. Takes his sweet time. He has a lawyer now. Has his lawyer got it across to him that there's no rush now we're into provisional detention, so pay no mind to edgy inspectors?

"It was Marcel's idea—he saw Manon in a locally made film he'd put money into and made a profit on, I might add. Quite adventurous, my friend Marcel… At any rate, Francine had been with us since, I don't know…'57, '58…but it was time for Francine to leave. She was our resident Arletty, very popular, but she was getting impossible and Marcel suggested Manon and it seemed like an excellent exchange: Arletty for Monroe. So we offered and she came in. The film business can be brutal on a girl who's all alone."

"Your friend Marcel has disappeared."

"Well, he's very old."

"Not enough to disappear. No one is."

"Then find him, Inspector."

"I intend to. What happened to Francine?"

"Don't know…lost touch. Back to Paris, maybe?"

"Marcel never mentioned his maid?"

"Oh, sometimes. Yes, he did mention the latest one reminded him of Francine… He goes through a lot of them… They don't seem to understand that he means no harm… With his stick?"

Thanks, Herméné. Merci, Gérard. Find the old man—shouldn't be too hard. We get an old Arletty fake instead. Yes, for sure it's one more thread…

That will circle but won't touch.

Repeat to a walking rhythm; pissed off. Proceed to your fitting at Ondine's…

3.

"Sein? Nothing much there at all," mumbles Ondine Duguay through a mouthful of pins.

"Except Mari Morgan." *Shh! Aliette—the mandate, ma belle; you're here only in your role as private citizen…*standing in front of the mirror in Ondine's work room. Her new camisole is still blocky, ragged along the hem—and already she's fascinated; the seamstress has found a steely blue silk that can turn silvery grey with the slightest move.

"I don't have to talk to you."

"Not yet…but Ondine, you know I can find out."

"Georgette knows nothing about it. My life, not hers." Squatting, circling like an awkward duck, pulling and pinning the hem at a level just below her buttocks. "…Keep still, please."

"I am."

Ondine tugs again, this time under the inspector's armpits. "Maybe you need a little more room around the chest…"

"Thank you."

"You're the type who'll grow before she shrinks."

"I hope so… Do you know Colette Namur?"

"Never heard of her." Her dulled old eyes remain engrossed in the job. She takes scissors and snips carefully at cross-seams under the corners of the lacy brassiere patches she's begun to fashion.

"Do you know Marcel Cyr? He was at the funeral."

"Disgusting man… One of the main reasons I ran from that place."

"Ondine… Does the goddess have something against men?"

"On the contrary—she loves them. It's one of her eternal problems."

"Tell me about it."

"That's all I know."

"Tell me for Manon."

"I told you, it's not my world any more."

Aliette has heard this one too many times before. The old were always excusing themselves from the battle, more often than not without just cause.

"That should do it…" Bony hands tugging one last time to ensure the thing hangs straight. "I can have it for you Friday if you care to pass by."

Aliette turns away and lifts the camisole up over her head, carefully, feeling pins scratch lightly against her back and breasts. There's the small service tree, alone in the untended yard. "Do you burn twigs from your tree sometimes, Ondine?"

"Sometimes. A little bit of ritual never hurts to keep your prayers going in the right direction, Inspector."

Yes, but which direction? And how far?

Walking home on a mellow summer's eve, *I think we'll definitely go for a run today*…and thinking of those Irish monks who'd caused such a fuss with the Latin mass. It was when the Church was "modernizing," after Vatican II—heady times, jetting priests in blue jeans around the world bearing a renewed Word and precepts of Liberation Theology. The good sisters at *Blanche de Castille*, her school in Nantes, had found it thrilling. Then those Irish monks on their forgotten island, coming out of hiding, resisting, insisting on the Latin. Some of the older sisters understood, or thought they might, and tried to explain it to earnest girls who needed to know. A lovely memory: old sisters, imparting a different kind of admiration. Because it was a difficult thing: Not simply ritual, but *faith* in ritual; that was the key to those monks' fierce stand. For them, that was the eternal and ever-necessary bridge.

4.

Alors, circling but not touching: this is a lot like spinning your wheels.

On the phone. The computer. Missing persons becoming missing pieces becoming abstract information—"out there" somewhere, hard to feel the relation to murder, much less a goddess.

Time is lost. Focus is diffused. Is she wasting her time believing that it matters?

Creating pressure on herself: should I stay with this or just go home?

The irritating heat is gone but impatience grows.

Professional hazard. Live with it, ma belle…

- 8 -

LIVING BY THE BOOK

Flossie tells Vivi, "Your job is to take care of them—but only for the moment and no more. They come here only for a moment. None of them can stay. They come here because they need to get out of their lives, but not for very long. Their cycles are not like yours…they're not as finely made as you and time can be so long and impossible for them… Marriage, jobs, getting old, it's all just day after day after day for so many of them. It plays on their souls. They get desperate."

Men? "Desperate for what?" Vivi's father had taken off before she knew what he looked like. She has always reckoned it was because her mother is so out of her mind.

"To get free of themselves," says Flossie. "They need to. You'll feel it. They ache for diversion, to get out of the routine. It's almost as if they're trying to break free of time itself… And that's where *we* live—us, here in Mari Morgan's. To them you're a strange woman in another world. When a man comes to you and believes he loves you— and it will happen, count on it—he might, but it's beyond his life. Resist it, Vivi, or you won't survive. But if you feel love, make it like a mirror. See yourself when you're working. That's what you have to do. Always see yourself, so you don't lose yourself in what you're doing. It's an art, but it's only that. We use it for something better."

"For the goddess?"

"…for ourselves."

Uh-huh? …It's confusing. Still, you had to listen. Flossie's so certain and love's something Vivi isn't sure of. Thinking back through her boyfriends, Hervé, François—it's true, they can seem desperate. They make such a lot of noise, it seems like they're going to hit you... And Jerôme, another one who was trying real hard just before she left, singing songs off the radio, insisting that he loved her. Cute, but it never stopped... And Colette's boyfriends: there was nothing in her mother's neverending trail of doted-upon lovers, soon to become despised men who weren't worth anything, to ever let Vivi know for sure about love. With Colette, she had stopped listening. But Vivi listens to Flossie.

They start her off with a man wearing glasses; he has a hairy belly and a *zigonnette* that reminds her of François'—round and fat at the tip. He doesn't say much, only that it was worth spending the extra money to get off the streets, and, when she's naked, that she's lovely. It's quick and nothing special. Louise says that's for the better. "Nothing special about it, nothing to remember, not even your first."

Then she has a man who says he knows the mayor and a lot of other important people.

And a man with poodles on his boxers who doesn't say a word.

And a man who comes as soon as she takes her clothes off—and leaves.

A Swiss who stands her on her shoulders and strokes the soles of her feet.

Apart from him, it's zizis and bellies. Not sure what else to think about when it comes to clients. Nothing, mostly... Vivi tidies her room. She feels a bit of a guest with those chintzy dresses still hanging in the closet. Is she supposed to wear them? She hopes not. Three times too big in the bum. Then she reads the verse yet once more: *I am the knot in every weave / I am the glow on every ridge...* She repeats and repeats it, trying to fix it in her memory. Like school, and to be honest she doesn't have a clue. But Ondine will be expecting some progress and she likes Ondine, so she'll try. She will, she'll try. Ondine's old. Strange. Sad. Yet Vivi feels something she needs. What is it? Ondine touches a place that Flossie misses. Sad, strange...honest? Vivi trusts her, that's what it is. Ondine's a comfort.

Because please don't think Vivi Namur is a stupid girl or, worse, some kind of natural-born slut. It's just that growing up with Colette, on the run and getting nowhere, she has a sense of place—the HLMs, and a corresponding sense of options. I mean, doing it for money? Physically it's no big deal. Easier than grinding away for hours and hours with Hervé; not like having to sit there talking about having babies with François when all you want to do is sleep; these men just do it and go away. As for "right"—*how old are you Vivi?*—well, it's just not a very useful question. Started when I was fourteen. That may not be right but it's pretty normal, at least where I come from…

And because Colette has been calling, worried as usual—she can never rest with her decisions—babbling about the murder and that inspector and maybe Vivi should come back home.

No way!

Flossie says she'll go and talk to Colette. Flossie says Colette will be fine.

…Now Vivi lays the old red book aside and goes back to her closet; takes the silvery one off its hanger and holds it against her body. Perhaps Ondine could alter it. It's cool under the light…might be sort of fun. Then Vivi checks her clock. And her appointment book. An American at eight. Flossie says Americans will love her, the way they always loved Manon. But Louise has told her Americans never spend as much money as it seemed they would.

Taking care of them: it really is a job.

2.

Next day Vivi's back in Ondine's workroom with the seamstress all over her, gangly arms, bony fingers, fetid breath, and pins and pins and pins. Vivi holds still, eyes fixed on the mirror. The lamé dress is being transformed, becoming hers. It would fit loosely, perfectly…it would flow. The effect is magical and she loves it already. "Ow!" Squeaked out as a pin pricks the back of her thigh.

"Hold still," mumbles Ondine. Three more pins are placed. "There," standing, stepping back. "It's going to be lovely."

"Like Manon?"

"No…" Suddenly vague; and Vivi watches the old woman disappear behind green eyes gone milky from too much needlework, hiding too far inside to even guess at. "Never like Manon."

"But she was lovely," says Vivi, smoothing the watery sheath, feeling a thrill as it shimmers and moves. Her American, Jimmy, saw it hanging there and he said, Oh yeah my Vivi, you have to wear that one next time please. "...Always laughing. At least that's what they tell me."

Ondine repeats it: "No." Vivi waits, gazing out at the lonely apple tree in Ondine's unkempt yard. Ondine asks, "How can you always be laughing? Manon was trapped and she was deeply ashamed because she walked right into it herself, laughing, as you say. Whatever you do in your time there, be realistic about it. Be careful with yourself. Don't lose track like poor Manon."

Or like Colette, sitting with her burning twigs and her booze, lost and so ashamed of herself as well. It's this thing about shame... "Did Manon never come to see you, to talk about it?"

"She did."

"Did you help her?"

"I...I tried...I don't know. It doesn't matter, does it? It's too late."

"But would he kill her for that? For being ashamed?" What a strange word.

"No!" Making a face, a crooked smile for a dense girl. "He wouldn't have known what she meant."

Vivi's not so thick—it's all these words these women heap upon her. But she senses it in Ondine now too. Shame sewn into regret. Because Vivi recognizes that same sense of ownership in Ondine's voice: *Ondine's* Manon, *Colette's* problem, *my* mother. Everyone had something they held close, even if it only hurt them...

She changes back into her jeans. They try the verse a few more times.

> I am a roebuck displaying seven tines
> I am a floodwater covering the fields
> I am a wind over a deep lake
> I am the tears of the Sun.
> I am a falcon circling the ledge
> I am a bramble hooked in the skin
> I am the perfection in every garden
> I am an enchanter—who else
> will set the whispering voice to song?

I am a battle-waging spear
I am a fish turning 'neath the surface
I am a call beckoning from paradise
I am a path where poets wander.
I am a charging boar
I am a gathering wave
I am the current inside the tide
I am a child—who else
sees through the unshaped sacred stone?

I am the knot in every weave.
I am the glow on every ridge.
I am the queen of every hive.
I am armour for every heart.
I am the tomb of every hope.

Vivi tries… But Vivi stumbles. It's just too far away.

Ondine tells her, "See the words!"

"It's not real… I don't know how."

"It's real. When you find the right person you'll know it's more real than anything else there is."

"But who's the right person?"

Does Ondine even hear a whining girl as she stares at the verse as if it were a door?…*into* it as if into the only face that mattered? "I don't know… Knowing these words will help you know. Learn them and be ready."

"Then how did you learn it, Ondine? Please…" Again Vivi waits as Ondine sorts grimly through the things in her mind. The waiting is the hardest part of these mornings with Ondine.

"My mother. My mother read it to me. She made me see it… She told me how she and a man were in love—she was about your age, Vivienne, maybe a little older…and they went to a beach along the coast where she grew up. It was in May, the month of the willow, a tree which loves water and is loved by poets. So they lay in a grove of willows and read it together. That was normal then, that both of them should know this verse. It was part of their lives, it was something they shared. And it was love that let her see it…"

What did she see, Ondine? Vivi waits, in the silent room in the silent morning.

"How the wind over a deep lake will speak of the depth, the myriad intonations in the face of the beloved…how life is as intricate as a billion ripples. How when a tear from the sun lands, it magnifies the heart crystal clear. How a bramble in the skin is a dark thought that won't leave you. How currents in the tide are the implacable strength of time, drawing people away from each other, changing the shape of faces and the sound of voices…"

Vivi is looking. Seeing? Well, maybe.

"Just a love story, really," muses Ondine, coming out of it, "but it's all there. Everything in the details of a life."

"How do you know? I mean truly know?" You have to tell me this, Ondine!

"Because when she read it to me and talked about it…about her lover, and love, she was happy. I was just a child but I could feel it. Go on…try again."

So, collecting herself, concentrating on the small tree in the yard because Ondine has told her apples stand for wisdom…when Colette would say that it sounded ridiculous; but now, with Ondine watching with those eyes…now starting to recite, each phrase coming with slow, deliberate care:

> *I am a roebuck displaying seven tines*
> *I am a floodwater covering the fields*
> *I am a wind over a deep lake*
> *I am the tears of the Sun.*

"Good…"

"*I am a falcon*…um…" peeking around for some help, embarrassed.

"…*circling the ledge,*" prompts the elder. "Go on…" Yet Ondine seems pleased enough.

"*I am a bramble hooked in the skin…*" Yes, maybe it's coming. Not just saying lines any more; Vivi's beginning to see what they're describing, the colour and the strength in some, the pain and the terror in others. But: "…*I am the tomb of every hope?* I don't know how to see that one. I can't. It…it makes me afraid."

"Fear is part of life," says Ondine, "and fear is part of love. But that's the secret. You have to imagine the beauty of everything. Even the beauty of dying. It's how the goddess shapes the world."

"Does that mean Manon was happy to die?"

"Of course not!…Don't be morbid."

"Then what?…please." The beauty of dying makes no sense. More dark words lost in the larger darkness of the one who spoke them; the sound of a person—Ondine—and not of themselves.

"It means death is a natural step in a larger existence… It means the fear that always lives with hope is only here, in this life and in the death that goes with it. That's the wheel. We're bound to leave it. We live to transcend it. Whatever else, Manon believed that…I'm sure she did."

I hope she did, thinks Vivi. Because the lesson's over for today. She gathers up the red book and a bag full of repaired things to take back to Mari Morgan's. "What was his name," she asks, "…the man with your mother on the beach?"

"Yvon."

"Was Yvon your father?"

"Yvon was killed in the war." At *Chemin des Dames*, in May of 1918, keeping the Germans out of Paris. "He might've been, except for that godforsaken war. But then I wouldn't have been me, would I? No, my father was a completely opposite kind of man…" Ondine smiles bizarrely at this long-gone twist of fate. It's something that touches Vivi's heart—part fear, part sympathy. Right now she can only shrug by way of reply; full to the brim, time to get out of here…

The bell tinkles. That gentle bell. "See the words, Vivienne. *À demain.*"

3.

Mmm, full to the brim, alone in the street, a tote bag full of repaired lingerie slung over her shoulder, the book held tight in her hand safe inside the pocket of her coat…

What is it, this thing called belief? What *is* that anyway? And how would I know?

Now Colette comes into it: Her battered face, her angry voice, all the speeches and complaints.

…Coming from your mouth it was all just names and words for so many years. Nothing in your life prepared me to understand…I know nothing of belief, Maman!…nothing.

Look at all the churches. See them pointing to the sky…Vivi's never been in a church in her life.

You spat on churches. You blamed churches. "Fucking patriarchal bullshit!"

(A stranger turns and stares at the muttering girl.)

And look at these other women, putes scattered on these corners, the ones who are gross, the ones who are dying. But that's not me…that's not what this is. They're alone. You see it in their eyes.

But Vivi is not. She can feel it, the way she's beginning to feel the words… *See* them.

Yes, she would learn that verse.

And I can cope with these men, their precious zizis and their horrid pot-bellies…

And I can watch over myself and keep an eye out for love.

Vivi Namur walks faster, stronger, moving clear of it—her first worry: the looks and thoughts of strangers. They don't matter. It's the verse. It's becoming part of Mari Morgan's. Turning the corner into the alley, she passes the sweet scents emanating from Erly's bakery and goes in the kitchen door. She's home…yes, and she wonders what Dorise has made for lunch. When they tell her that her mother, Colette, had been found dead in her bath that morning, Vivi's busy mind goes blank.

9

THAT PROVISIONAL FEELING

St. Peter, monitoring the gates of Paradise on behalf of the god of the Church of Rome, does not accept suicides. *Point final.* Mari Morgan is more lenient; although you should probably expect to be sent back to try your life a few more times in various reincarnations before being welcomed. The goddess wants you to get it right, but in your own good time. However, before trying their luck at either entrance to eternity, suicides, falling into the death-by-violence category, must first go to the police morgue. It's usually no more than a formality and rarely the concern of the Police Judiciaire. And a razor to the wrists is not very original—like the woman herself. But Aliette Nouvelle had recognized an opportunity as she'd looked down at Colette Namur stretched out on the stainless steel bed.

Raphaele Petrucci says he found wine, "and not much else at all, actually," in her stomach.

"No beer?"

"Yes, she probably had a beer too."

"No ergot remedy?" Just a guess.

"No."

"Milk?"

"Sorry."

"Mmm, didn't think there would be…" This is neutral shop talk in the back of a cab heading to the depressing circle on the northern edge of town; it wouldn't do to continue the more personal discussion leading to his presence on her hastily assembled team. The inspector, the pathologist, Jean-Marc and Charles from IJ. The latter are along willingly; Charles Léger is in fact eager to smell that smell again if there (as she has insisted it will be). Raphaele was bribed:

"Charles will come. Jean-Marc will back his partner's judgement. You have to come, too!"

Raphaele had reiterated his basic position. "But I didn't smell it."

"You might have!"

"People hear about these sorts of impulsive adventures, Inspector…I don't need people saying I'm incompetent."

"No one's impulsive. Like you say, it's a subjective thing. As a professional team we agree it's a possibility and we need to have a second look." …A second sniff.

He'd turned the knob and steamed a cup of milk. She'd accepted a cappuccino and told him it was good…she needed him onside in this.

He'd said, "I'll come with you if you come with me."

"Where?"

"My place, Saturday night—pasta with a three-cheese sauce you'll never forget."

"But that's extortion. That'll do you in before incompetence."

"No, it's an invitation."

"It's not fair!" Feeling heat spread through her ears; hearing that other voice: *Whoa! Why so angry, Aliette?… you losing something here?*

No matter; it fell off him like water. He'd asked, no blush at all, "Really, Inspector, how long are we supposed to ignore this thing?"

"Which thing!"

"Us."

Incorrigible. Improper… And those unavoidable Latin eyes. Such is the give and take of the modern workplace. What are you going to do about it—file a grievance? What he can't know is she's hedging her bets; that she has that plane ticket west for Saturday noon, but will cancel if this plays out the way she thinks it will… *Yes?* Yes, of course. *Well, it's another example of the give and take of the modern something, no?* Mmm. For now, she has him…them. And having made an "urgent" call to the Palais, she's sure there'll be at least one more.

Another part of her is thinking of picking up her new chemise from Ondine Duguay tomorrow and showing it to Raphaele on Saturday after supper. *That would definitely make you feel better...*

The cab drops them at the top of the circle. She leads them past the messy children, the dulled-out adolescents, the acquiescent mothers, the shuffling papas. They gather round the arborite table, poverty's dull centrepiece, stained with spills, littered with spent matches, glasses, three emptied bottles and a quarter of another. Inspector Nouvelle has her nose in a charred dish, nodding "uh-hmm, yes..." to IJ specialist Charles Léger. This is the power of positive suggestion. As Charles bends to take a whiff, the pudgy face of Chief J. of I. Gérard Richand appears at the apartment door. Bowing slightly, she says, "Monsieur le Juge...thank you for coming." And a minute later, "Commissaire..." as Claude Néon walks in, having in turn received a curt call from Gérard demanding what the hell?...and looking more than a little embarrassed. There's no real reason for any of them to be there. Suicides are for the *SU*.

Still, it's gratifying to see how quickly those in charge can respond when they get worried.

These two distracting latecomers instinctively hold still as Charles Léger sniffs again. He offers a flat scientific nod indicating yes. Jean-Marc Pouliot lingers over Colette's ashtray for a full minute. He extracts a sooty morsel, tests it on the isolated end of his finger before stating, grave and absolutely professional. "Ah yes, I do remember that."

Now Raphaele Petrucci takes a turn...

Claude asks, "Why exactly are we here, Inspector?"

"We have a second violent death of a person connected to the cult at Mari Morgan's. I have statements and letters from Colette Namur attesting to that connection, and statements from my three colleagues here attesting to the possibility of physical evidence which links the two deaths, and which may shed important light on the circumstances surrounding the murder of Manon Larivière."

"And what evidence would that be?"

"Smoke—from the burning of apple twigs."

"It's got this sweet tinge to it," adds the pathologist, thoughtful (beautiful!); "hard to mistake."

"All we need now," Aliette explains, probably a little too like some cheery Girl Guide leader organizing the next activity, "is the camisole and a thorough analysis at the best lab money can buy and I'm sure this case will take on some extraordinary new dimensions." Far too cheery. Pushing her luck. Her little victory…*low-key, Aliette!* Because so often a case is a series of little victories over the system and its keepers, and they have to be gently won.

Gently? Fine, you got it…

Yet the moment seems inevitable vis-à-vis the shadowy methodology of Inspector Aliette Nouvelle. Neither Claude, now their de facto "leader" by virtue of his presence, nor Gérard, who authorized the release of Manon Larivière's body and effects, perhaps prematurely, and hates the thought of a mistake, has any choice but to also take a whiff of the ashes in the dish. Then Claude and Gérard leave, neither of them happy. It's Thursday afternoon and Gérard's wife has ordered him to get home early to pack the car. And Claude knows he'll be stuck with whatever the Judge is thinking.

Raphaele Petrucci leaves, too. "Merci, monsieur," in her measured, professional voice. But he has performed perfectly and knows it. His warm smile says she can expect more of the same on Saturday night.

Charles collects the ashes and sets about testing his machine's reading against Colette Namur's clothes; back to science now, it's not as if we'll convict on the vagaries of the human nose. Jean-Marc beckons from the bathroom. The attending *SU* cop has pointed to the message scrawled in blood on the rim of the blood-stained tub.

…Three words? First one mostly washed away; or is it just a bloody smear? The second looks like *eau*; water? Or maybe *beau*? And then *maeu*—or is that *marn*? …*maev* maybe? *Beau muet*? Beautiful silent. Silent water… *Beau muer*? Beautiful to change…as in *transform*. No—Colette Namur could spell, if nothing much else, her letters to Vivi prove that. Her grammar was not so bad either. A name perhaps. *Mari*? That fits. No—feminine: it would have to be *belle*, not *beau*… *Beau mauve*. A lovely mauve…what? Sunset? A nice thing to write before dying. But why? The inspector can make no sense of it. She tries to imagine: the steam, the water turning pink. A woman in her bath.

Dying. Private, warm; and slow…time to prepare for a transition, time to drift away.

And was the goddess waiting?

What…? remnants of a bloody prayer traced by a lazy finger softly seduced by death?

Leaving it to an equally puzzled Jean-Marc Pouliot to ply his skills, she goes out to talk to the neighbours.

It takes a while to work her way around the circle, through the men who don't know and couldn't care, and all the mothers and their complaints about Colette's very bad example and how she always seemed to believe she was never really one of us… And none of these circle-dwellers has any real idea where young Vivi's gone: Been sent off to some school or something? Hah! More likely an abortion. Colette had told different stories all around the block. She's probably just run away like all the others… Maybe she'll come back now Colette's gone. Then again, looking around, why would she? A boy called Jerôme is swinging on the squeaky swings in the middle of the filthy park, headphones on, crooning along with the radio. Dopey, even happy looking where his peers have perfected scowls to complement the gelled spikes in the flame-coloured hair, the bolts through the oily nostrils. Maybe Jerôme's a bit on the slow side, or maybe he's a budding poet; shutting down his music, he brags of never missing a day on the swings since he was eight.

Aliette agrees it's quite a record. They chat as he swings by… He misses Vivi… He confides he loves her despite the fact that Rachelle…that's her over there on the teeter-totter, watching through menacingly kohled eyes…despite the fact that Rachelle has gone the distance and had a bolt inserted in her tongue.

"Why would Rachelle do that?" wonders a curious inspector.

"Pour la pipe c'est formidable!" (It makes for incredible head!) explains Jerôme, hopping off. "Rachelle really loves me. But I still have this thing for Vivi, I really do. It's like destiny or something, you know?"

"Everyone has one," notes the inspector. Even the ones who dwell in these HLMs…

The last Jerôme had seen of Colette was yesterday afternoon, walking back from the store with some bottles and a woman; "…a cool woman with cool clothes. Fox face, sort of, could've been a probation officer or social worker but they never look so cool, you know?—the six hundred-franc blue jeans from the boutiques in Basel?"

Which tells the inspector most everything she needs to know. The *SU* had collected the blade and would keep it till the file was closed, or turn it over to IJ, if requested. But the blade's tin-foil wrapper is still on the table, in plain sight with the rest of the detritus of Colette Namur's last day. Now it's sure Colette's friend's prints will be all over those bottles, that wrapper, but not the blade; she wouldn't have touched the blade…so surely that this friend will have no qualms admitting she'd been there. To try to help Colette. To offer some guidance through another rocky time. You have to have friends when things go bad. Women have to stick together. Aliette can hear Flossie Orain's smooth voice as if she were still sitting there, helping Colette work it out.

Aliette reads the note again; it was in an envelope addressed to Vivienne Namur lying on Vivi's bed:

> Vivi. I did my bit. I'll see you when you've done yours.
>   Love, Maman.

Poor Colette. All that remains is to deliver it. Flossie's still blameless, Flossie's safe. Who needs to kill when all you have to do is talk—over a lot of wine and possibly also a beer?

Walking away from that dead-end circle, going into the high street to find a cab, she looks back. Yes—*dwellers*, too far from it all to ever be considered citizens. It's their murmurings as they sit with their young, all life revolving around the tiny park, the constant creak of the rusty swings, creaking fruitlessly like a one-note message from a distant outpost, sending…sending, but receiving nothing back to bring the outpost closer to the world: swinging, swinging—their message, their diversion. Colette Namur had "saved" her daughter from this, then had gotten out.

And so back to Mari Morgan's. A man with a briefcase identical to her own is arriving at the same moment and holds the door for her. A gentleman. Someone might have thought they were a couple: a handsome and successful couple with *his* and *hers* cases, arriving for an evening of something different at the end of another day downtown.

But Martine is there to greet this man and they head straight into the bar. While Aliette stands watching another man. This one's struggling without success to move Louise out of his path and mount the stairs. "But she needs me!" protests the man, several times. Aliette hears the accent. English or American, it sounds like.

"No," says Louise, "she needs *us*."

"A client," mutters Flossie, suddenly at the inspector's side. "Vivi's American. Some get like that." Stepping forward, she takes control of the situation; Louise stares at Aliette for a strange moment, then heads back upstairs. Flossie's polite but firm as she guides the man out, advising, "Give her a few days, monsieur. She needs time to think…" Then, voice altering, "Of course if there's anything else we can do for you…"

Then a quiet tête-à-tête with the police.

"How is she?" asks the inspector.

"Best left alone to think it through."

"Colette might have been as well."

"You would think so. She begged me to come."

"With a razor blade, Flossie?"

"I always carry one, Inspector…been too many places in my life where it's made the difference between a few words and much worse. I took it out to make a point."

"What point was that?"

"To challenge her into taking some responsibility for her decisions. Colette Namur always followed along like a sheep, then blamed everything on the big bad world. She was hard to admire. You have to let a person have her own life and fate can be mean—and so you try to help. But after a certain point…I got mad. I told her she should have the courage of her convictions or there was no point. Which is true, no?" Aliette Nouvelle won't answer that and Flossie Orain's frank gaze is transformed by an exasperated sigh. "I didn't think she would go that far."

"You thought she might be saved by her convictions."

"Colette missed it. She missed on everything."

"You used her, Flossie…you used her terribly, somehow, to murder Manon Larivière. I'm going to prove it."

"But how could I have?…and why would I?"

"I'm not sure. But people *are* desperate and they *do* follow along like sheep. I think you talked Colette into killing Manon. An initiation fee? The only way into this place for Vivi? Her little bit for the goddess? I don't know, but I will find out."

"Please don't be absurd…not today. Even if I could, Colette could never do such a thing."

"Not alone. Probably not alone. That Francine—pretending to take care of the old man who was Manon's friend—"

"Who?"

Aliette can't help but smile—but sadly, feeling tired, sick of it. "Doctor Cyr's non-live-in?"

Flossie's eyes don't waver. "I thought she was Léonie."

"No, Flossie…Francine. They've both disappeared."

The smile coming back is ironic. "Well, at least that's halfway reasonable."

"Yes," agrees Aliette, "far too reasonable."

"I don't understand."

"I think you do—and I'm certain you talked Colette Namur straight into that tub."

"Inspector Nouvelle," pausing…thoughtful, "sometimes belief has to be stronger than feelings. It's the only source of power. Why do you think I gave you those letters? I could have burned them. I gave them to you, freely. Do you think I didn't feel her pain?"

"I don't know what you feel, Flossie. Here's one more letter," taking it from her pocket, "but it's not for you. Are you honest enough to deliver it?"

Flossie takes the letter. "All my life," she says, suddenly a step closer, confiding like a long-time friend, grotesque in her presumption, "one thing I've never been able to cope with: the weak ones who latch on… They latch on and keep telling you how much they love you so you'll let them drag along behind. It drives me crazy."

Aliette steps back, away from the hand that reaches to touch hers. "I'm not a weak one."

"I know that. I think we have a lot in common, you and I… You say you don't know how I feel. Well *that's* how I feel. I wish you'd stop thinking this way. I can't see how it will help anyone."

At this moment Aliette would like nothing more than to just smack Flossie across the mouth. And add a few carefully chosen words. But she won't. Undignified. Police work is a human game, a highly civilized one; in the end dignity can be the deciding factor… No, as the gall of disgust, possibly even hatred begins to tie a knot inside her stomach, the inspector simply thanks her adversary, while her eyes say something along the lines of, At least now it's plain. Then she takes her leave. Gracefully.

Aliette Nouvelle: graceful.

Flossie Orain: fading back behind the opaque mask as she softly closes the door.

2.

An exhumation order for the remains and effects of Manon Larivière signed by Gérard Richand is on her desk when she gets back to the office to do her report. Good; she was pretty sure it would be. Still nothing on the missing car, its elderly owner or an ex-Arletty look-alike. Jean-Marc Pouliot is still fooling around with three-word combinations that might befit a last farewell from a bloody tub. But one small step: we'll get our Marilyn Monroe's underwear back. Is that worth missing the plane for, her family, the beach, a rest? It will have to be. She goes home and calls her maman, tells her, far too businesslike (only way she can manage it), that they should not expect her at Belle Ile.

Next morning the inspector sits beside Claude in the back of his official car, following a police hearse out to the grave site. Early, 7:30; they dig at 8:00, before any funeral guests have a chance to witness the lurid and always fantastic front-page act of digging up the dead. We don't need that, thank you… Claude's not talking to her. Pissed off at the way she worked around him. Not that it matters. All that matters is the mandate from Gérard. The back-hoe and two men arrive for work at the regular hour, unaware of their task, sleepily expecting to dig another grave. Working in the other direction does not bother them though, until, thirty minutes later, when they hoist the box out of the ground, sweep it clean and slide it into the back of the hearse. Something's not quite right—she can see it on their faces. She asks the *SU* cop who drives the hearse, "What's their problem?"

"They were saying either she rotted at record speed, or it's empty."

"Oh Jesus!" exclaims Commissaire Néon an hour later, when the latter is confirmed: there is no Marilyn Monroe facsimile in this box, no elegant underwear either.

Inspector Nouvelle is rocked as well, but not completely surprised. The bottom keeps falling out of this one at every turn... Mmm, and the bottom is falling out of her commitment to find an answer for a woman who got trapped inside a star.

So they had to steal her body back. How creepy can you get?

She sits at her desk with nothing. She was going to call and cancel her flight, stay on the job and track a goddess, uncover her nature, the compelling thing that lives in a goddess' heart. But now... They're so tedious, these people with their little beliefs. They must be little, the way they hide them away: little beliefs, too precious to withstand the light of day; and they must be tedious, tedious at heart, the way they all fall into line. Hare Krishnas smiling on the streets of Paris. Moonies getting married en masse in a stadium. Residents of a fortress in Texas following their gun-loving leader into the flames. Citizens of Jonestown—and their dogs!—hiding in the jungle, lapping up that deadly Kool-Aid. All together, brothers and sisters! And just last fall: the burned-out bunker of the Order of the Solar Temple just down the road in Switzerland, so elaborate in its crimson accoutrement, so rich and pure of vision. All ashes. Did those believers make it through?

Manon Larivière. Colette Namur. Cut from the same sad cloth, no? Asking for it, no? Hate to think it, but Flossie's right: fate *can* be mean, and all the more so if you give yourself completely. Dying for something called belief? Tedious and pathological. Well, *allez-y,* go for it, sisters! And what a silly Aliette for thinking they needed the likes of her. Gazing out at a sunny sky, she's on that plane to Nantes. And not... Wavering between a sense of duty and futility, burdened with this feeling of throwing good energy after bad, disgusted by a world full of half-brained sheep.

Does she really care about stupid prostitutes?

What about useless mothers on the edge of town?

We have a man in provisional detention. The men who run the system perceive a pattern in this man's life and logical reasons for him to be there. Herménégilde Dupras is their solution to the crime and the best way in to the roots of their sense of the larger problem. And we have an inspector in the grips of that provisional feeling. It crops up when she's stalled. When she knows she's got nothing solid on Flossie Orain. Is the journey through all the lies and the sheep—yes Flossie, they're a pain in the ass and there are always too many, milling around the way sheep do, blocking the way to the truth—is that journey worth the trouble? There'll always be another Marilyn Monroe fan. Legions of Colette Namurs. And you certainly don't need a Herméné to run a Mari Morgan's. Who learns? What gets better? Mmm, this one's not worth it. *Stay on that plane, Aliette.* It'll keep till I get back. *Oh yes, the goddess keeps.* Whatever's left of it...

There's lots left—or it wouldn't be a journey, would it?

Right. A journey. Merci. She collects her things and heads straight out. Walks it, down to the Palais through the excellent morning. She should call, but can't wait for official channels; she'll knock on the door instead. She'll be on that plane tomorrow.

Marcel Cyr; that first day: "Here's to the next part of her journey."

Could he actually dig her up and drive her to the coast in that lovely car, put her on a ferry and take her across to Sein? You would need your non-live-in as a helper for a trip like that. We're talking ten, twelve hours, more like a day in that old car; even a Marilyn Monroe would begin to reek something horrible. And why in the world? Yet all signs point that way.

3.

Not Gérard's door. Gérard has escaped—he should be somewhere near Lyons by now, his kids presenting arguments for their lunch. Nor the door of any junior J.of I. who may have been left with the file. Aliette climbs the marble stairs, turns right instead of left on the landing, and hustles along the solemn hall. The offices of the Procureur occupy the other end of the top floor. The better end, known as *le Parquet*, referring to the magistrates down on the floor representing the interests of the community as opposed to the magistrates up on *le Siège* (the bench), independent of interest save service to the written law. But not Michel Souviron's door either. Michel has also escaped—from what she hears, he usually goes camping in the Alps. Michel, pleasant and accommodating as he is, would still likely tell her to go back to Gérard, or if he did let her in (after a good long wait, because that's Michel's quiet way of making sure we don't lose track of who is who), he would somehow make a joke of it and tell her no. Aliette has thought this through. If Gérard or Michel cry foul and they remove Inspector Nouvelle from the file? Well, wait till September…

"Can you help me?"

It's Substitute Proc Cécile Botrel who lets her in without a wait, who's in charge of this one during Michel's absence, who's not at all put out by the inspector's request. Nevertheless:

"I'm sorry, there's still too much of a gap. Nothing to support it." The inspector's second try at an interpellation order to be served to Florence Orain. "He said you might come calling with just such a request and forbade it expressly. The risk. He meant the fallout, not the legality, of course. But that's part of his job. Mine too. I won't second-guess him…I like it here."

Very up-front, this Sub. Maître Botrel is in charge, but, as she admits, not completely. "I had to ask," shrugs Aliette… Yes: Her smile, smart eyes, simple hair, bookish lenses, no adornment in her ears, minimal makeup, there's a synchronicity between her pared-down presence and her straightforward manner that attracts. Despite the refusal, the inspector finds herself buoyed up by this woman. An ally. Hard to come by when competing duties lie between.

"…But I will rewrite your mandate to include the locating of the missing body, obviously. To include, but not necessarily be tied to, your search for the car and Marcel Cyr…" jotting notes; "the same to apply to the locating of one Francine Léotard, aka Léonie Brandeau. Include InterPol alert; a car like that's a treasure, could be headed anywhere. I assume you've a network up and running on this."

"Yes, but I'll need an assistant to work it when I'm away. If you could suggest it to my boss."

"I could… And I'll send introductions if you find yourself working on someone's else patch."

Merci.

"Do you think it's likely? I'll call this afternoon. I'll tell them you're coming and make sure they welcome you with open arms."

"Please, I wouldn't call anyone just yet. I'm not certain and I apologize for that…"

"Don't apologize."

"Maybe there is no connection. Maybe this Doctor Cyr is a very strange old man and that's all there is to a missing body. If I were Flossie Orain, that's what I'd say… I'll be very quiet. Likely mostly on the beach. What I mean to say is, it's down on the books as my holiday." No point playing games with someone who seems open, willing, even eager to try things.

Cécile Botrel says only, "A holiday is good for the soul."

Yes, purify it a bit; get rid of this sour sense of things. "But I will go to Sein; it's just up the road. It all starts there—at least according to what I've been hearing, and I have to go and see. I'll call you if it's turning into work."

"Fair enough." The Substitute lays her pen and notes aside. "I appreciate your frustration, Inspector. Body snatchers don't help the matter. And I do see your inclination to have a better leverage with Florence Orain."

"Do you?" On the record or not, I need some back-up here.

"When we went in there, after you… It's just a feeling you get from a person, isn't it? Apart from the way she worked Michel, I was quite spooked by her intelligence, frankly."

"Yes…"

"She doesn't need to be there, doing that…she could be sitting here, easily, if she had wanted."

"Well, she has a cause, doesn't she?"

"The goddess?"

The inspector offers a bitter smile. "Her brothel is ground zero."

"She said that?"

"Yes. And she more or less admitted she handed the blade to Colette Namur…challenged her into slicing her wrists."

"More or less?"

"Like you say, she could be sitting here if she'd wanted. She knows exactly where the lines are."

"Did Colette Namur want her child back?"

"I don't think so. She idolized Flossie Orain all her life. Call it separation anxiety. Flossie helped her deal with it. A true sister."

"In any case, Colette Namur's a tragedy but she's out of the game. It's still this unknown Manon Larivière."

"We know she had headaches." This is a cop in the act of mocking her own lack of results. *Stop it, Aliette—work with this woman!*

"And that she appears to have been killed by a man who—"

"—whether you like him or not appears to have had a genuine affection and no real reason!" The inspector rolls her eyes, takes a deep breath…this by way of begging pardon for interrupting in such a manner; pardon is granted with a nod; the inspector repeats what her gut will not stop telling her: "It's Flossie. And some or all of the rest of them. Somehow."

"Fine. That's the way you're headed—let's stick with that." Cécile Botrel sits back in her chair, considering it. "Killing their own… You'd think it would be men—if we're talking ground zero." And now a wry smile, musing, "…the poor goddess."

"You're laughing?"

"Not in the least… I—well I've never been the kind to burn twigs, but I…"

But it's Aliette Nouvelle who has to crunch the smile. Call it incredulity.

The Proc catches it. "But I'm a lawyer?" She allows a quick laugh to emerge, to show she can live with incredulity. "Yes, and I love the law, the logic…better word is reasonableness. The goddess keeps me grounded when the abstractions glow too strongly. Fairness, not power… It's inclusive. The state needs fairness as much as the defence, no? And I don't feel you and I are in competition the way some of my colleagues might. You and I, we circle around truth and a fair solution. It's not set in stone. The goddess seems to be a reflection of that and this lawyer happens to be more comfortable with her than any of the other choices. That is, if spiritual predilection is a choice."

The inspector is bemused, as always when people start telling her, unbidden, about their lives.

"And you?" asks Cécile.

"Oh…" For Aliette, the question is like a balloon floating in the air: one tapped at it when it came near, one waited till it came near again…with no deep need to grab onto it. "I never really think about gods or goddesses. I hope there's one who likes me…" Folding her arms, feeling her cheeks warming. Embarrassed. Why? Because this woman is willing to share some feelings over and above her professional opinion? "I mean, should the Pope capitulate on female priests or should a doddering old church just quietly die? I think about it once in a blue moon but never more than that… Be sad if it died."

"It's too rich to die," argues the lawyer. "And ordination of women wouldn't take away the politics of hierarchy. People would still fight and make deals—all that tiresome noise when it's supposed to be about the sound of eternity. Personally, I can live without churches."

Simultaneously, both women make gestures as they face each other, waving away a church that has grown too old. *Bon*, we connect through silence, even in offices. *I do…I like this woman.* "But, no offence, Maître, there's never been a matriarchy. Matri*lines*, yes, lots; but matri*archy*…" shaking her head at Cécile Botrel, "no proof at all, I'm afraid."

"I'm not offended. And I don't need proof." Confident lawyer eyes fixed on those of a skeptical cop.

"A lawyer who doesn't need proof? What then, if I may ask?"

"Some stories. A feeling. An approach to life that grows from one to the other. Forget the philosophers, the logistic proof on any side of it—god, goddess, however you conceive of it. Philosophy, logic, history, anthropology, myth or theology…all very necessary, lots of it beautiful, but none of it can cross the gap to faith. Only the poets can build that kind of bridge."

"At Mari Morgan's they have a verse. And a motto. And…" it occurs; "a model of a cow." Hm.

"*Voilà*. Stories and a feeling is all it ever is…" A big bright smile sent across the table. "I'm a lawyer. I know these things."

A partial smile coming back. Oh yes? "I've been wondering…if there *were* a goddess ascendant, in our minds, the culture…wherever— whether there'd be any prostitutes at all. Perhaps human beings would be different. Perhaps love and attraction would occur in a different way." She shrugs. "…I haven't got too far with that one."

"There are reputable psychologists out there who'll tell you that prostitutes *are* the goddess. But," her tone falling back inside its official timbre, "it's not prostitutes or a goddess, Inspector, it's a murder. One human being killing another. This is what we're here to solve."

"You're right…" Actually chuckling for the first time in several days; "I guess everyone needs a clear-thinking lawyer occasionally."

"And I'll pretend that's a compliment." Standing, like Michel, like Gérard…reaching to shake her hand. "Enjoy the beach. I hope you see something miraculous on Sein."

5.

Aliette goes back to her office and confirms her flight. Assistant Inspector Patrice Lebeau taps on her door: at her service. Merci, Cécile Botrel! She briefs him on Marcel Cyr and his bogus maid, the classic car…asks him to keep an eye on the premises and movements of Ondine Duguay. She clears her desk. Waters her cherished shamrock, promises it Monique will come in to take good care. She smiles a modest *au revoir* to Claude.

Claude, unsmiling, says, "*Bonnes vacances…*" Adds, "Leave a number with Monique."

"I will."

She calls her mother to announce the change of her change of plan.

"Are you all right, dear?"

She probably deserves that—although from the very first declaration that she would become a "detective," Maman has been consistently leery of her elder daughter's chosen career. "I'm fine. Things are just a bit tense at the moment."

"A good time to come home then. We look forward to seeing you."

"Merci. I love you…"

On the way out, stopping at Monique's desk with watering instructions and coordinates for Nantes and at Belle Ile—there's an envelope from *Le Parquet*. The note is printed on official stationery:

> Inspector, Messieurs Léger and Pouliot of IJ have sent along the results of their work yesterday. This morning's developments mean I can't comment on its evidential value. However, where Monsieur Pouliot can offer no solution to Colette Namur's final moments in her bath, something did occur to me which may be of interest. Given the context of your investigation as it appears to be evolving, you might want to consider that 'Maeve,' an Irish name and still quite popular, was the name of a legendary Celtic queen given to war, dirty politics and much sexual subterfuge. Maeve was one of those who knew all about power. I have no idea if she was actual or not. Interesting character, though. Tuck it away.
>
> Faithfully, Me. Cécile Botrel, Substitute Procureur.

C'est beau Maeve?

She takes the long way home and stops at Ondine Duguay's. She feels the seamstress may be more forthcoming now—out of fear if nothing else. And she wants her new top, if not for Raphaele Petrucci's pleasure (no, she hasn't called him yet to break their date; wasn't in the right frame of mind as she left the building; but she will, she will…) then for whichever man lucky enough to meet her on the beach at Belle Ile. Mmm, now she knows for sure she's going, Raphaele is fading. Now it's a stranger who admires her, who holds her hand and guides her through his airy rooms overlooking the ocean toward his simple bed…

"Something's not right with the goddess… Eh? Ondine? Want to talk to me yet?"

Not yet. Aliette's package, wrapped in tissue and packed in a much-travelled shopping bag, is duly handed over. She doesn't open it. She waits for Ondine.

Whose eyes, red and strained behind bifocals, will not meet hers. They're looking away, out the window at the small service tree, growing heavy, dropping its fruit in the shadows of the long neglected yard. Finally Ondine says…whispers is more the tone, "We have to be strong. So strong. Everything is changing."

"Madame, we have to be superwomen. But if we don't make the grade it doesn't mean we have to die."

"Everyone has a role to play." As if repeating a catechism.

"Right," snaps the cop. "Now why don't you go over there and tell it to Flossie Orain!"

"I don't… I can't…it's not my world."

"Will you stop saying that! You're still here in the world with the rest of us…you're not helpless! You brought the goddess to those women. It's you who knows what she's supposed to be. Tell them! If not for Manon and Colette, then for the sake of Colette's daughter… Tell Flossie. Tell Louise—they're not doing it right. What's *your* role, Ondine?"

Ondine trembles as she ventures to speak. An inquisitive look—like some mistreated animal: why are you doing this to me? Biting down on her bottom lip, she manages to squelch the tremor. "I make their things. Aren't you going to look at the thing I made for you?"

"What if I went to Sein? What do you think I'd find there? Would it help me understand the problem at Mari Morgan's?"

"Nothing… Rocks. A beach. The sea. Stars in the sky…"

"What about love? …Ondine!"

"I don't know what's there for you! …I found something spiritual at a time when I needed it. Don't you blame me for it!"

"I wouldn't. I won't!" *Calm down, please, Aliette.* "…But what do you need now? It would be good to have someone to talk to, wouldn't it?"

"And stop treating me like a fool! I've had enough!"

Aliette believes her. She asks—simply, "Do you want me to bring Georgette?" Ondine only stares at the package. So she opens it. Soft… Yet such a cool steely blue, holding it close to her eyes in front of the mirror. And the edging is an intricate calligraphy any lover could study for hours at the table of her body. The AN monogram stitched in royal at the right thigh: it's Aliette's and no one else's. It *is*

Aliette—it's the thing that waits inside. "It's lovely. Perfect…" Trying to smile, taking out her wallet.

"Thank you." The compliment; the payment. Ondine seems lost as she smiles back.

So that an inspector feels like crying. That provisional feeling. That urge to get away.

As for Georgette: No group on Fridays; and anyway there's too much packing and buttering up of Madame Camus, her landlady, getting an absolute promise not to forget to feed poor Piaf, let him out, let him in, yes of course he loves to be scratched… For Georgette she composes a brief note to be left under the wiper of the old VW Westfalia van sometime in the middle of the night:

> Your sister needs you. AN.

And Raphaele? *Don't be such a chicken, Aliette. Call him…* I'm not! I will. Tomorrow…

6.

Tomorrow arrives. Saturday, August 15. Assumption Day. It's well flagged on any calendar and any girl schooled by the nuns will mark it, at least in passing. The cab driver is instructed to stop for a moment at the pathologist's apartment door. Good strategy: a plane to catch—no way she can sit there making excuses for too long. *Is this called sexual subterfuge?* But he's not there. Damn. Probably at the market getting those three cheeses and other nice things for tonight.

Oh well. Another note:

> Sorry—duty calls me westward. Please forgive… Perhaps when I return?

But how to sign it? Aliette? Aliette Nouvelle? Your friend, A. Nouvelle? Inspector Nouvelle?

Oh god… She goes with the friendly, but not overly, AN.

Assumption Day. At noon the skies are clear. She's feeling virginal in the original sense, i.e., independent, free of it all, for a month at least…at least for today.

And so she flies away.

3RD PART
PERSONNE POURSUIVI...
PEINE JUSTIFIÉE

In search of the mind that guides
the murdering hand.

"By ancient tradition, the White Goddess becomes one with her human representative—a priestess, a prophetess, a queen-mother."

—Robert Graves,
The White Goddess

10

A LINE ACROSS YOUR LIFE

Time draws natural lines across the course of a life; but an island in the middle of nowhere will tend to bundle time into itself. This is how the goddess sees it. While Aliette flies west in a jet, ultimate destination Sein, Ondine gets there first by memory.

It's a Saturday in September, 1943. Ondine Duguay rides out from the port of Audierne on a slow trawler toward the light at Raz, and the Ile de Sein six miles beyond. She has taken a bus from Quimper that morning and is on her way to do business with one Angélique Ménou, the woman who makes the tallest, most intricate *coiffes* in Pauline Brekelien's shop, a *dentellerie* in the Rue Sainte Catharine. She's almost twenty. She's been with Pauline, at first as an apprentice, attaching and mending for her keep, since stopping in Quimper just before the outbreak of the war. She's lonely but used to it; these Breton people are odd and it's odder to think her mother had been one of them. She has often had to wonder why she left Georgette and came out here all alone to find an answer for her mother's life. Because it doesn't seem she's found it… But she has learned the lacemaker's trade to Pauline's satisfaction, and has also discovered a talent for managing money. Which is the reason she is on that boat, travelling as Pauline's agent.

The sun is bright, but the sea wind chills and she tucks her skirt snugly round her knees. She pulls her jacket collar up and huddles on the back deck, watching seabirds swooping and squawking in a trail along the boat's wake. Being out on the water gives a sense of freedom.

At the wharf, soldiers of the occupying army had scrutinized the papers and belongings of the seven women passengers, just as they had checked every basket, sack and crate destined for the remote island community. A gunboat has escorted them to a safe channel. There are long guns couched in embankments along the shore, ready to blow them to pieces if need be. There'll be a small garrison, guarding Sein in the name of the Reich, waiting to greet them when they land. Guarding an island of women; in June of 1940, after the defeat, the men of Sein had all—113 of them—sailed off to England, answering the famous radio call of the exiled General de Gaulle.

There's a girl who's used to boats, moving from passenger to passenger, offering apples. Back at the dock Ondine had watched her overseeing the tallying and loading of a dozen bushel baskets. She's clad in the usual drab layering of grey skirts and an apron favoured by Bretonne women, a stitched collar and brooch her only adornment. What sets the girl apart as an islander is the black, winged, helmet-like bonnet concealing her pinned-up hair. A *jibilinen*. Ondine recalls the hats worn by the Papal Guard, seen once in a postcard. As she draws near, Ondine hears a tune—a girl's soft whistle under the wind, and recognizes a song heard on Sunday afternoons in town as the men quaff ale and cider and clomp around in their wooden shoes in front of the taverns. *Le Pommier enchanté*…The Enchanted Apple Tree:

> Dans le mitan de mon verger
> Je possède un fameux pommier
> Qui donne tant et tant de pommes
> Lidoric lon laire
> Que tout le monde en peut manger
> Lidoric lon lé
> Lidoric lon lé
> Tout le monde en peut manger!
>
> In the heart of my orchard I have a special apple tree
> It gives so many apples that everyone may eat
>
> But when you climb this tree to taste the fruit on high
> It is forbidden to come down 'til all the fruit is gone.

One day inside my orchard Death came by for me
"O Sir, try an apple while I go to make me ready."

Now grey Death is my own prisoner up in my apple tree
Eating one harvest of apples while the next surely grows.

With a modest nod, the girl proffers the fruit. For a moment Ondine glimpses her plain bronzed youthfulness hidden under her costume—and behind the reticence an outsider naturally shows. "Merci, mademoiselle." She has heard, often during the winding, gossipy course of the day at the shop, and quite pointedly as Pauline sent her off on this trip, that the women of Sein are a strange and not so friendly lot, ferocious and cunning in their vindictiveness when it came to quarrels—"Anything you bring back is on consignment; don't you dare advance her a single sou!" And deeply, darkly superstitious. "The only boat you'll ever see the likes of her in is a basket, with her rake for a mast and her apron for a sail." Meaning Angélique Ménou was a witch, probably all her sisters too. Strong words; because Ondine could not imagine any women more dyed-in-the-wool skeptical and fervent in their attachment to the "old ways" than Pauline or the others at the shop, or, for that matter, almost any woman she might meet in the streets of Quimper. They're good women (hadn't they accepted an orphan from Nevers?) but they're a breed apart. The collars and bonnets worn by all the women and girls on festival days, and by some of them every day, are Pauline's stock-in-trade…

It's coming up four o'clock as they skirt the shore from the south-east. Sein is flat and treeless, hardly two miles long and less than one mile wide. "We call that one Nerroth…" The apple girl is beside her, grey eyes shot with a brilliant silver as she squints into the angling sun.

"Excuse me?" says Ondine.

"Those rocks." Pointing to a formation. To Ondine it looks vaguely like someone reclining, reading perhaps…with her knees folded up. Then the girl points to the next clump at the tip of the next cove. "That one's the Pig. And over there…" pointing to the north, "the Cat's Tail."

Ondine squints hard but the stone creatures elude her. So she points at the big light. "What about that light: is it on the island? Maybe I'd like to walk to it."

"Ar Men? *Mais non, madame…*" with a gruff chuckle, not very girlish at all; "Ar Men is as far as the moon. Between the light and our island there are a thousand dead men and boats."

Ondine shields her eyes and looks again, but the tip of Sein and the stretch of sea are impossible to separate. "It's hard to tell distances out here."

"It's true," agrees the girl. "But it's a nice thought—to walk out on the sea…"

A small crowd waits as the pilot brings the vessel to berth against two huge tires slung along the wall of the quay. Several women are wearing the odd cylindrical headpieces, the coiffe, some more than a foot in height, miniature towers of the most exquisite lace patterning, pristine and medieval. Most of the others wear the sombre *jibilinen.* The mail is distributed before anything else, directly from the gangplank. Two of the women—standing, strangely, right beside each other and both of them wearing the high coiffe—begin to wail in despair, one…then the other, as they open their sad notices. Everyone, including the two German soldiers, pauses to watch.

Ondine feels a tug on her arm. She looks into heavy-lidded, sun-washed eyes. The woman is stocky, maybe forty or forty-five, and one of those wearing the more practical black bonnet. Beneath its brim is a broad spoony face built around thick lips and a wide mouth. "You've come from Pauline Brekelien." Stated in a flat tone that conveys no trace of welcome.

"Oui…Madame Ménou?" Extending her hand. "My name is Ondine Duguay."

But the woman glares, somehow affronted. "You know the Holy Mother sees all the way from Paradise to Sein. She knows my work is the best in all the Finistère. You won't get one piece of it without hard cash—first!" With that, she turns and walks off.

Ondine grabs her bag and hurries after. "Madame…in this war economy it's very difficult for a retailer like Pauline to have a lot of cash on hand. We go from month to month… Pauline has the best reputation in the biggest market! She gets the best price… You get the best percentage!"

Angélique Ménou stops, sizes her up again, looks away and spits on the cobblestone. "She owes me a thousand francs."

Ondine takes bills from her purse and hands them over—efficient, honest, and with a smile. With another smile, not quite as certain, she says, "Now you're liquid."

The woman scratches at her nut-brown nose, snorting crudely. "I haven't been liquid for thirteen years…since the eve of Pentecost, when my dear ignorant François decided to go out fishing."

"Something happened?"

"Of course. He was caught in a storm and lost."

"I'm sorry."

Her heavy mouth juts, her thick lips press and curl, ironic. "Oh, he's out there somewhere."

Ondine is not sure how to respond, but at least now she knows she's welcome, more or less. She follows Angélique Ménou off the quay into a street barely broad enough for a wagon to pass. They proceed in silence, turning tiny corners, passing in and out of the dimming light till they come to a door in rue Paul Goardan. The house is clean and deceptively large, two levels, built in an *L* shape. The door hiding the back stairs fools Ondine—until she is shown through it and up to her room. Another oddity is the bed set partially into the wall, like a berth on a boat or a crypt in a tomb. The room faces west and a ray of evening sun highlights the heavy, well-oiled woodwork. Charming evidence of her host's creative hands can be seen in the curtains, the doily under the basin, the bedspread and pillow case.

Left alone, the traveller peers out the window. For the second time she sees the tall figure of the Ar Men light, and now its flat twilight glow. She hears a clank and a lowing. A white cow, a healthy size, stands in a makeshift stall of straw fashioned under the eave in one corner of the yard. A small vegetable garden is doing well in the centre of the yard. Now the girl from the boat appears at the gate, followed in by the old pilot pulling a stevedore's cart containing the baskets of apples. Angélique emerges from her kitchen and greets the girl with a brusque kiss. As Ondine watches the unloading of the apples, the girl goes in and out of the house in obediant response to Angélique's commands…it becomes clear that the girl is Angélique's daughter. Then, the unloading done, the pilot and cart departed and her hosts having gone back inside, Ondine rests in silence, save for the sporadic clank of the cow's bell and the soft hum of the wind. The wind: she realizes she has been hearing this sound from the moment the boat's engine stopped and she set her foot on Sein.

The girl's name is Dorise. Without her cap, her black hair is thin and shapeless, parted at the side like a boy's, hanging just above her collar. She's fifteen. "She has her father's face," says Angélique.

Supper is a potato-and-barley broth, a flat bread with fresh butter—which is a treat—and a glass of milk. They eat in silence, for which Ondine feels responsible. "How did you manage to get all those apples?" she finally asks.

"I trade my tickets and save them till the harvest… The Germans allow them at harvest."

"But all for you?"

"That's none of their concern."

"What do you trade?"

"Butter and milk."

"We're lucky," adds Dorise, "we have Céleste. We don't need much else from the mainland."

"Céleste…" repeats Ondine. "She's pretty." Because neither Angélique nor her daughter are.

Mentioning the mainland reminds Dorise that she has brought mail along with the apples. Fetching the opened envelope from her jacket pocket, she lays it by her mother's plate. Angélique wipes her bread in the last of her soup as she reads.

Dorise begins to clear the table. "My brother Yann. He's older than you. You're…?"

"Twenty in December."

"Oh. Well then, you're twins. He went with the rest of them."

"Now he's in the British navy," mutters Angélique, rueful, as if it were the most absurd and unreal thing that could have happened. She lets the letter slip from her fingers. Sits staring into her empty bowl.

"Very brave," ventures Ondine.

Brave? Angélique grunts. Brave has no meaning on a flat piece of rock called Sein. "I would like Herr Hitler to come over here for a brief stay before he conquers the rest of the world. I would sit on his face and show him what was what, and I think everything else would be fine after that."

Dorise is filling the sink. Ondine sees her cheeks grow red from her mother's remark…and she feels her own doing likewise. Blasé, Angélique rises from the table. She offers no coffee or sweets. Not even an apple. Beckoning her guest to follow, they leave Dorise with the dishes and go through the dark hall to the salon.

The room is dimly lit by lamps on side tables. The walls are a white brick, enhanced against the dark wood of the furnishings. In one corner stands a blue cloaked Virgin, almost life-size, her sorrowful eyes at a level with the wainscoting. Ondine sees pictures of the two men: the dead husband, and that must be Yann, in his sailor's suit, with his mother's thick mouth and concave features. Brilliant sunny eyes…Yann is handsome; she's happy to be his "twin." Other photographs show older people and babies, Dorise with a group of staring girls and a stolid priest on their Confirmation day, and a younger Angélique dressed for her wedding. But to business. The merchandise is laid out across the divan and two side-tables: four dozen new coiffes all in the tall style that is Sein's trademark, but with varying patterns in the needlework, and with delicate single, single-split or double lace tails attached. Ondine puts her fingers on each item, marvelling at the work and wondering how to get safely back to the subject of money. Angélique, meanwhile, takes a bottle from the cabinet and two thimble-sized glasses. She pours one for herself and one for Ondine, takes a sip from hers, then sits like a bishop, waiting.

Ondine, polite, wets her tongue. She's not much of a drinker. Had she been, she might have recognized something akin to a diluted Canadian rye buffered by a taste of apple. It's the hint of apple flavour that allows her to dip her tongue a second time…and then a third. She can't say she likes it, but it's important to be gracious.

Dorise does not join them… But they never do get around to money. Ondine's questions about Angélique's facility in the craft of lacemaking turn, easily and inevitably, into snippets about herself: Pauline, the shop and her life in Quimper…then to shy, muted thoughts about her mother's death…her father's less than honest life. All the while Ondine carefully samples the apple-tinged liquor. Soon she's talking too much but there's much to be told. About her sister Georgette: how she was as tall as Georgette—had matched her year for year, but everything else was slightly less so, from her breasts to her hips to the shine in her hair…how Georgette's had an auburn sheen that glowed almost red after she washed it, but her own's this chestnut colour, a little finer and it does not blow around her face in the extravagant way she would like…and Ondine hears herself telling Angélique Ménou how she and Georgette had argued bitterly about the things their poor mother had believed, and how she'd left her doubting sister and travelled to the Finistère. "All alone…I came all alone, because it can't be true that she has to be in hell. That's not fair. It's not her fault she lost her hope and died… Could it be?"

But why would she know—this tough, crude woman from Sein?

But Ondine cannot stop spilling out her heart that night. Nor can she take her eyes away from the image of Yann the sailor. Thinking, He looks so good to me…strong!

"He was a virgin when he left here," murmurs her host.

And thinking, Did I actually hear her say that?

When Angélique announces, "You will wear one of my coiffes when we go to mass tomorrow," and standing, signals the end of the day, Ondine goes to her room feeling as if she's been stopped in mid-flow. Mid-dream! There's much more in her heart. Sitting on her bed looking out at the night, bemused, enjoying the lingering effects of her drink… A sliver of moon glides north amid countless stars. Sein's own light is down, by order, but the beam from Ar Men is long and bright, swinging through its rotation, filling her face for an instant, then moving on, leaving dappled waters behind it. She hopes the British Navy can see it. She closes the shutters.

Another dull clank…clank of a cow bell. Céleste is stirring in her straw bed in the yard below. Ondine wishes her good night, rolls into her pillow and drifts off to the hum of the endless wind.

Clank, clank…clank. It comes through her sleep. Dorise is standing by the door holding a lantern. Ondine pulls her jacket on over her nightdress and slips on her shoes. "It's the men," whispers Dorise. Ondine thinks, But aren't the men all gone to the war? But as they go marching into the night, she's feeling something like a soldier herself, following Céleste. Céleste has been given the lantern and it swings from her horn… Clank, clank…clank, out past the end of the road and along the path by the seawall, down to the beach.

The Ar Men beam is down now too. A veil of emerald glows in the sky, woven in patches through the rolling mass of cloud, its reflection glittering on the black face of the waters. Dorise stands in the edges of the surf, looking out to sea—anxious, expectant. Ondine is delighted to see that Céleste has been joined by friends of her own kind, all carrying lanterns and bells, moving in random patterns, bells clanking, sporadic, noisy, their lowing blending with the wind. Ageless menhirs are scattered in the shallows, pointing to the heavens, saluting the magnificent light. Then Dorise waves into the darkness and the wind seems to rise. Ondine feels her hair lash and dance like it's never done as she moves along the foamy steps. Now Dorise is waving frantically and running to the point. The wind whips the sea into a beautiful chaos. There! …A boat is approaching!

A small boat with a single light swinging from its spar rocks into view.

Ondine can see the outline of a man…one man alone, and he's afraid and confused.

Ondine wonders, Who could be fearful at such a moment? Look at Céleste and her friends: a marvellous sliding twinkling configuration! What could a sailor possibly fear approaching such a sight? It must be even *more* beautiful for him, out there…like stones on the necklace of a giant seductress, refracting rays and glints of colour as she turns in her bed, beckoning calmly through the rising wind, the running clouds, the leaping spray. But the closer he comes the more she understands. Strong and brave—or feckless…he needs to know and is coming to find out. He needs to…he must! Even as the rocks rip his vessel and the boards below him begin to crack apart, he comes ahead, compelled, a man without choices, jumping desperately for the shallows, his tattered shirt tails flying like wings.

And now struggling out of the water, close to dead.

As he lies at her feet he finds the strength to reach and touch her coat.

Ondine kneels, then lies down beside him, accepting him. He nestles against her warm belly there on the beach and she combs back his hair with her fingers, cleans the sand and seaweed from his face. She knows him; it's Yann, the brother who had gone to war, her "twin." For some reason he loves her. Ondine knows by the way he touches her. And Dorise has gone, the sea has settled, the clouds are breaking up, the spectral green of the aurora fills the sky completely and makes the water shine. She and Yann listen to the bells on the lowing friends surrounding them. There's a face in the firmament: a woman, huge, watching them, pleased that it should happen. The wind hums on and on.

2.

Next morning Ondine wears the high coiffe to mass. All the women do. And, like their sisters on the mainland, the women of Sein have, in honour of Sunday, exchanged the plain grey *tablier* for aprons embroidered with bead work and colourful strands of ribbon. Dorise has put on a loosely netted black cord shawl over a blue velvet tunic top. Angélique wears a blue-violet amethyst in a gold-bordered cameo. After mass, walking up the lane toward the head of the island, these traces of colour are vibrant set against the stark stone cemetery wall.

The day, which started bright, is turning blustery. They walk head-on into northwesterly gusts. Ondine clutches at her unwieldy headpiece to protect it from buckling. Neither Angélique nor Dorise raises a hand to shield hers, so she cautiously lets go. The starched lace holds. Still, it's like wearing a sail… A lightness has remained in her head and the morning appears with striking clarity; but she's anxious, needing to say something about what she had seen or dreamt the night before—not at all sure, so vivid had her adventure been. Ondine looks out past the meagre gardens and the small fields beyond where barley and potatoes are grown, to where a gathering of cattle grazes on a yard-sized pasture under the greying sky. She sees a flat, barren piece of earth bounded by jagged rock and black water. No one should live here. The stone is too hard and the sea too sinister. And the light, Ar Men, standing in the waves: this morning it's a drab and lonely signpost, halfway between here and nowhere, waiting for Saint Anthony to find it. "So isolated," she muses.

Angélique says, "It's what we know."

"I think purgatory must look like this."

"*Qui voit Sein, voit sa fin,*" is the defiant reply. "That's what they say, isn't it?"

Ondine nods. Yes, she has heard them say that: *He who sees Sein sees his demise.* Then she tells Angélique, "Last night I went to the beach. With Dorise and Céleste… I met Yann, your son."

Angélique turns, bleached eyes probing. Ondine, in turn, looks to Dorise. To back her up? Dorise lowers her eyes in the submissive half-smile that marked her in the kitchen the previous evening. She walks on ahead to loose Céleste, who has been tethered since breakfast.

"It was a dream," says Angélique, expressionless, like a judge.

"It was like a dream. I saw a woman. And the most beautiful sky."

"Mari Morgan."

"Who is Mari Morgan? I felt she loved me. Both of us…Yann and me."

"She's a messenger, a deliverer. Like Saint Christopher. She shows us the way to our fate."

"Your death?"

"No—our fate. Our reason for living. We don't die…although most of us have to go through death to find our fate."

Ondine tries to weigh what she's hearing. "I don't know what that means," she answers.

"Were you frightened?" asks Angélique.

"No, I wasn't. Not at all."

"I don't know what it means, either…not for you. Each of us sees a different spark out there in the night. Each one welcomes a different sailor…"

Ondine's look of disbelief is spontaneous.

"But didn't Pauline Brekelian tell you about these things? About Celtic ways?"

There's impatience in Angélique's voice. She's angry. Or worried? It's not clear to a visitor. Ondine shakes her head, wary: some things; not these things. "Is it wrong, my…my dream?"

Angélique ignores the question. Walks slowly on. "We believe a person tries her life several times. There is no punishment, there is only the next life, and the next one after that, on and on until it's right. Then you don't have to come back. Then you've met your fate." Her brow is knitted up as she stares at the ground in front of her. It's as though she were explaining it to herself, insisting, "You have to have an active spirit! You have to keep going forward, and strive to be good to finally find it… Now Yann." She stops on the sand.

And is suddenly sobbing into clenched fists, almost silent, but deeply, her shoulders racked with the exertion, the tendons in the back of her neck pinched tight.

"Angélique?" Ondine is frightened of the pent-up forces inside this woman. Yet she is not rebuffed as she puts both arms around Angélique's broad back and holds her. "What is it? Tell me, please…" She feels the pain of grief releasing itself from inside the woman's heart, hears the meek, girlish weeping… It doesn't last long. Ondine becomes aware of the wind again. "Are you all right?" Loosening her arms, easing away.

"He's been killed."

"Yann?"

"There'll be another letter for me when the next boat comes. But not from him."

Everything in Ondine's heart denies it. No! What are you telling me? "I don't understand."

Behind the teary pools, Angélique's eyes flash half-bright. She points toward the water. Céleste stands on the crest of a cluster of rocks. Dorise, her face transfixed in a dumb smile, is pointing too. It takes Ondine a moment—she's inclined to smile as well at the sight of a perching cow… It suddenly comes into unmistakable focus: the shell and brow of a turtle. Céleste is showing her *la Tortue*, a rough megalithic figure, now undeniable.

A cow standing on a turtle? After the wonder, Ondine feels confusion verging on fear beginning to churn in her gut. "She was leading us. It was Céleste who took us here to the beach. She…and the rest of them…" throwing a glance in the direction of the heath, where eight other cows feed; "they brought Yann in through the storm with their lights. Their dance."

Angélique Ménou nods, confirming this notion, but offers no explanation. Instead she says, "I'm going back. I want a drink." She walks away from Ondine, hunched and tired as she steps up the sandy incline to the gravel path.

Ondine catches up with her. "Please…you have to tell me what happened!"

"I don't know what happened. He's dead. That's all."

"No! You don't know that. I'm the one who saw it! I was with him. He didn't die. I was holding him! Me! What happened to *me?*" And now anger supplants her fear. "You have no right to put me in the middle of your…your—"

"My spell?"

"What is it that you drink!" Ondine is shouting at her. "What did you do to me! They told me about you!" Angélique trudges on, steely faced, ignoring. "Stop and face me!"

She does. "Of course they told you about me." The wind folds itself around her voice, calm, low, implacable… "About all of us. They always have. That we're witches? That we transform ourselves and control the wind?" It seems to Ondine, searching her eyes, struggling to fathom friend or foe, that the woman is mocking, bitter. "They tell stories but they don't tell what they mean. That's the shame of it. Our stories are their stories. We have the same blood. But over there, they're stuck fast on the wheel, trapped by time and all its busy circumstance. Like your mother? I'd think yes… Here on Sein we're almost lost, as close as you can get to nowhere…but at least we're still partially free of the things that make them lose sight of themselves. That's the most important thing: we don't have to live in thrall to time. Time is in *us*, and if you believe it—and live it, the stories remain pure. And your soul will find what it's looking for."

Ondine complains, "But I'm not one of you!"

"Something in your life brought you here. You saw what you saw." Angélique shrugs; it is not hers to explain. She walks on.

But it is. It has to be. Ondine feels used. Tricked. "Is it a drug?" Demanding, grabbing Angélique's arm and holding tight.

Angélique makes a sour face. "It's a drink," is her curt reply. But she has to tell and they both know it. She frees herself from Ondine's fingers. "It's just barley and the mould from the little bit of wild rye we manage to keep. And apples, from them…" looking eastward with ironic eyes, "for immortality. And sweetness. You want a person to like the taste of it."

"Yes…?" Tell me more.

"We call it *Maeve.* She was one of us, a Celtic queen. Her son was a brown bull calf who defended her against her enemies, but then he killed himself by smashing his brains out on a rock, maddened with pride for all his prowess and bravery… I thought you said you weren't afraid."

Ondine won't speak till she knows more.

"We've always used the rye fungus. It's called ergot. It helps ease a heavy menstruation and it brings contractions, to stop the bleeding after a birth. I'm sure they've used it where you come from. Your mother never said?" Ondine shakes her head. And Angélique shakes hers: a mirror filled with things felt but never known. "Well, it has always been there and it has always helped us…helped us be women, you could say. If you leave it a bit longer, and cure it right, with some barley or potatoes, well, then it helps us in other ways."

"How?"

"Visions. It shows us what we need to see to go back inside the stories that are in our blood—so we can be who we are and not who the priests or the politicians or the wars or all the machines would have us be."

Ondine has no reply to that… They walk back past the cemetery. Ondine looks behind to see Dorise and Céleste following in a meandering way, just now ascending to the path by the sea wall. "Does Dorise know all this?"

"Yes. But differently. She's only fifteen…hasn't been with a man yet. She's not a traveller like you. But she's the one who gave me the clue."

"What clue?"

"When she asked your birthday and said you and Yann were twins…I knew I should give you a sip of Maeve."

"And you think he's dead."

"I know he is." To her, it's a matter of fact.

Ondine bites her lip as she hears the truth in this woman's connection to the ground where they walk, and to the sea surrounding. "I'm sorry," she murmurs.

They return to the dim salon, unlit and even more shadowy on a cloudy morning than the previous night. Angélique pours another small glass of the liquor and passes it.

Ondine asks, "Why are you giving me this?"

"Last night was for me… Today it's for you. But you won't see Yann again." She looks sadly down into her small cup. Raising it, she sips; then raising it again, this time to Ondine in a toast, she swallows the rest in one shot. She closes her eyes and relaxes into her chair. From behind those eyes she asks, "Don't you want any?"

Ondine wonders if last night's confiding and trust had been real at all. Tomorrow morning she would be on the boat, headed back…*over there*. "Do I need it?" She's still wearing the tall coiffe. She reaches up and touches it, running her fingers along the grain of lace. Turning to the blue-gowned Madonna in the corner, she looks for help in the thing she knows: "What about her? I thought you loved her. I thought she inspired you…your beautiful work. Aren't you ashamed to betray her with this? I…I don't feel right." Staring at the drink, unclear, unsure; afraid.

"I do love her," says Angélique. "Would I allow her in my house if I didn't? We all do. It was us women who carried the stones to build her chapel. She's one of us."

No… It feels wrong, a sin, to say that, then drink this thing they called Maeve.

"Don't hide from what you saw…what you heard," is the woman's challenge. "There is a second existence. It's beautiful…no?"

Leaving Ondine saddened because she's unable to turn away, unable to *not* listen.

And Angélique watching as if she knows well the curse of mixed emotions. "Don't feel guilty, Ondine. That's the last thing she wants of us." Gazing at the mournful icon in the corner, she says, "She had her miraculous child far from here, but her name, Mary—she comes from the sea." Now sighing heavily through her nose, gross but endearing, almost a chortle; "…in a way, those grim grey Jesuits brought her back to us when they finally found us and taught us to sing their songs. Did Pauline Brekelian ever tell you the Creator's holy spirit is female and that she moves on the face of the waters? Did she ever mention that Celtic heaven is the sun itself, caused by the shining together of all pure souls? *Le Sid*. She never told you of *Le Sid*?"

"No…" She never told me. Nor did my mother. No one ever did.

"The church of Rome took away the beliefs but it left the lore. But a truly religious person heeds the stories and songs as closely as the scriptures because they existed before the scriptures were written and they remain after the scriptures are gone… First there were nine priestesses, right here on Sein, all of them virgins. They could tell the future…and they could control the wind. Now any man worth his salt would try to make it through the storms to find out from those virgins… No?"

"I'm not a virgin," whispers Ondine. A girl and her sister out travelling alone will find boys and men wherever they want to, and have some fun before they go their separate ways.

"Virgin has little to do with your body. That's the one the priests invented. It's how you think, and how you feel. Isolated. Self-reliant. I think you might be."

Ondine looks at the glass in front of her as her life is being described. All that searching for the happy thing she had heard in her mother's voice… This woman was giving her something that was looming, inevitable, in her life.

"Between here and heaven is a vast purgatory, but it's not the dismal place you learned about at school. You saw it—in the north. It's a place of hope, a beautiful emerald sky, where the dead are gathered and re-formed, to start again. That's the real story, the deeper one, the one that's full of life—and I have no qualms if I drink to celebrate it. I need to celebrate it…it's *my* life. It might be yours as well."

Why? asks Ondine once more…asks it with her eyes as she picks up the glass.

"Because she loves you. The goddess loves you. Look at Céleste: she takes you out and shows you around…la Tortue."

So Ondine tastes another sip of Maeve. And she sits with Angélique…and Dorise when she joins them, until mother and daughter disappear into the privacy of quiet tears and memory. Then she wanders out and finds herself walking alone by the shore. Angélique was right; the presence of Yann is vague, just the image of another boy whom she had known…before.

As if a line has been drawn across the fabric of her life.

But it's easy to see all the shapes on Sein now. All the colours too, in the sea.

11

THE DREAMIEST SONG OF THE SEA

Slightly more than half a century later, a sun-browned Aliette watches Sein take shape in the distance. Her father is dozing, oblivious to the chop and spray. Maman pulls the binoculars from the picnic hamper and adjusts them. Her sister Anne is in the cabin getting chatted up by their boatman.

"Witches and seaweed," was her mother's laconic comment the night Aliette had announced her intention to go to Sein.

It was followed by her father's decree: "We'll all go. A day trip."

"I really should go alone."

But Maman, putting aside her usual skepticism about her daughter's job "with the police," had dug out some books and together they'd read up on the Cult of the Sun, curses and human sacrifice, shape-shifting…how Sein was celebrated in antiquity as the dark home of nine Druidic priestesses and thought to be a kind of way station between this life and the next; how its megaliths were believed to be the doors to the underworld and the Celtic paradise which lay beyond; how the isolated community was the last in Christian Europe to be evangelized by the Society of Jesus. "It's a shame you weren't interested in this when you were children. Your grandmother knew a thing or two about it…"

Yes, and if Mémé were alive, no doubt she'd be along on this excursion too.

And Anne, too often less than focused, had spent an entire morning on the phone figuring out connections, arranging for their own private water taxi across. Today she'd roused them at 5:30 a.m. to ensure they made the first ferry from Belle Ile to the mainland.

And Papa (I'd rather be sailing!) had shopped painstakingly for the exact wines he believed they would need as he'd planned their lunch.

Everyone's helping the inspector out on this one and she loves them for it—she honestly does; but it creates a disorienting time-warp effect: zoom…back to the middle of girlhood. It has nothing to do with investigating a murder. No, it happens every summer, in one way or another. It's the problematic part of a family holiday for an adult child with no family of her own. It can leave her feeling outside of time and going nowhere.

Going nowhere? Going to Sein. They had taken the bumpy regional road along the coast, through Audierne, past hydrangea, deep violet and bridesmaid blue spilling from the stone window bays of roadside houses, then west across the plateau where fields of grass running down to the strand were topped with yellow wildflowers glowing richly in the early sun. Descending to the wharf at Raz, they'd passed a shrine depicting the Virgin receiving a sailor at her knee. Now Aliette takes the binoculars from Maman and peers at the flat speck of land: 6 miles out, 15 acres, 20 feet at its highest point, 348 registered inhabitants. It would be lost if it weren't for the presence of the Ar Men light… Closer in, the rock formations in the tide waters along the shore are foreboding. Those would be the doors to the way to Paradise.

Distracted by a classic car, she hadn't thought of a simple plane. Assistant Inspector Patrice Lebeau had called to say that a very old man travelling under papers for one Michel Nobletz flew to Nantes with a connection to Quimper the very afternoon Manon Larivière was buried. Monsieur Nobletz had checked a good-sized box through freight before boarding. Thanks to Maman's research, the Nouvelle family now knows Michel Nobletz was the Jesuit missionary who came across to Sein in 1613 to teach the Holy Word and found people still practising the Cult of the Sun… Aliette can see Flossie Orain smiling at the symmetry in the choice of an alias for Marcel Cyr. No one at Quimper airport has any notion where the man and the box were headed. Yes, they remember him; that box reeked terribly, like rotting apples. A man with a truck had met him at the gate.

Doesn't matter; this must be the place.

Their boatman is called Yvon. Yvon Nicolazic. He steers through a cut and into the harbour, slows, shunts them into a space along the quay between two trawlers.

Disembarking, Anne says, "Yvon knows this Angélique Ménou. He'll take us to see her."

"I'll go alone." What has she been telling him? To Yvon: "That would be good of you."

Maman intercedes. "After our lunch."

Yvon waves this off. "Angélique would be delighted. Come for an aperitif…all of you." Brash, he takes both sisters by an arm.

"Excellent idea," gushes Anne.

Maman won't have it. She tells Anne, "Your father has gone to a lot of trouble preparing our picnic." Taking her girls back from the presumptuous boatman, she tells him, "We'll eat first and explore your lovely island later. We will meet you here at four o'clock as stated in our contract."

"It's not my island," says Yvon.

Hamper under one arm, blankets under the other, Papa leads his family away.

Anne is telling Maman, "He's nice!…you don't even know him."

"Neither do you, dear—and that's the point."

Anne and Maman clash often, especially where it concerns Anne's taste in men. Aliette plays both sides, depending. Right now she can see Anne's: Yvon the boatman has a flinty-eyed beauty that fits the day.

2.

Ondine Duguay's bleak description of Sein was somewhat out of date; the islanders had since discovered that serving lunch was better business than catching it, and today the crescent-shaped quay is bustling with visitors off two large tourist boats out of Audierne, noisy, perusing menus posted on the colourful facades of a dozen cafés, or gawking and pointing as they wander in and out of the tiny lanes leading to the homes and the rest of the island. The Nouvelles, eschewing the crowd, leave the quay directly. They head past the church and onto the path toward the big light at the northernmost tip.

Once past the village, however, Sein is indeed a flat and barren rock. There are no animals grazing or vegetables growing in the patchy yards bordering the gravel path. Nor is there a single tree to be seen. Anne asks a woman carrying a basket full of seaweed, "Where's the beach?" The woman gestures behind her with a disdainful shrug for the tourist. There's no beach, only the embankment, a ribbon of slime-laden shelf…and the bouldery formations, many of them tiny islets in their own right in low tide, forming a protective line along the edge of the sea. The only suitable place for a picnic is the grassy ground surrounding the hut-sized, long abandoned Chapel de St. Corentin. At least there's a wall to let them get out of the wind. "And we do have a lovely view of the turtle," comments Maman, folding her coat and sitting on it.

"What turtle?" asks Aliette

"That turtle." Pointing toward a formation studding the waters below the base of the light.

"Oh yes!" exclaims Anne.

"Isn't that intriguing?" Papa is unrolling the blankets, commencing to lay his picnic spread.

The inspector squints. "Where?" Feeling left out. She's supposed to be the leader here.

"Those rocks…just there…" says Anne, making an arrow with her arm.

"A dolmen?"

"A turtle."

Aliette can't see it.

For lunch everyone receives a paper plate containing *crudités*— a selection of broccoli, carrot, celery, green and red pepper—with a dollop of ravigote mayonnaise on the side, and one *pain bagnat* stuffed with a tuna, basil and tomato spread. This is supplemented with jars of spiced olives, green and black; four cheeses, the pepper grinder and a baguette. They sip a silky Nuits-St-Georges with their sandwiches, a coarse St. Chinian with the cheese. For dessert, a pear goes well with another slice of the creamy-tart St. Agur. A bite from a bar of Zucher dark chocolate and a sip of coffee from the old thermos are optional. It's another perfect meal and Papa accepts their congratulations with a not-so-humble nod. Aliette expects that now, in time-honoured tradition, he'll stretch out and fall into his snooze mode.

Not today. Her genteel father gets to his feet, announcing, "I'm off to explore." And he ambles away, first to inspect Sein's light.

The women sit, feeling the sun, stomachs full, hearts quiet, harmonious. Aliette is staring empty-headed out to sea when she sees the turtle. She sends a grin in the direction of her mother, who had been first to see it; but any impulse to speak is, for the moment, absent. It's the wind. She feels its steady whisper wrapping her in a cocoon that might keep her there for an age, leaving her alone, weather-worn, with no style or colour but merely grey, old…forgotten—and yet utterly distinct like that rock creature reposing in the waves. Happy turtle. It appears to Aliette's dreaming eyes that Anne and Maman are sensing the wind as well, that they too are practising a prayer of solitude, preparing to be timeless: nine virgins…now three Nouvelles.

"Yes, she wants to see you…" The voice cuts through the reverie. Yvon the boatman stands in the wind, ten paces away, lank ends of oily hair snapping against his eyes. He brushes it back…and brushes it back again, posing there.

"She wants to see me?"

"Angélique…she's waiting to see you. She says come and have a drink."

"You'll take me to her?" Standing…

"You can find her," says Yvon in an offhand way, then he steps over the unmarked line and into their area. He sits on the grass, within knee-patting distance of Maman, smiling at her as if to say, I'm not dangerous.

Maman only stares dumbly, still somewhere else in her post-prandial meditations.

While Anne leaps into action. "We have chocolate and coffee…" opening the hamper, "a pear…and there's a good glass of wine left if you don't mind drinking from the bottle."

Aliette asks, "So?…where?"

"Go straight back to the church but turn right at the blue gate. Keep going past Fernand Crouton then turn left at Paul Goardan.

Hers is the white with the green trim." Yvon turns to Maman. "I have children too," he informs her. "You can't really protect them from anything, least of all love."

Aliette picks up her coat. With a hint of a smile—good luck!—for Anne, she leaves them. Anne will need it. Maman could hold her own.

3.

The door is open. Aliette goes in. "Angélique Ménou?" A nod. "Would you be the mother of Dorise Ménou, now residing in…" It's difficult to see gaunt Dorise in a face so fleshy, brown and wrinkled. Closing in on ninety, guesses Aliette. And weirdly regal in the intricate cornet of lace which she wears tied under her chin with a bow: ten inches tall with bibs attached to the base, curving out and down to the nape of her neck.

"*Oui, c'est moi.* Sit down." Her voice is rich, if a trifle woozy. Resting on a side table at her right hand is a plastic tray with a bottle and two glasses, each containing an ounce or so of a clear liquid. It seems she has started without her guest. A four-foot-tall plaster Virgin stands behind her, doleful eyes averted as if trying not to watch.

"My name is Aliette Nouvelle, Police Judiciaire. I'm—"

"Drink with me." Angélique lifts her glass and sips the offered spirit.

"Thank you… I've just had lunch. I'm interested in the whereabouts of Marcel Cyr."

But Angélique Ménou is not. She gestures toward the other glass. "Maeve. I make it myself…it will open your eyes to the goddess."

Maeve… *C'est beau Maeve.* The inspector holds the glass to her nose and instantly recognizes the fermented grainy vapour tinged with apple; but much stronger than the cloudy stuff from Dorise's kitchen. "Merci," replacing it with a gracious smile, "I've already had half a bottle of wine—and I've seen the turtle! I don't think I should push my luck… This is the same remedy Dorise makes. Or something else?"

"Maeve is Maeve. She can be a cure…or a host. Drink." She does so herself and finishes off her glass. "I don't think my Dorise has ever had a man," she mutters, licking her lips, gross. "I think she fell in love with that Ondine Duguay… I wonder if she'll come home to bury me."

"Of course she will… What happened when Ondine came here?"

"I only met her once. She came to tell me my son was dead. She loved him."

"I'm sorry. Were they married, Ondine and your son?"

A slow shake of her head. "He never even met her until after…" a thick hand concentrating on the task of pouring herself another shot.

"After what?"

"After he was dead." Now toasting her visitor in a perfunctory manner. Drinking.

Oh Lord, this is not what I need… "Where is Marcel Cyr?"

"Drink with me!"

"I won't drink with you, madame. Please stop… Dorise is involved in a murder." Will that help clear the woman's mind?

"I think you're too proud."

"Did you hear what I said? Your daughter and Ondine Duguay are involved in a murder. I need information. I need—"

"Are you a horse?" asks Angélique.

"I may as well be," says Aliette

"Epona…yes," filmy eyes assessing; "you're one of hers… Now I see it. I'll bet my Dorise knew the moment she saw you. Go back to the mainland. You can't be so proud. Not out here."

"A woman was killed. Her name was Manon. Dorise says she was her friend. This drink you make is involved. Your goddess…all of them! That makes it worse, no? Why would they kill their friend? Madame Ménou? Why would the goddess allow that? And I know they sent her out here with Marcel Cyr. You must try to tell me what…what…" What *could* this Angélique Ménou tell her?

"There was no murder," says Angélique. "She wanted to be with the goddess."

The inspector tries again. "Someone killed her. The goddess was there."

"It is what she wanted!" Insisting, almost lucid.

"But Marcel Cyr… How could he be part of it?"

"He made a bargain. He kept his side of it."

"What kind of bargain?"

"What do you think? They gave him what he wanted—what he lived for." Angélique imbibes more Maeve and repeats it. "There was no murder. Yes, he brought her here…" And another taste, eyes boring into Aliette's. "He and Céleste, they took her out and delivered her to Mari Morgan. This was what she wanted."

"And then?"

The old woman shrugs, her energy spent. "I don't know. I'm old. I was sleeping. You'll have to ask Céleste…" Her mouth drops open.

Aliette has seen the same thing in Ondine Duguay. Blank passivity; that posture of inevitability shaped by a past that must—has to!—preclude her from the here-and-now. Aware of the stillness in this room, this house, she asks the wizened lady, "Are you alone?"

"Since my husband sailed into the arms of Mari Morgan fifty years ago. Maybe sixty. Before the war. Do you know how long that is?"

Aliette shakes her head. Too long. She knows it's futile, but still she asks, "Where is she?"

Out back? The inspector moves through the silent house. She sees a white cow tethered in the walled-in yard. Yes, well… And returns to the shadowy room. An interlude: the woman watching her like some old dog, waiting; while the inspector considers the regal bonnet…it was beautiful work, and the dissolute remains of a life beneath it, a caricature of the horrible witch glorified in the disappearing lore. "Tell me…please try to tell me one thing: was Ondine Duguay a good person?"

"Good? What is this…good?"

"Good. You're a mother—you would have known."

"Mmm…" A foggy rumble from far inside, defensive, responding almost in spite of herself. "Yes, she was good… She saw Mari Morgan. What else could she be?"

"I don't know… It's why I'm here."

"From corruption, sweetness," says Angélique. As if just now remembered. And cueing her to drink again.

"Merci, madame." Aliette leaves, closing the door behind her.

There's a girl coming along the lane, about eleven or twelve, still skinny with straw-coloured hair cut off in bangs above her eyebrows. Aliette's hair had been like that once. The girl passes her without a glance—so many tourist faces in the course of a summer that's almost done. Aliette turns as she hears the girl knock at the house she has just left. When there's no answer, the girl knocks again, harder. Aliette can't help calling—quietly, "Angélique's not very well today, I'm afraid. I doubt you'll raise her right now." The girl only nods: she knows. She takes five more steps, unlatches a gate in a wooden wall and goes in by the back way.

Aliette finds her way out of the labyrinth of lanes and onto the main quay, walks through the sun and crowd to the far end. Heading back along the path to the picnic site, she steps into the cemetery and searches till she finds a stone for *François Emile-Marie Ménou*, and his dates, and the inscription *Disparu en mer*. Beside is a stone for *Yann Théodore François Ménou*, also *Disparu en mer*. The epitaph is on many of the stones bearing male names: these were sailors of one sort or another and they all had disappeared into the sea—into the arms of Mari Morgan. She stands in front of Yann Ménou and thinks of Ondine Duguay. Crying. Ondine, frustrating as she cries to be unburdened of responsibility. Ondine, who is a good woman, according to the mother of this long-departed sailor. "What else could she be?" Now an inspector has to wonder just what kind of answer she could have possibly expected of old Angélique Ménou.

Deliverance. Eternity. Love. How can one generation know what the next will do with its stories and beliefs? Here in this isolated place, so barren in its present…deeply elaborate in its past, life was as literal as chilled soaking flesh, and, Aliette senses, as veiled as the dreamiest song of the sea. Life was fate. Fate was a woman who lived in the sea: Mari Morgan, who sang the sounds of deliverance, eternity and love into the hearts of ones such as Angélique.

The sea; the heart of Angélique—both these unknowable places. An inspector has to believe Angélique is not malevolent. Just decrepit. From corruption, sweetness? We can only hope. But this drink. This drug? *C'est beau Maeve…* A cure; a host. Was it, layered in drab medicinal pretexts, a concealed weapon? She wonders if Manon Larivière's cloudy remedy had been masking a deadly ecstasy. If Colette Namur had been even more powerless than she'd first surmised. If Ondine Duguay had stopped at Sein half a lifetime ago and let a strange woman's potion induce her into falling in love with a ghost. And had she kept her ghost and brought it home? Why?

The goddess whispers: *Because love is love and we need to keep its stories.*

And when the story fades—as it surely has in Ondine's soul; what dark residue remains?

The sea is a mottled sheen of black and silver lit by streams of a westering sun shot through holes in the broadening cover of cloud. Aliette dawdles, watching the waves and stones, lulled again by the one-note song of the wind.

4.

"…you see, the last time I was born under the sign of the oak and I despaired of ever moving on. Then the war came and I went to join it and bam! less than an hour after the shooting began I was dead. One shot and gone—blown apart, and ready to be remade at last. Mother Nature would not let me move on. She had boxed me in. I was freed by a war, by something I had never believed in at all and that's the wonder of it. A paradox bumped me closer to the edge of the wheel. It's frightening when you think about it. A man could look at paradox and easily forget about believing in anything. And then his children…and the next generation after that. What kind of world would it be?" Yvon bites into the chocolate and chomps down on a last mouthful of pear as Anne and Maman consider this large question. Tossing away the core, he tells them, "Now my birthday's in September and the apple is my tree, and—"

"—and the apple means immortality," says Aliette, stepping forward, taking a place on the blanket beside her mother and sister. Her own birthday (thirty-six on the 27th) was just last week.

"Yes," without breaking stride, like a schoolmaster acknowledging a latecomer; "…and now my work is on the sea, where there
are no trees at all. Just Mari Morgan, waiting for me."

"Oh…?" Maman sucks on her lips, perplexed.

"But that doesn't mean I don't need another good woman,"
says Yvon, with a smile for Anne, "to take me through to that last day.
More children, too."

Anne doesn't say a word. How could she?

Aliette asks, "You've been enjoying yourselves?"

"I suppose we have," says Maman.

"What's the difference," asks Anne, tentative, "between being
remade and…and dying?"

"No one dies," says Yvon. A statement of fact.

"Then between being remade and not moving on?"

"It's something in your heart."

"Oh."

Yvon checks his watch and rises. "I'll tell you about it on the way
back." That's a promise. To Aliette he says, "Your mother tells me you
work with the police."

"She shouldn't have."

"Why?"

"Because it's none of your business."

"I think you don't have enough respect for your mother."
Aliette makes no reply. None of them do. They sit in a row and watch
him. To Maman he says, "According to our contract, the boat leaves
in thirty-five minutes. Maybe you should find your husband."

Maman looks around briefly and agrees. "Yes, maybe I should."

Ignoring Aliette, he offers a gallant thanks for the snack to
Anne.

But now all heads turn as a white cow goes striding, fifty yards
away. The creature's heavy movement is momentum incarnate, as if
falling perpetually forward, heading for a sunlit patch of green beside
the lighthouse… A young girl follows ten steps behind, running to
keep up.

"Salut, la belle Céleste!" calls Yvon; *"…à la prochaine!"* Only
Aliette realizes he's calling to the cow… "Maeve will give you a head

of steam," he adds, with a sly smile for the cop. Then: "I will see you on the dock…" looking up at the sky as he walks away.

"What were you talking about?"

Maman is on her hands and knees, gathering bits and pieces of the reopened picnic. "Yvon was telling us about his previous lives. He's 350 years old, broken down over eight different lives. He discovered the original icon at Auray…found it buried in the mud when he was plowing his field. He says it was Anne la Noire, the divine underground mother, and that the priests took her away from him and painted clothes on her so she could be a properly presentable Saint Anne. Poor man says he's been seeing the ghost of a naked woman ever since…"

"Mother!" Maman's droll report undermines Aliette's fragile sense of Sein.

Madame Nouvelle stands, groaning with the strain on her hip. "Do you think I'm going to risk alienating someone like that out here on this godforsaken place?—*and* with someone as irresponsible as her…" a cool glance at Anne, "encouraging him at every step? I don't want to die where no one knows me… Your father's probably been cooked and eaten by now."

"You were fascinated," snipes Anne.

"I didn't say he wasn't interesting…so many of them are, aren't they? He does seem to have a wonderful respect for his old maman. That touched me, I admit." Then, squinting as she scouts the distance, "…Where *is* your father?"

Aliette demands, "But why did you have to tell him what I do?"

"I couldn't think of any other reason to give when he asked me why I'd come to Sein."

"And so you told him about the case?"

"Just the broadest of outlines, dear."

"So now the whole place is going to know."

"Perhaps not. It's not his island, remember…"

"There he is," says Anne.

Papa is approaching from the eastern side. It seems he has circled the island. He has found a stick of some sort—is using it as a staff. The end of it glints as it catches the sun for a split second with each stride he takes toward them.

They gather round and examine the elegant black lacquer, now more than a little scratched, the gold knob and tip…it has to be gold; brass would have been stained green from the salt. He'd picked it out of the rocks. "Up by the light…it was just sitting there waiting for me."

Aliette turns it over in her hands. The cow is now standing across the way, like the proverbial statue, her nose pointing straight at a cairn to the left of the light, half submerged in the rising tide.

Yes, everyone's helping you out on this one, Inspector…

But the boat is leaving at four.

5.

Would Substitute Procureur Cécile Botrel make good on her promise and ask police bosses in the Finistère to help an inspector from the east? She would. Aliette waits an hour, then calls Monsieur Varney, the Divisionnaire at Quimper, who passes her along to Monsieur Armez, Principal at Audierne. "A boat to Sein with a diver? It will be our pleasure, Madame Inspector… Well, as soon as you can get here in the morning."

She gets back into Papa's car and onto the early ferry across to Quiberon, and heads back up the coast. At ten past eight she leaves the dock at Audierne with one Inspector Brisson, a diver and a man at the helm who's supposed to be an expert in the shoals. A stiff wind, a brilliant sun… Just before noon they find two bodies on a shelf in a grotto at the head of the island. Manon's luxurious chemise is in tatters, permeated with salt. Marcel Cyr has one spindly arm protectively around her. How? There's no evidence on his body implying he was forced to be there with her.

Part of the deal, Aliette—you can ask Céleste.

Sure; watching as the two corpses are floated out… An old man came to Sein. To die. To die willingly? Between the likes of Angélique, Céleste and this drink they call Maeve, she reckons there's no answer that will ever make sense beyond the boundaries of Sein. The place is only rocks and sea; you had to include the sea as part—not separate; and in so doing, an event such as Marcel Cyr in a grotto with a murdered plaything becomes uncanny.

They find a third body in Angélique Ménou's salon, half a glass of Maeve still on the go beside her. Sad, but not too; ninety-two years old; a hard life but a good long one. "We'll never see the likes of her again," says the father of the girl who lives down the lane. Aliette agrees. Angélique's time is past due. As a priestess, she's obsolete. And quite likely even on the witness stand she would have kept on talking according to her own way of seeing it. Fueled up with visions, perhaps, but not much use to the court. Aliette returns to the mainland with Maeve instead, and two waterlogged souls on loan from Mari Morgan.

That night, back at Belle Ile, a small miracle: "It's marvellous," says Anne, where she stands with Maman and Papa, looking north from the kitchen door, up at the amazing dance of green-gold light in the northern sector. "And rare in these parts," adds Papa. "It occurs when the solar winds are trapped by the earth's magnetic field. It usually needs a much more northern climate than this." Joining them, watching with that shared sense of wonder, Aliette thinks maybe what it needs is *her*, coming to collect one her own.

The last day, after rolling off the ferry and before heading down to Nantes, the Nouvelle family takes a short detour by the cathedral in Carnac at Aliette's request. "I just want to look at it. Just for a minute."

"At what?"

"The horse…in the frieze over the front door."

They stop. Maman pulls out her book. "In the Celtic tradition the horse stands for loyalty, ennobling the man it carries on its back, accepting to obey him but not to be his slave. The horse is the funeral animal, the one who carries pure souls to the Beyond. The relationship between man and the horse is not a confrontation but a collaboration, a union based on equality. The horse is not the one who brings death, like the bull; it is the one who submits to death with its master. It dies with man in man's wars because it has tied its destiny to man's…"

Anne asks, "What about woman and her wars?"

Maman only nods, continuing, "The Celtic horse goddess, Epona, the mare, is also called Rigantona. She is the Great Queen, the Mother Goddess."

Aliette gazes up at the image of the horse bearing the Virgin, and the line of colts following. "Why is it all so incoherent? Makes sorting out the angels look like a piece of cake."

"Because it's so old."

"I'd rather be a horse than a cow." It's the kind of thing she could say there in the car…with just them.

"Then you will be, dear," assures Maman.

"Yvon says I remind him of Anne," says Anne.

"Anne dear," advises Maman, "it's the last week of the holiday, it's the best time to enjoy yourself. But I want you to think of next week as the beginning of a new year. A clean slate. Time to start over. New clothes, a new attitude. Maybe a steady job…"

"A new boyfriend?"

"Not him. Please."

To keep things fair for the two girls in the back seat, they stop at Auray, home of the mother of the mother of Christ (at least according to the story). Saint Anne held a rosy apple in her right hand; with her left she supported her daughter, the Virgin, sitting on her knee holding, in turn, her own blessed Child on her lap. "The last time we were here the two of you were like wild horses chasing each other around the place," remembers Papa. "I was just waiting for you to knock something priceless over."

"So was the guide," recalls Maman. "We were asked to leave."

Neither Aliette nor Anne can remember that…

Back at Nantes there are three messages from Maman's friend about a bridge night, two from Yvon Nicolazic, obviously not too conversant with the machine, and one from Monique back at the office: it's urgent, it's concerning the Commissaire.

- 12 -
TRICKY TERRITORY

A *partouze* is a sexual encounter involving more than the usual couple. A threesome, a foursome…*une partie de debauche* is how Petit Robert defines it. We have to believe it's the last thing on Interim Adjunct Commissaire Néon's mind as he goes walking into Mari Morgan's the night Inspector Nouvelle's information arrives from Audierne. So the missing body of the murdered pute has been found, as well as that of Marcel Cyr, regular client and close friend of the suspect Dupras? Good. Claude goes walking into the brothel excited in the way any cop will be when he has something that might provide an advantage. Yes, it has occurred to him that Inspector Nouvelle acted behind his back. But she has the support of that new Sub Proc Botrel; and none of Claude's counterparts at the other end have seemed at all put out by her presence on their territory. Whatever she's done out there, she's done it right—found her own way in as usual. Claude Néon, each day a little less the neophyte Commissaire, is learning to live with these irregularities, and, he hopes, to work with them. *Alors*…walking in, in no way under cover and with no intention of making any kind of fuss that might get him sued over the privacy rule; just a smile on his face and a major secret up his sleeve, ready to play the game. If he could engage the one Aliette has marked as the leader, why—she might say something that could close this thing.

"It's the Commissaire, n'est-ce pas?"

"Oui, Claude Néon. You are?"

"Florence Orain…this is my colleague, Louise Lebraz."

Shaking hands. The redhead is quite something.

"Is this business or pleasure?"

"Just stopping by to give you an update. PR is becoming very important, no? My inspector's off on other business just now and—"

"Yes, we've missed her. One begins to feel close to one's inspector."

"The fact is," explains Claude, "the inspector has done her bit, for the most part. The thing's pretty straightforward as far as our work goes: some interviews, coordinating forensics, reports to the Instructing Judge. There are some loose ends, but it's mainly in the hands of the court now… Oh, and the psychologists."

"The psychologists?"

"They're looking quite closely at the prisoner. Has a lot to do with how the Procureur presents his case."

"Ah. And how is he doing?"

"Don't know…" Keep that smile, now: polite, casual. "Not my business… Basically, I just need to see that the seal is still on the room and—"

"We haven't touched a thing…" Leading him through to the back.

"It would be nice to be able to get at the books," says Louise as they peer into Herméné's empty office. Two strands of yellow tape bearing *SU* Commissaire Duque's signature still bar the way.

"I don't see what harm it would do," says Flossie.

"Sorry, mesdames, but that's the rule."

"And where would we be without rules?"

"Hate to think…" Taking a peek through the glass doors opposite, into a darkened dining room. "This is a nice place."

"What were you expecting?" Louise again; her tougher tone reverberates in his lower parts.

"I try to steer clear of expectations, Louise."

"And does that mean everything's a surprise—or nothing is?"

Yes: A bitch. But he could buy her, couldn't he? If he wanted. "I bet you're a surprise."

"You don't know the half of it, Monsieur le Commissaire."

The other one, Flossie, offers, "Would you like a drink?"

"Sure, why not? …Be able to say I've had one at Mari Morgan's."

"Tell your girlfriend," suggests Louise.

"What's your problem, madame?"

"What are you doing here?"

"Just looking." And smiling.

"What a shame." The redhead walks away.

Leaving him with Flossie, arms folded, an impish grin on her face, a satin choker with a tiny silver bell around her neck. Fine; that's who he's come to talk to. Isn't it? It *is* disorienting around a place like this. "Everyone wants Louise," she says, taking his arm, jingling faintly as they head back out to the front and into the bar, "but I think we should start you off with something a little easier."

Which takes the wind out of his sails… Didn't it, Claude? Yes. Afterward Claude could distinctly recall the feeling of losing his footing at that moment with Flossie Orain on his arm. A sense of time, a sense of purpose… "Look, madame, I said I'm just—"

"I know…" Laughing gaily. "Don't worry, we'll find you exactly what you need."

"I'm working!"

"But so am I, monsieur." Sitting, sweeping her hair back from her neck…her white neck with that bell; leaning toward him, confidential. "Two professionals. Eh, Claude? Have a drink with me."

Are you supposed to get up and walk out? No, you have to go with it and hold your own, and especially when you're the Commissaire. The place is full; that is, eight men sit quietly, nursing drinks. And a smiling Claude, hi guys! makes nine. Recognize any? Can't tell; things are moving quickly here. "Thanks…" Sipping at something like a fruity Scotch. "Homemade?"

"Dorise, our cook. Chin chin, Commissaire." Clinking glasses. "See anyone you like?"

No one appears to be "with" anyone. The women seem to circulate, from the bar to a chair or a lap, to chat or flirt…then they'll drift out to the front for a word on the phone or back to the bar to fetch a refill…then back to the tables, each one letting each man have a touch, a whiff, a whisper, until his senses lock onto something desired. Then the man Flossie says is the accountant from Hôtel de Ville leaves the room in the company of a short one with carefully coiffed black hair who looks something like Monique, his secretary. Hm. And that

Louise looks to be settling in with the eldest of the evening's guests—
a psychiatrist apparently, retired now, Flossie says he used to do a lot
of consulting to the court but it must've been before Claude's time.

If an old man can handle her, why couldn't I?

"Only you know the answer to that, monsieur…"

"What?" But I didn't say… Then a girl he has not yet seen
comes into the bar. Young, in a dress that's more of a jumper: tight
bodice, short, to mid-thigh; a midnight blue under the dim light, with
tiny sequins glittering in random waves. He marvels at the soft oval
face of an ingenue framed in swirling hair. She passes him without a
glance and sits with a guy on the far side of the room. Also young; hair
and coat look foreign.

"That's Vivi…that's her American."

"She's—"

"She's new."

"Ah…her mother's the one—"

"—the one who died, yes."

"It's tough."

"She's a strong girl."

Claude imagines her strength. He asks, "What do you mean,
her American?"

"Her regular."

"That mean exclusive?"

"Not at all. But tonight it does."

"Ah." He sips his drink. It's good.

"What about the case, Commissaire?"

"Claude."

"Claude…" Flossie smiles and rings her tiny bell.

It rings in Claude's mind, a tiny sound tugging at him as though
each moment were beginning to stretch. What *about* the case? And all
your responsibilities? Claude is stuck for a reply. This ringing is
growing, splintering his varied feelings about the case into a detailed
breakdown of the fragments of his life: work, loneliness, choices…this
is love, this is obsession, this is duty…this is what you are, this is not
who you think you are…where's the balance between those honest
mistakes and the wilful pretense? A man will wonder, with or without
a drug in his brain. By that point Claude knows Flossie has given him

something stronger than whisky. *Now* does one get up and walk out? Claude is not inclined to. The girl and her American leave the bar hand in hand. And now Louise, on the arm of the old shrink. Somehow they fit together well. That old man is going to have fun…

"Fun is mostly in the mind, Claude."

Jesus! I didn't say a word. Did I?

"Maybe you should meet Céleste."

"Céleste?" Heavenly name…heavenly sound, and surrounded by ringing.

"Our cow… Surely Aliette told you about Céleste."

SurelyAlietteSurelyAlietteSurelyAliette… Something in the inspector's report about milk in the morning, a cow in the kitchen. "I never did like cows, me."

"Oh, she's beautiful… Dorise says Aliette loves her. You will too, Claude. Everyone does."

SurelyAlietteSurelyAlietteSurelyAliette… This is work. This is for the case.

"What do you want, Claude?"

"I want to laugh."

"Like Herméné laughs?"

"It might be important."

"I think it's crucial."

"For the case."

"Absolutely. It's why we're here."

Like a drunk unable to remember how he made it home, driving by pure instinct and rote, must have stopped here, must have turned there, haunted by the thought of it, his mind hot-wired by the thing Flossie has fed him, it's a trip to a place well known but the way is not describable.

But it leads through Flossie's bed: "Is it you?" …as she settles on him, high on his chest, looking down, inching closer still.

"It looks like I'm the only one left, monsieur. And Céleste… I think you're going to love her."

He remembers fragments flipping into ever new configurations, kaleidoscopic, with no sense of going from A to B and beyond; but inevitable, no way round it, into Flossie, who bends to give his nose a friendly lick before shifting higher and smothering him with herself...*through* Flossie—Flossie's voice, Flossie's bell, her feel, her smell and on to a connection with this presence he knows but won't dare define beyond his body's sense of pleasure. Céleste? She's the best! extraordinary!...welcoming Claude Néon to a place beyond condition or restraint... "It's not believable."

"If you don't believe it, you won't laugh."

Yes, all right...belief is essential. Because she looms above him. Because he's pinned. Because the pressure's all in degrees of softness. Pressure from both ends.

Both ends of what, Claude?

My life?

"I'm going to make you laugh." Shifting gently, nudging him deeper and deeper into the pillow.

Because it's not logical to be afraid.

"...laugh just like a baby. Come on, Claude... *Come on, Claude!*"

He remembers her voice...someone's voice—it no longer sounds like Flossie, no longer *feels* like Flossie, modulating, blending back into the sound of breath; and reaching up, blindly, across the wide terrain of her belly, completely sure that he believes it, and feeling happy—like an infant captivated by pure good. And laughing.

Once. Ding!... The laugh reverberates, shaking him, it seems, apart.

He is found by Erly the baker the following morning, crawling half naked and delirious in the back alley, a note tucked into his sock: This man should wash his face. After basic questions at the brothel, Assistant Inspector Patrice Lebeau had decided it was best left for Inspector Nouvelle. Tricky territory; it's her case...

2.

"Group sex. Obviously he wasn't ready for it. Scared the hell out of him." With the help of child psychologist Jean-Paul Blismes, Claude has been able to build the beginnings of a story about a cow. "They latch on to these primal images. Like the kids. But it's a start, eh, Claude?"

He's in a highly nervous state when Aliette visits the private room at Hôtel-Dieu. Mildly catatonic; *catatonic*: marked by stupor or muscular rigidity, alternating with phases of excitement. Post-traumatic Stress Syndrome is the official diagnosis. J-P Blismes usually works with young offenders but was given the Herménégilde Dupras file because of Chief J. of I. Gérard Richand's interest in the suspect's early history; and so he also seemed like the logical man to see about Claude, "given the common fact of Mari Morgan's, you see?" …But it's more rewarding working with a case like Claude's. "…I enjoy the challenge of reconstituting his mind." And because, J-P confides, he and the man in detention are getting nowhere. J-P maintains it's classic denial. Trouble is, Monsieur Dupras agrees, saying J-P refuses to accept that his late father used to come to Mari Morgan's once a week for years. "It's just not true… I mean, don't you think my mother and I would've sensed this in my father?" Result: impasse; highly frustrating. "…and with Papa gone and Dupras' delusions, I doubt we'll ever know."

Aliette can't deal with the life of Jean-Paul Blismes. She asks for some time alone.

"Be gentle with him."

"Oh, the Commissaire knows I'm the most gentle cop around… Don't you, Claude?"

Claude's eyes flit. Monsieur Blismes withdraws, somewhat reluctantly.

She sits at his side and pats his jittery hand. "What happened, Claude? What did she do to you?" She can see he wants to tell her. But it's stuck inside. "Was it for the fun—or for the case?"

"Mmm, mmm, mmm…!" This rising to an odd squeak.

"Don't worry. I believe you."

He watches her, wary.

"Then tell me this: Is it really the best sex around?"

The barest trace of a smile pulls at the corners of his mouth.

"She gave you something." Yes. "Was it Maeve? …Did you hear anyone talking about Maeve?" Removing a jar from her briefcase, unscrewing the cap, she holds it under the Commissaire's nose. "This stuff?"

He sniffs it…and then again. Yes.

"Hm. And did you see the goddess, Claude?"

He's trembling again, frantic fingers going for the sides of the bed.

Aliette *is* gentle. "But don't be afraid. If you did, that's wonderful! What's she like?"

Claude grunts, squeaks, wanting to tell.

"Yes…tell me. Beautiful, I bet. Come on… Just say it."

"Mmmm…mmmm!"

"I'm listening, Claude. Tell me she's wonderful. Tell me your life will never be the same." The inspector holds his hand in hers—no need to be frightened, keeping her eyes locked on his. "It's only me…Aliette. I'm here."

Big frown; so worried…

"Smile."

He tries.

"Yes… What is it?" Bending close to hear.

Claude manages a broken whisper: "Are…are you a…a cow?"

Aliette keeps hold of Claude's hand. "No… Actually, I'm a horse—apparently."

- 13 -
TWO MINDS/ONE KNIFE

Bravo, Flossie Orain! A big display of spite and power. What else could it have been—except pure provocation? Claude Néon is not the one she wanted to touch. Claude is not the one who has seen her true face. It's not his case. This one belongs to Aliette Nouvelle and Flossie Orain is taunting. To what end? Is her power meant to impress? If she were honest, with her instincts if nothing else, a person had to live in the here and now and respond to the situation. No islands just for girls. Angélique Ménou is dead—had been dying for a long time. Sein is a relic. The retrograde is not the eternal; no connection. If the goddess takes her meaning from the place where she resides, the path the goddess had taken from the life of Angélique Ménou through Ondine Duguay and on to the likes of Florence Orain was from an image in the heart to a notion in the mind. Surely the challenge was keeping her in your heart as you opened your mind.

But in the absence of a heart? Seen in Flossie, the goddess is the will to power and not much else. Flossie's beliefs have taken her far past any instinct or vision, no matter how right or urgent. Flossie, and the women of Mari Morgan's who support her, have acted against themselves and not merely the law.

But does the inspector have any more proof that Flossie Orain is the killer of a woman who made her living offering a crude two-dimensional illusion? Aliette has two bodies in cold storage downstairs. A sample of Maeve is in the vault. Raphaele, polite, not pushing it, mentioning only that she looks well rested, has confirmed, "Yes, this is the same substance as the remedy but condensed to essentials. It would definitely produce jarring psychoactive effects. Yes, the remedy could mask the drug."

But Manon Larivière was killed with a blade.

There is a law against giving a person a drug then ravishing him till he can't think straight, let alone move. Probably more than one, if you start to take it apart. Would Monsieur le Commissaire proceed against Flossie on those grounds? Not likely. Reputation; the ability to even talk about it in a coherent way. And Aliette does not think that she would blame him.

Who will say something to collapse the wall around the pute? …Just a pute and nothing else.

Bitter, bitter, bitter! How quickly that warm sun and sea air disappears from one's disposition.

The phone buzzes: Monique…"*Oui.*"

"Two ladies to see you."

"Names?"

"Both Duguay."

"Both?"

"Sisters—quite tall?"

A moment later in reception. "Bonjour!" …Shaking hands; this *is* a surprise!

"I got your note," says blithe Georgette, as if that will explain everything.

> Your sister needs you. AN…

Well, good. "Come into my office. Please."

"Who is this person?" Georgette, perusing Aliette's work space for the first time, is stopped at the poster depicting Johnny Hallyday performing on the street in front of the mural of the Acadian deportation, one of the more colourful corners of Nantes.

"Johnny Hallyday." Georgette shrugs; she hasn't heard of Johnny. "I was there," adds Aliette. "Sit, please. Can I get you anything? Some coffee?"

"Tea."

The order is placed. She faces the sisters. Quite tall indeed…willowy. But while the elder is robust and defiant in every flicker of those forest-green eyes, the younger is spindly—and afraid.

Georgette says, "Ondine needs to talk to you."

Aliette asks Ondine, "About the case?"

"Yes."

"Very well," taking pen in hand; "Georgette, if you wouldn't mind waiting outside."

"She knows it all," mutters Ondine. "I'd like her to be here. Please."

"There are certain rules…procedure."

"I need her to be here." Yet the sisters remain apart and impassive, neither making a move to touch the other; but Aliette already knows the Duguays are not the kind to be holding hands.

"All right." Putting her pen aside. This can be a visit. No depositions till after it's out.

2.

"Manon came to me…often, before that night. I left Mari Morgan's hating all of them, only wanting to never have anything more to do with them. But after a time they began to come back to me. I suppose Flossie was right…we were attached because of what we'd shared."

"The goddess."

"They needed something. It turned out to be me who provided it…" Still barely a mutter, as if she's ashamed: "the goddess was the only reason I was ever in that place."

"Not Herméné Dupras?"

"I was lonely. I'd spent my best years living halfway between my own life and my mother's. I came back here to face something I should have faced years before. He's not a mean man… He told me what I needed to know. We stayed in contact as I set up my little shop. He saw my skills and put them to use in ways I'd never imagined. Then he offered me a position. I saw something that looked like the power and respect I'd never had. More than any shopkeeper would ever have. I was flattered. And I was flattered by his kind of affection for a while. I suppose I needed it. It got in the way of seeing things clearly…" Glancing at her sister; her sister gazing resolutely away. "But after I understood the man, it was them—the girls. They needed me and he came with them. That's why I would never listen to better advice. Herméné was only pride, never love."

"How did it begin—the goddess, at Mari Morgan's?"

"I was there, with Herméné, and running the place, more or less, and thinking I was happy… I talked to them. I told them about the customs I'd seen on the coast…and I read to them from the red book. A book: to show them it was real…more than just some woman talking."

"But did they respond? Were they interested? I mean, that kind of woman…"

"Is never what she seems, Inspector. Never. Not once in all the years I was there did I meet a girl—a woman, who was like the one the clients thought they were getting. Especially not poor Manon. At least not then, when I first knew her… Yes, they responded. They had all been girls once—some had never stopped being. They liked stories. They liked the images of love…" Ondine sits straighter, gathering some strength. "And there's nothing about guilt in that book. It was different from the rules they'd grown up with. It was good for them to believe that even the kind of women they were could be creatures of destiny. If that was so, then there might be a way of assuming a bit of grace. Real grace. Not the kind they put on for work… We talked about things like that and read together. One of them found a model of a cow and we put it in the kitchen… I called it Céleste. I changed the name on the door. I put the motto up in the bar."

"OK…" Watching her; a view changes with a deeper background. "But was it only for them?"

"And for me… It was also for me. I badly needed to keep something alive. Something that had happened to me."

"On Sein?"

"Yes."

"Is it true you only met Angélique Ménou once?"

"I spent one weekend there. That's all."

"What was it that happened?"

"Love."

Georgette blushes. Ondine sees it and blushes, too.

"What about this drink: Maeve? Did you bring that from the coast as well?"

"Dorise brought it, years later. I mean, as a remedy…"

"And you shared it with your girls."

"It's useful."

"But they have it—the stronger thing that Angélique was drinking. Flossie has it, I'm sure."

"I tried it again… I asked Dorise and she made it. For me." Ondine pauses; her face is pinching in on itself, reddening. Aliette lets the silence rest while the woman finds her words. "I tried it with Herméné. To see if we could…to see if I could find what I'd…" Trailing off. Obviously she had not.

"Then he's the one who gave it to the girls."

"He tried it with the next one. With all of them. Then Flossie—she took Maeve and used it."

"For sex?"

"For everything. For everything that we were about… It's so powerful."

"This idea of a cow…how could she have—?"

"From me! …From one night of making a fool of myself with Herméné Dupras."

"And so you left Mari Morgan's."

"Knowing they were using it that way was more than I could stand."

"What did Herméné have to say about it?"

"He thought I was jealous. He knew nothing about the goddess or anything to do with her. He couldn't have cared less. To him, Maeve is just a drink Dorise knows how to make. One more way of having fun… Please forget about Herméné Dupras."

Aliette grabs her pen, regardless of Georgette's presence. "Herménégilde Dupras did not kill Manon Larivière."

"No."

She scribbles a note. Then, "Who did kill Manon Larivière?"

Ondine Duguay closes her eyes, takes three silent breaths. "Do you know what it's like to lose track of your life, Inspector?" It's not the kind of question an inspector will usually answer. Ondine opens her eyes and sees this. She says, "Manon was so delicate under that wretched blonde disguise. And in such pain during those last days. The pain of despair. Hopeless. And this morbid confusion... It never stopped."

"Her headaches?"

"Her life. It was changing. She was not as old as most women usually are when it comes, but—her condition, her headaches, her heavy bleeding—she was into the menopause and it upset her. It scared her."

"I've heard of it happening. But you would think someone in her situation might welcome it. The bleeding, the migraines, they can all disappear. It would be a relief, no?"

"Only physically. The problem was her life...her idea of herself."

"We all go through it. They say the eyes finally open."

"She was no longer a big blonde full of jokes and the promise of magic. Her life—the one she had devoted herself to so completely, so absurdly—was over."

"But that was an act...not a physical thing."

"No..." Ondine is sad to have to say it. "Physical was all she was, all she knew how to be. We would talk about the goddess and she would take every word into her heart. Manon loved her. But it was filtered through this shell she thought she needed. A taste of Maeve every day with Flossie's blessing only made the shell that much harder. A very simple girl, Inspector. She thought she'd found an answer in the idea of someone else's life. Her way to be special. She knew everything about that woman and nothing about herself. Her only connection to herself was her body. This change that was happening brought it home to Manon that her ideal had killed herself at thirty-six...that there was nothing for her to go by when Marilyn Monroe's life changed like hers was doing because Marilyn Monroe had never got that far. Her life couldn't show Manon what she should do... Manon was lost."

"So she came to you. What could you do to help her?"

"Not much. Urge her to leave it. And commiserate. I knew the feeling... She was like someone who could have come from me. Like a daughter I might have had."

"What do you mean?"

"I understood her fear—that her life had disappeared somewhere. I, mmm…" Bending forward and rubbing her temples, straining to find more words for the police. "Inspector…I learned how to use my hands and it made me feel that I had something. When a man took my talents and used them like they'd never been used before, I was seduced by that…by being special…" Casting another woeful face in her sister's direction. "But my hands could never make me special enough to bring the right person into my life. It was certainly not Herméné Dupras; that was made clear every single day. But I had trapped myself. I couldn't leave it…so I gave myself away. I gave myself back to a memory, to one moment in a young woman's dream. And when the dream was over…I knew what Manon was feeling. And she kept saying the only thing left for her was to go and be with the goddess. I knew that feeling too."

"On Sein? I found her there… Her and Marcel Cyr. Was it him?"

"He was only her guardian. He made a bargain—to deliver her… We had to send her. To finish it." Bleak face; tears are pressing to get out… "It was what she wanted."

Aliette waits on the edge of this woman's darkness, watching that befuddled thing creeping back, clouding it. "Finish what? …Ondine? What are you trying to tell me?"

"About devotion? Perfecting faith? Sacrifice? …Flossie says belief is only made pure with—"

Georgette explodes. "She's the one! She perverted it completely! She used you for her—"

"It's not Flossie. It's me. I'm the one."

Georgette stands. "Let's stop this! We should have a lawyer!"

"No…" Ondine looks away from the offered hand.

"Yes! You're in no condition to—"

"Georgette!" Aliette interjects. "Let her speak or you'll have to go."

"You have to help her!"

"I have to find out what happened first!" In a more appropriate tone: "Please remember where you are…and that you came here of your own accord."

Georgette does not like to hear it. She sits, glowering as only Georgette can.

Aliette asks Ondine. "Who killed Manon Larivière?"

"I did."

Aliette cannot make her pen move. "*You* did…how?"

"With a knife… It was for me to do it. It was my responsibility. My fault. My mistake. My terrible, terrible mistake…" Tears are streaming now; yet she sits there unflinching, needing to tell.

All Aliette can do is ask, "What happened?"

Ondine relates the events of the night of August 5th.

3.

The weather has been impossible. People's nerves are frayed. When Flossie appears at her door, Ondine stands there mute, on edge, as if looking at a stranger. "You must come, Ondine. Manon needs you." But she's been expecting her. Looking into those sparkling umber eyes, Ondine has to admit part of her had been hoping for this summons. Those have been unspeakable hopes but she can't deny them. Manon's confessions and fears have turned to troubling hints about redemption, and of how she might resolve it all. It's Flossie who has planted this notion; if you know Manon at all, that's not hard to see. Manon's been saying these words, but she has always only been a vessel. The worse it was becoming for Manon Larivière the more clear was the voice of Flossie Orain coming through the complaints and the longing… Intimations of purpose. And service. Ondine had begun to understand she would be called. She would be needed.

It's good to be needed. Ondine has been waiting, still, passive, for too long.

They walk through the streets in silence, at an urgent pace, faster than is comfortable for old joints only slightly lubricated by the steamy air. But that's how it had always been with Flossie, urgent. Those early days…Ondine had been so impressed by her. Her and Louise. Impressed and intrigued: they were educated—Flossie with a Philo A baccalaureate, a degree in History and a term at the Law Faculty, Louise with the B bacc and two years of Economics. They were big readers, good talkers. They were thinkers. What were they doing at Mari Morgan's?

"Dropping out and going to war," was how Flossie put it.

What did that mean to a seamstress? Had the two new girls been in the streets of Paris in May of '68? Were they involved with one of those German Maoist factions that liked to plant bombs? Ondine could never quite grasp the world they had come from. But what *was* clear, in the way they talked and their manner of confronting the world—clients, Herméné if he said the wrong thing, even someone like Erly the baker next door—was that they understood perfectly the machinations behind the values sustaining a place like Mari Morgan's. They'd come, they said, to "ground zero" because it was simply the best place from which to break it all apart and find something new.

They had embraced the goddess—wholeheartedly!

They had been equally delighted when Herméné introduced them to Maeve.

"*Le minou n'a pas besoin de carabine!*" proclaimed Flossie, returning from the library loaded down with more books containing dusty stories that picked up where Ondine's old nameless red book had left off. Some showed the goddess in her guise as a ruthless, fearless fighter: Maeve, a politically astute queen who played heroes off against each other, in her bed and in her battles, always keeping her sizable territory shifting—liquid, you might say…always ready. *Pussy doesn't need a gun…?* "They're only stories, Ondine. But they show us everything we can be…*have* to be, when the time is right." Then Louise would turn around and show her a plan for profit-sharing, or a salary scale equating Ondine's share with Ondine's efforts, and Herméné's with his.

Impressive and intriguing. And disturbing, being pulled forward so drastically by this energy, this attitude—then being pushed aside. Ondine could never be a part of it. She had walked away. But they would not let go…kept coming to her: repairs to a garter belt, more pretty things. These things were also part of the new design. She had complained: is that all I'm good for? I'm your *teacher*. Is there no role for me now?

But Flossie had kept one. A special role—only for Ondine.

...They go in the back way, all in a rush after ten—no, twelve years away, Flossie holding the door, ushering her through the empty kitchen and into the cool room where the apple twigs burn in a dish on the unadorned table. Her old work room. It's exactly how she'd left it. As with everything they did, Ondine has to admire the way they've concealed it, filling in the window, extending the wall behind Céleste and making it a seamless structural support, the room itself a forgotten closed-off space which opens only to hands that know exactly where to touch. But why? Surely not for the sake of Herméné Dupras... Why are they hiding her like this? What had they done with the goddess?

"Protecting her," says Flossie, closing the wall behind them; "...keeping her safe, pure. In a world like this, a woman like Manon needs the goddess to be pure and clear." She takes the jar and a glass from the old cabinet and brings it to Ondine. "She can't go on, Ondine... Too miserable. Too hopeless. She's reached the absolute end of all her hope...August 5th is the day. She believes it's the only thing she can do."

"I know."

"Then you know she needs you to help her."

Ondine confronts Maeve, the hand that offers, Flossie's earnest face. "How can I?" At that moment she does not feel anything but a weightless curiosity as to how a person could do it. She had been thinking about it. As the need and the request had become clear, Ondine had been trying to conceive of doing this thing. Now, confronted with it... The release of one's deepest self into the act; in many ways it would have to be greater even than the victim's. And from a farther distance than an executioner's. And from a stronger place than a murderer's. All those things, combined in one act. How could she do it? How could anyone be expected to?

"She will show you," says Flossie, handing her the glass.

Ondine accepts it... Would she do that? Would the goddess take her as a priestess and take her out of time? After all this time alone in a dingy shop? Two minds. It's difficult to find balance on a muggy night... No! She tells Flossie, "Manon doesn't know what she wants. She's being morbid. She needs love and help. This is not the time for—" For a moment, in the vague light of the small sanctuary,

Ondine hangs there confused and intimidated. Where are my tape and scissors? She'll make something new and exquisite, just for Manon. *That* was her role… Looking around for the things she needs.

Flossie lays a calming hand on Ondine's arm. "It's the ultimate gift. It means the most. It gives the most energy. It's what she believes she is meant to do. An active spirit, Ondine… A purpose for everyone. It's what you taught us."

"I can't."

Flossie asks, "What do you believe you were meant to do?"

Make underwear? Left unsaid, but Ondine knows Flossie. And Flossie knows Ondine.

"This…" Ondine reels, remembering, feeling the quiet coolness of the room where she had worked and taught them, breathing the sweet scent of the smoke, sharing the verse, the ideas, the goddess. I made this place. I helped some women who would never have known it find some integrity, a bit of meaning; it's what I believe I was meant to do. "Nurture an active spirit," is what she hears herself whisper.

Flossie says, "I know you've been waiting, Ondine…waiting to move forward. None of us can stop until we're off the wheel. The only way to move is to do the real thing our fate says we're meant to… You know this is where your life has brought you."

"You do it."

Flossie smiles, with love—or something so much like it to the eyes of a needful Ondine. "Not me…not yet. Drink. Maeve will help you."

Not you, not yet: a strong woman, still young and alive to the world, many things still to do.

And me: is this where my life has brought me? Ondine knows she has brought this moment upon herself, invited it…by hiding, by sitting in the past and only waiting—waiting for the goddess to show her the next thing. But if I turn away, where will I be? What will I have to show? Show *her*… Thus Ondine tastes Maeve again after so long away. It's the same as before, burning, leaving layers of flavour on her palate and down her throat. It's the same as the first time, on an island at the edge of the world.

Closing her eyes, she bends toward the meagre trail of smoke rising from the dish of burning twigs. She stays there, in wordless prayer…empty prayer, losing track of time, letting the smoke infuse her being. And Flossie lays a caring hand upon her head.

Finally, looking up, through changing eyes—Maeve is working… But where is Manon?

"She was here, with Dorise and Louise and me. We burned some twigs. We shared Maeve. We made sure we understand. Dorise was helping her with her hair…"

Ondine can see it: Dorise with Manon, preparing. She can see Dorise's raw hands holding the silver brush, brushing the unreal platinum hair. Dorise afraid—but also in awe. And her grey eyes, the eyes of a homely fifteen-year-old who had believed completely in another, better existence. And Manon believing it too, to save her soul.

"It was beautiful to see," says Flossie. "I could feel the goddess there with us, so proud, grateful for this gesture… She's waiting for you, Ondine. She's with Herméné…"

With Herméné?

"Don't worry."

No? Why? …Then she understands.

Flossie nods. "It may as well be him."

Practicalities. When push had come to shove, Mari Morgan's had always been defended in the most practical of ways. Now an unseen door to protect the goddess. And Herménégilde Dupras to protect Ondine. Yes, it may as well be him… And the others? What of the others?

"They don't know… Ondine, it's between Manon and the goddess." And those of us who will understand, those she needs to help her go through. It's only Dorise, Louise and Flossie who have adjusted their movements on this special night—Louise is out in the front making sure, Dorise is watching the back stairs, it's safe and quiet, it's the best we can do for our friend Manon…

But these worries are fading from Ondine's mind. Already she can feel Maeve lifting her away from the concerns of one brief night in time.

Flossie proffers the book. Ondine sets it on the table, touching it, bemused. Yes, Maeve works differently on an older woman's mind. Ondine feels her…but it's as if she feels her come and go. Has the space between herself and the goddess grown smaller with the years? Is she with her already? Mmm, two minds returning to one… The book opens at the verse. Ondine sees the words and follows them…

Flossie takes her hand. The wall swings open slightly and together they go out.

Manon is unaware. She's at the bookcase, examining the photos gathered there, many of herself, feeling them, going from one to the next, searching… Ondine waits, watching her, letting her feel her way. Herménégilde Dupras is slouched over his desktop in a formless heap. The sight of him's a jolt—the face of the goddess dims. No! Ondine can't dwell on Herméné—won't allow him into her fate. Not now. Far too late. It's Manon. She's the one who's trapped here. She's the one who needs to leave. Ondine moves closer. The red book is still open in her hand.

Manon senses her and turns. Her face and hair have been done as if for work. They were always made this way. Manon has not changed, not even for this night…she had insisted that she could not. Even as she'd poured out her despair at what she believed was the end of her useful life, Manon had refused to consider shedding that mask. She holds a knife and comes to Ondine with a halting step, as if walking in the dark, looking but not focusing, face trembling like she'll shatter. "Please, Ondine. Maeve can only give me so much courage." Hearing it, here in this room where Ondine herself had spent so much time helping build a playworld around Manon… Ondine trips inside herself again—she thinks she sees what the men must see: this is where the charm turned hot, Marilyn Monroe's lonely heart opened wide.

…But, finding strength, Manon whispers, "Read it to me." A humble request; while passing the knife into Ondine's hand; "I want to be inside the verse. With her…Ondine. Away from this."

Ondine begins to read for Manon—slow, deliberate, the same care for these words she'll give the most intricate hand-embroidered hem. And reading so, each line allows Ondine to see more clearly. The situation…and its necessity. Manon is an inch away, pressing closer, keeping her hand…now both, now tightly, on Ondine's right hand as it holds the knife, pressing its point against herself, against the silk covering her body.

A silken thing that Ondine had made? Wavering…

Looking up and into Manon's eyes, that notion is the last one. Ondine reads for herself: Each line brings her closer into alignment with something original, infinite. So Ondine disappears from herself. Only the words remain. In a voice. Inside the faintest scent of apple smoke.

Manon is a woman without a future. But the golden-haired acolyte is luxuriant, full in her presence, giving herself fully, insistently, willing it, the merging of her life with that last line.

"*I am the tomb of every hope.*"

A sound…a woman's sound. Pain. The sharp surprise of it.

The knife is now inside her. Feeling momentum, Ondine presses further.

Then lets go of the knife, not like a knife but a handle on a door.

Manon sinks down, carrying it with her to the floor.

Ondine hears a voice—Dorise? or Flossie or Louise—say simply, "From corruption, sweetness."

She remembers a hand on her shoulder…and blood seeping into the material of Manon's chemise.

After that, the heat again, outside, as they hurry her away.

- 1 4 -

On Secret Doors and Waiting

The inspector lays it out—raw, cool, mean; it's the only way: The act is central, but Ondine's part is marginal and highly mediated despite her tragic claims. She is an outsider. She's an old woman—just a seamstress. It's not her world anymore. She was used by someone younger, stronger, far more dangerous. No, what would be the point of arresting Ondine? One's sense of justice, not to say the goddess, will be skewed. Can you live with that, Ondine Duguay?

Or is there a way to effect some change before reaching legal closure?

Your move, Ondine… Not that I expect much from a helpless old lady. Who would?

Ondine leaves with her sister, empty, leaning on her sister's arm. Will a tired seamstress respond to one cop's bitter assessment? It's a challenge, and a gamble. Aliette feels the presence of Georgette may improve the odds… She folds the deposition sheet and puts it in her pocket; for all intents and purposes it's still clean. In the beginning was the word, no? This applies to legal process as much as to the notion that the goddess takes her cue from the environment. Can the goddess do much good at all from behind a secret door? Surprise me, Ondine… Stand in for me, Georgette.

She leaves it and heads home. But she can't walk away from it. Such a useless cop!

Up through the anger comes that voice, conciliatory, trying to tell her no one's perfect:

Her house is full of many mansions, Aliette; didn't the good sisters ever tell you that one?

Yes.

Of course they did… And most of them are reached through secret doors.

She doesn't buy it. A secret door in the kitchen. *Quelle conne,* Aliette! How could you be so stupid? No one gets fooled by a secret door any more!

Au contraire—everyone does, every day.

I should have guessed!

But you're a professional—you don't guess.

I could have known. I touched it. I went right over and touched that model cow.

Because you thought she was beautiful.

There's no excuse for not seeing it… A cow. So literal. How blind!

Please! …Give yourself a break here. Secret doors are basic to the job. Secret doors opening to a labyrinth of elemental passages. It's the world you live in. It's why you have the job you have…You, the inspector: the things you recognize—just…just a glimpse, a clue—and move toward. How do you arrive if not by means of secret doors? But don't expect each one to open just like that—just because you happen to be standing in front of it. It doesn't work that way, ma belle… Nine years on the force? You should have come to terms by now.

No! She doesn't want to listen. Or it could be that she can't; professional identity is on the line here. She tells herself: You should have sensed it. Deduced it! It's in the logic of the place…in every move they make. Finding it could have saved Colette Namur. Kept that girl Vivi from ever setting foot inside the place… She asks herself: Are you truly the best we have to offer? Do you really deserve all that supposed freedom to pick and choose and come and go as you please? And pretending you deserved the top job… Bullshit! Just a sham. A secret door. Pretty pathetic, Inspector. Etc. Etc… Too much anger. Hard to think clearly as the waiting begins.

She's not the only one who's bothered by developments. Arriving home, collecting her mail, there's another communication from Substitute Procureur Cécile Botrel. Through the post? Because her boss Michel Souviron is back on the job? And this one's not on official *Parquet* stationery…

> I trust you will treat the attached with discretion and not for the purposes of work per se, but more, perhaps, for research into why we are the way we are—some women, that is. —CB.

The attached being a copy of a printout from an *RG* file on Florence Orain.

RG is *Renseignements Généraux*, the internal branch of the secret police, to which Aliette has no access without a mandate (and even then it's never easy). *RG*'s notes echo Aliette's: Flossie is known to be involved in prostitution, minor drugs; but included in the reference to the incident during the Papal visit to Paris are two items from a juvenile record. These describe charges related to acts of church desecration perpetrated by the subject when she was fifteen. Altar trashing. The attacks were marked by the subject's tendency to scrawl quotations. A fragment from Matthew 19:

> …and there are those who have made themselves eunuchs for the kingdom of heaven? (sic).

And one from Corinthians 7, Paul's defence of celibacy:

> …but the married man is anxious about the affairs of the world, how to please his wife, and his interests are divided.

RG, ever thorough, is apparently keeping watch on the lady, in an effort, one had to suppose, to avoid further possibility of catastrophic embarrassment for Mother France viz. a Holy Father with a lump on his head or worse. As usual, *RG* was itself breaking the law; this information ought to have been destroyed when the subject had reached the age of majority. Maître Botrel is taking risks to help her.

"Just calling to thank you."

"Don't mention it."

Enough said. Stay discreet for both your sakes! But the inspector likes her. She wants to talk… "How in the world did you come across Maeve?" Maeve belongs to mythology—not the secret police.

"Oh…sometimes when you love someone their name sits in your mind like a neon sign. I was going through IJ's report on the message on Colette Namur's bathtub and it was right there in front of me. My girlfriend's name. She's Irish…teaches chemical engineering at *la Chimie*."

"Ah." *Ecole nationale supérieure de chimie:* top-level chemical engineering school, one of a medium-sized and mediocre city's few national points of pride. Must be a smart woman. Then, connecting three seconds too late: "Your girlfriend?"

An embarrassed pause sensed clearly down the phone line… *Aliette!*

"…I thought you would have known. Legal circles in this town are small, to say the least."

"No…no, I didn't know… And I certainly didn't mean to—"

Cécile remains lawyerly matter-of-fact. "Maeve was for you, Inspector, because I've met Flossie Orain and I know you're going in the right direction. The thing in your mail…well, that one's for the Commissaire. When I interviewed him, he managed to tell me bits and pieces of what she did. I felt ashamed, frankly. And angry. So facile…"

"Yes."

"It's difficult… Political, professional, personal; they tend to get mixed up, don't they?"

"Yes."

"People should be reasonable, no?"

Yes, Maître. Merci. Good to know you're still with me. This will make the waiting easier.

On the other hand, October's *Marie Claire* has also arrived. It features the *Marie Claire Guide Amoureux,* a detachable supplement with colourful illustrations and accompanying descriptions of twenty different ways of making love:

The Accordion—he's on his knees; she's on her back with her knees up and practically touching her nose…we're all scrunched up here. Like an accordion. "Sure. I'll try it…"

The Amazon—looks like Olympic wrestling. She's got him down (on a beach in the picture) on his side; she's got one of his legs lifted so his knee's up around her breasts; she holds it there, pinning him, the nexus of her soft weight at the stiff centre of his gravity. Applying pressure as required. "OK…"

The Twist (No 2)—*Marie Claire* says this is a position where the woman can explore her more lascivious side. She lies on her back (beside a slice of watermelon with the ocean in the background) and puts both legs around one side of the guy, who is on his knees; thus they join from a less-than-centred geometry; and she twists. "Yes, that could be lascivious."

The Wheelbarrow—she lies at the end of the bed and sticks her bum up in the air. He picks up the wheelbarrow and goes to work. "I would love that so much, Piaf…"

The Jockey—he sits on a dining room chair; she sits in his lap, facing him. "Hmm…" Because there's a horse running free in the back of her mind now and it won't go away. But in this one *she's* the jockey, he's the horse: "not quite what I'm looking for…"

Leafing through, Piaf warmly at her elbow.

The Rider. (*Position classique*) is another in this sub-genre of her-on-top-of-him. A woman who needs tenderness, who may not be sure of herself, may be shy when it comes to this position evocative of images of prostitution. If she can conquer that and learn to play with her fantasies, this position is the source of great pleasure. Conduct your own sensual game at your own speed. Move around, vary the penetration, touch the man, look at him, embrace him. Men like it when the woman takes the initiative. Other features: lying on his back, the man has better control over his ejaculation, and this makes it better for both of you. Right, but it's still the wrong way: sitting on *him*, the generic *she's* the rider not the horse… And why would *Marie Claire* say this one's a classic in one breath and tie it to images of prostitution in the next? Have they got a problem? Or is it the generic *us* that has the problem and they know we'll react to the word? Reverberations up and down our lives…"We'll have to write a letter to the editor. Eh, Piaf?"

Ah… Here's one that reverses the proposition and comes nearer her instinct's wish.

The Tractor (*Le Remorqueur*)—She's the machine; she's down on her hands and knees, tending forward, pulling the load, so to speak. *"On ne parle pas des chiens ici, mon Piaf…"* Not talking *doggies* here, Piaf; nor wheelbarrows; not at all: he *sits*, flush to her behind, his legs draped round her haunches, the tractor driver. He just sits there. Steering. As engine and chassis it's her job to provide the means of motion. This appeals to a pony's needs. "Tractor's a lot like a horse… Eh, Piaf? I mean look."

This sort of information will make any waiting harder.

"Hello, Raphaele? Aliette here. Remember that three-cheese sauce…"

"Come on over."

Saturday night, she puts on her new camisole, slips out through her secret door and goes. It clears the mind, momentarily. But (inevitably): Is this right? Is this a relationship? He cooks beautifully. Does exactly what she tells him to do in bed. Does amazing things with his tongue. Drives that tractor as well as you could want… Mmm. Doesn't make noise. (Neither does she.) Doesn't insist on sharing a shower. Could be the perfect man. The only problem is that she feels no real need to go down to the basement for coffee on Monday. Or Tuesday. That's not part of her desires. *Nothing's perfect, Aliette.* I know. Don't rub it in. I don't need it… *But it's horrible when you know it before you even finish eating that great pasta. No?* Please! Give it a rest. People need. People try…

I never rest. I just change shape, ma belle.

A week after Ondine Duguay's visit to the offices of the Police Judiciaire, Assistant Inspector Patrice Lebeau reports that she has disappeared from her domicile. Inspector Nouvelle, staying calm, sensing progress, says to leave no stone unturned.

And luckily there's other work. Two cases are passed along, the trans-border kind she usually handles. A murder in the city's Turkish enclave: two families fighting over fruit stands at the market; or could it have more to do with the market in forging illegal papers and avenues of entry for fellow countrymen? And a heroin merchant from the burgeoning park in Zurich, two hours down the road, is said to be about, looking to expand his trade. Aliette gets right to both of them. Business as usual; good to be busy.

Being busy, other things come to her.

Feeling like a screw-up for letting the old woman slip away, Assistant Inspector Patrice Lebeau passes by almost hourly now and catches a boy in the alley peering through the fence behind the missing seamstress' shop. René, almost ten, lives across the way. He admits there are sometimes good things to see—"like sometimes ladies in there trying things on." As if the cop will understand. Patrice says he'll think about dropping the peeping charge if René can tell him anything more interesting he may have seen. "Well," racking his memory for something more interesting than ladies trying things on; "back in August, when it was so hot? …there were a lot of them, all dressed up, and this old man… They were picking up the apples from the old lady's yard and putting them in the back of this big old car."

Like this car? Showing a picture of a '49 Citroën TA. Yes. And René's mother remembers seeing it too. She brings her child down to the commissariat and they both sign depositions. "Never seen so much activity in that place," she adds, recalling that stifling August day; "thought she made undies and the like." She's more than happy to help the police and guarantees them her René will soon grow out of his urge to peek.

This information prompts concern at the Palais de Justice over the fact that Ondine Duguay had been to Inspector Nouvelle's office shortly before her disappearance.

"But before her disappearance there was no reason to hold or even talk to her. Her sister is my friend…she was trying to help where she couldn't. It was mostly a personal thing. Between them. Me, I sat and drank tea."

"Mostly?" prods the Judge, looking tanned and well-fed from his five weeks in the south.

The inspector shrugs. "No mandate, Gérard. I asked, monsieur—and you said no."

Gérard Richand rolls his eyes and heaves a sigh. Business as usual for him now too.

"We touched on the case, of course, but I didn't write a word. Really—just a tea party with two old ladies."

What with the seamstress running, René's revelation, the bodies, the drug, and whatever-the-hell this thing is they're saying happened to Néon at the brothel, Gérard is feeling more than a little out of the loop. It's not a feeling a Chief J.of I. enjoys. Gérard throws his weight in certain directions… Once again it's amazing what can happen when the ones with the power actually start to care about something; in three days there's a call from Germany. Francine Léotard has been apprehended while strolling along the Lindzerstrasse in the Lower Saxony town of Oldenburg in the company of one Christophe Giguerre, a respected car-parts manufacturer from Lille. It's one of those situations where you don't ask whether German police methods are ahead of ours or behind; all that matters is that the next day Marcel Cyr's classic car is found in a box on the dock just down-river at Bremerhaven, due to sail for Leningrad in four days' time.

Bravo! No fine object of beauty and most especially one made in France should have to spend the winter in a Russian gangster's garage. We look forward to seeing Francine and Christophe…

Feeling better about almost everything here.

Almost, Aliette?

Well it's painful trying to tell a man you don't really want a man who does everything you tell him to… They start saying things like why did you keep telling me exactly what to do? Clouds the issue. Becomes a vicious circle…

And Georgette, problematic at the best of times, is watching her. Waiting. Expecting.

But even Claude, still wobbly, still resting, but slowly finding his way back from his trauma, seems receptive to her proposed plan of action. Claude's initial reaction was much the same as hers: "A secret door? Unbelievable!" Then he'd said, "Although maybe I'm not surprised."

Three weeks…turning into four. Aliette's tan fades and disappears.

- 15 -
I AM THE QUEEN OF EVERY HIVE

Thursday evening is a rare free night for both Flossie and Louise. It's Louise's monthly break for four or five days. It's the night Flossie usually receives Christophe, her regular from Lille. But Christophe's in Germany on business and Flossie has let the space remain unfilled.

So they share a slow supper alone in the dining room.

Louise seems far away, staring past Flossie's eyes. Flossie asks, "What is it?"

"We had a sideboard exactly like that one at home," says Louise. "Stained green maple…same stain, same copper work on the panels, same fittings…English, mid-nineteenth century. Papa found it in Antwerp…so strange where things end up."

Flossie regards the stately sideboard, the crystal carafe and wine service set on a silver tray on the right side, the rosewood cutlery chest on the left. All from Herméné's mother's place. Most of the better furnishings adorning Mari Morgan's are. "You never told me that."

"It was like my secret," murmurs Louise. "My deepest darkest secret. My personal challenge: to sit here and not feel it… It was uncanny—Maman's silver was the same weight as this. She had her initials engraved on every piece. Part of her trousseau. Some nights, back at the beginning, Maeve could make me think I was home."

"Maeve loves a challenge…"

"Or that I was married…that this was my dining room, that the life was exactly the same. The one she'd planned for me. The one she demanded. It's lucky we don't have a piano…I don't think I would have been able to stand it."

"You're a musician?"

"I was supposed to be. She made that too impossible. She was too perfect. It's why I had to get away…"

"I always thought it was your father and his righteous money."

"I had lots of reasons. I guess we all do… I guess some of them are closer to the heart than others."

Flossie says, "After all this time and you never told me these things…"

Louise is perplexed. "I know. It's like I closed a door and left all that on the other side."

"I always tell you everything."

"Do you? How does one ever know? …I suppose I couldn't relate it to you and me."

"I feel a kind of vertigo," says Flossie, "like I'm sitting in mid-air."

Louise smiles across the gap. A wan smile: I love you but I can't help you; got my own thing here and I need to work it out; "Ondine says I should go see my mother before the end…"

Flossie nibbles an edge of Muenster from the tip of her knife, swallows the last of her wine.

Louise ponders it. "I don't know… I know I should. But I know I can't."

"It's been too long," says Flossie.

"Ondine says I should come to terms."

Flossie rises, goes to the sideboard and takes a decanter from the bottom shelf. And two tiny china cups, each with a gold leaf rim around the lip, a painted dragon swirling intricately inside. Filling them, she places one in front of Louise. "Here. Come to terms."

Louise says, "No…" her mulling grows darker; "not tonight… Ondine says she's still my mother, even after she's gone."

"Do you really need Ondine to tell you what you feel?"

"It's a comfort to have that perspective… I didn't realize how much I've missed it."

"You sure she's not a sentimental old woman?"

Louise emerges from her reverie. She tells Flossie, "She has nothing to be sentimental about. Not any more. You know that."

Flossie sips her Maeve and makes a mawkish toast. "I am the queen of every hive…"

"Flossie… Don't. Ondine's only doing what she can. It has nothing to do with you and me."

Flossie can't help it. She takes the untouched cup from in front of Louise and drains it too. She smiles down into it, eyeballing the dragon and quotes another line. "I am an enchanter—who else will set the whispering voice to song?"

"Please…we have to let this take its course."

"I just wish she'd mind her business."

"It is her business," says Louise. Gently. Wistful. Louise's clients would never guess.

2.

Speaking of business: J.I. Jamms III, MBA, *Représentant commercial, Le Monde de Mickey* works for the French marketing arm of the world's most famous mouse. His mom calls him James-The-Third; as instructed, Vivi Namur just calls him Jimmy. He has been parachuted into the Republic as line-coordinator of a marketing blitz aimed at ensuring that every French family with kids will make the pilgrimage to the new theme park going up just east of Paris (*le grand projet de fantaisie*) at least once. There are excellent stock options tied to Jimmy's numbers and he works hard, travelling the regions. But if his bosses back in California knew he was here with Vivi, he'd be gone in a second. Mari Morgan's is not exactly a family values kind of place.

Although Jimmy's bosses might understand his inclination. With her halo of dark curls, pert nose, teasing smile and light brown eyes, Vivi looks fascinatingly like a certain pubescent TV star who is now old enough to be Jimmy's mother but lives forever in reruns on his company's own TV network, frozen at the most magical moment of a girl's life… A very lucky find.

When first informed of this miracle, Vivi had said, "It sounds Italian—Annette."

"No, no, my Vivi—she's about as American as you can get."

"But me, I am French…"

"Of course you are…" But tonight Jimmy has brought something he'd like her to wear. A hat—a black felt beanie with two plastic "mouse" ears attached. A brilliantly enduring marketing tool created by his employer, it was part of the uniform worn by members of the original TV "club" that brought American children running straight home from school throughout the '50s.

Here's your shirt (with your name on the front),

Here's your ears (one of these caps)

…Now you're an honorary Mouseketeer!

At which point the lucky guest would receive a big kiss. If the one bestowing it happened to be the girl-star with the smart little body, nine-to-thirteen-year-old boys all over America would quiver. A wonderful new feeling. Jimmy has watched the reruns and quivered too.

The girl, the ears; they represent a major thread through Jimmy's life. "Please—for me?"

But something's gotten into her. *"Non!"* And to get the point across once and for all, she shoves Jimmy and his stupid hat away so hard he rolls half out of the bed.

"Damn!" in English, slamming his fist against the floor to break the fall. "Good, Vivi…just great," rolling back beside her. He holds it up: "You made me break one of the ears."

"Good, yourself!" snapping it out of his hand and dropping it in the waste basket beside the bed. The famous ears now rest atop a pile of damp tissues and used condoms, things Jimmy would rather not look at, let alone risk touching. "I am not interested in your cheap toy… This girl you talk about, I don't know her."

"Come on, Vivi. You know the rules."

"Je m'en fous." I don't care. She gets up, squats over the bidet, pees, turns on the hot water and begins to wash herself. Which means Jimmy should leave.

"It's just a hat, for God's sake…a game!"

"No." She begins to dress. "I am not here for games."

"Voyons, Vivi…" Get real, girl. "…of course you are." Jimmy retrieves the ears. He puts on a smile and offers them again. "I mean—

we've been having some real good fun, you and me. Like pals, right? I'm starting to feel you're my friend… Here, just put it on for Jimmy and we'll forget this ever happened."

"The goddess doesn't want your mouse around here."

"Goddess? What the hell are you talking about?"

"*Rien*…" Never mind. "Can you please leave me alone now?"

"Vivi, this is the most famous mouse in the world!"

"*Va-t-en*, Monsieur Jamms." Go away.

"Hey…"

"Now."

"What is this shit? I paid good money. You make me very sad, Vivi…" Stomping out, shirt and coat over his shoulder.

Well it makes her sad too. Has she lost a loyal regular? A good-looking one, who's more her age and also kind of fun. Who was nice in a way no one else was when Colette died. Is her attraction to Jimmy the reason she feels she needs to draw this line? She knows it's wrong. She's finding the attraction difficult—it leads to affection and it's not easy forbidding herself to like someone, to learn to let him touch her body without letting him touch her heart… It seemed so easy at the beginning… A hat? Flossie says it's part of the job. Just do it and don't think twice.

Oui, oui, oui, Vivi knows the rules. She's having trouble with the rules.

Whatever happens in your life there, don't lose track of yourself. Ondine has told her this. After Colette, Vivi knows she must believe it. So why does she have be some Annette? …Stupid hat! And you probably shouldn't have said that to him—about the goddess—either, my girl… Oh *oui*, the mistakes are piling up.

Is she eating too much? Flossie says Dorise's cakes are for the pleasure of their clientele…

And the girls are telling her Flossie's not pleased that she's been leaving her nightly sip of Maeve untouched. But who needs it? …For the goddess? After hearing Ondine's story, Vivi had to tell Ondine, "There are so many drugs. It's nothing new. There's no green sky, no glittering sea."

Ondine (crying again) had agreed. "You're right: Maeve belongs to Sein and nowhere else."

But Maeve's here. She lives in Mari Morgan's. It's almost like she's Flossie's friend.

She wishes she could talk to Flossie, but Flossie is not… What? Not who Vivi first thought she was. Not who Colette always said she was…

Oh là là. Why is this happening? …Heading down the back stairs to the kitchen, nothing to do now—Jimmy paid for all night, feeling hungry, angry, mostly worried. Flossie's going to have my ass. Vivi finds herself some food, some milk. Pushing the lever under Céleste's belly, she slips through the wall to visit Ondine.

3.

It's been almost a month now. Vivi had been out back one morning, hanging sheets on the line to dry in the September sun…when Ondine came walking up the alley with another old woman. "This is my sister." Vivi could see it. Hear it too: Ondine's sister looks at Vivi and mutters, "What are you doing with your life?" Then she hugs Ondine and walks away. Ondine goes in the back door and straight over to Céleste. Dorise almost faints. Ondine tells her, "You have to help me. She's got someone watching me. I can't stand it… How does this work?" pushing and prodding at Céleste's belly. Dorise hurries to help her. The wall opens. "Let me stay in here." "But what will Flossie say!" "She owes me this…" Vivi and the other girls had gathered, watching the two women standing in the musty chamber. Who would ever want to? Like living in a tomb. But there was a chair…and candles to read by, cushions to lie on. They heard Ondine murmur, "Yes…this will be my room again. It's only right." Then Louise had appeared and shooed them away.

Ondine hasn't budged. It has to do with Manon, obviously, though no one dares ask. Flossie has told them, "Just say you haven't seen her, and mean it…like with a client." Vivi's prepared to do that for Ondine. It does not seem right that Ondine would be in trouble. What could an old woman ever do? She had tried to help Manon, hadn't she? …But that Inspector has not been in to bother anyone.

And in a month the room Flossie calls "our sanctuary" has been transformed. In Vivi's first days and weeks in the house it had been lonely…scary! sitting in there in the dank stillness, staring at a wispy stream of smoke and trying to think about the things they said she was meant to think about. Goddess things. Now it's Ondine's work room, brighter, cluttered with a bit of life, and the best place to sort through the problems that come with trying to get along at Mari Morgan's. This room is becoming second nature, an inevitable part of each day. Vivi believes this is the thing Colette imagined. The good thing. Vivi feels it… It's not Flossie, it's Ondine. With Ondine there, behind the wall with the goddess, it makes everything different.

> I am the knot in every weave.
> I am the glow on every ridge.
> I am the queen of every hive.
> I am armour for every heart...

Someone's always in there with her, with something to fix, some time to spare. Josiane was there twice on Tuesday; Vivi knows because so was she. "I know the verse now…" Taking the red book from her pocket (…don't know if I understand it, not sure I ever will; but I think I have it in my head). She had to wait yesterday morning while Ondine and Sophie discussed something. Something major; Sophie was wiping away tears when she finally came out.

Even Louise, last Sunday morning, sharing a cup of tea. Vivi had joined them… She had backed out, not wanting to disturb, but was invited so she got a cup, sat and listened. Louise was smiling as she related long-ago demonstrations of impossible piano exercises. Smiling? It was almost tears. It was the edge of affection. It was something Vivi hadn't seen in Louise before that moment: "…just impossible for a seven-year-old girl to get right. She showed me, over and over—the upright face, perfect posture. I think I was too proud of her to concentrate… I never learned. She was trying so hard. Too hard, daring me to match her… But she lost me, as soon as I was old enough. When I was sixteen, I hated her for all that pressure. I left. Then I lost her. What a shame, the things we waste …"

"Go and see her before the end."

"No…too late. No point."

"You have to."

"I can't…"

Talking about her mother. Hearing it…*seeing it*, this is good for Vivi's heart.

Tonight Vivi goes in to see Ondine, to try to tell her about Jimmy her American client, the problems he brings to the situation.

Dorise is there tonight. She's singing. Some refrain…strange words:

> Ahès, breman Mari Morgan
> E skeud an noz, d'al loar a gan…

"What's that?"

"Bretagne…my mother used to sing it to me."

The one who lived out on that island. Who had just died…"What does it mean?"

"Oh, something like…*from this time forth, the enchantress sings to the moon.*"

"Mari Morgan."

"Yes."

That Dorise would sing! A little voice, pure and light. Dorise appears fully now, a woman living far beyond the boundaries of those pinched shoulders, that starched white smock. Vivi sees a lifetime shaped by the smile shaping the singing of the song.

She thinks, Ondine told me I would see something that would help me believe.

A small revelation for a girl from the housing projects…

And Ondine hums too.

4.

Later on, the place is still. They've all gone up—for the second time, to sleep. Hungry again, Vivi goes back downstairs for another look at Dorise's apple strudel. But: Don't want to eat too much! Flossie had been quite clear. I'll work it off, Flossie, I'll work it off… Vivi eats her strudel and gulps a glass of milk. She whispers a second goodnight through the wall to the old woman hiding in the room behind Céleste.

There's a shuffling and scrabbling at the top of the back stairs…a clinking sound behind it. Jimmy Jamms comes lurching down and sprawls on the kitchen floor, practically at her feet.

"Jimmy…what happened!"

Flossie follows close behind, her nightgown falling open. All she has on under it is a velvet choker with a tiny bell. It's the first time Vivi has seen Flossie's well-kept body. Colette's—loose and chalky at the end—flashes clear in her mind's eye as Flossie grabs Jimmy under his arms and hoists him up. "Don't stand there," she hisses, "get the door!"

Automatic, Vivi rushes to open the back door. Flossie drags Jimmy. He passes right under her eyes…looks up at her but does not see. Vivi has seen that before, too many times back at the HLMs. He's out of his mind. Really out of his mind. "Oh, Jimmy…" Hurrying after.

Flossie leaves him lying by Erly's trash. "Shh!"

"But—"

"Leave him!" Flossie takes Vivi by the wrist and pulls her back into the house.

"But what happened?"

"He came into the bar causing a big scene…wouldn't let it go, so I took him up and gave him his money's worth… Stupid man." Flossie pauses to catch her breath. She sighs, energy draining, massaging herself below the eyes. "What are you doing talking to clients about the goddess, Vivi? Why can't you just do your job? We don't need problems like this. The clients…the other girls, no one wants to see it."

"You hurt him…" Pulling the door open.

"He'll survive…" Pushing it shut again; "just forget about him."

"But I care about him!"

"No you don't. You do *not* care about a man like that."

"How do you know what I feel!"

"Shush! I don't want to hear any more about it…is that clear?"

"Flossie!" pulling on the door; tears beginning, "…you hurt him and it's my fault. I have to do *something*…"

"No!" Flossie's hand clamps down on her wrist once more.

"Leave me alone!" Vivi rips free. "…you're worse than my mother!"

Flossie steps forward and slaps her face. "No!" Then twice more. "I'm not! Never say that to me again. Your mother was nothing but a feeble fool!"

"No!"

"Yes," says Flossie. So coldly. It's a fact. "Now go to bed…and get it straight, Vivi."

Next morning, when Vivi goes in to talk to Ondine about it, she finds Louise holding still while the waistband on a pair of leather slacks is adjusted. Both women are dismayed to see the swelling around her mouth. She tries to lie—because of Louise. "One of my clients…having trouble at work."

Louise says, "She didn't mean it, Vivi. Try to forgive her… Flossie feels everything is her responsibility… She loves you."

Flossie loves her? She dares to ask Louise, "What did she do to him?"

"It wasn't her—it was Maeve. Flossie is not a bad person. She's got things on her mind."

Like what? …But don't ask!…not your business. Something from before your time…

Ondine holds her peace, working away with her pins.

And Vivi works that night, sore mouth and all.

- 16 -

VOICES OF MARI MORGAN'S

"Bonjour, Flossie."

"Salut, Inspector. It's been a while."

"Yes. A lot of loose ends...taking me every which way."

"So I understand."

"And now Ondine Duguay."

"Ondine? Is she all right? We haven't heard a word in weeks."

"Missing."

"No!"

"We have to talk."

"Of course. We'll sit in the bar."

The place is tranquil, coming up noon on a Sunday morning, but things are bound to pick up after lunch. In the course of her ongoing relationship with her "cousin" Myriam the junkie hooker, Aliette has learned that Sunday afternoons are the busiest time of the week in the pute trade. Men tend to get restless, lonely—whatever you want to call it.

"Can I offer you anything...a beer?"

"You never give up, do you? Friends is a fantasy, madame."

"A guest is a guest, Inspector."

"I suppose it's true... A beer would be nice." Flossie goes behind the bar...returns with a mug full of brew for Aliette, a Scotch on the rocks for herself. "Merci...day off?"

"No, but it's still Sunday. Chin chin..."

"Chin chin."

Flossie faces the inspector's eyes. "So: Ondine."

"How long since you've had contact?"

"Seven…eight weeks. Since Colette, as a matter of fact. It happens like that. Then suddenly we'll have a load of things for her to do."

"She was at the funeral?"

"Yes."

"You talked?"

"Not too much."

"Not too much?"

"Nothing much to say…we're more or less strangers now."

"But Vivi…the other girls; I was given to understand she talks to them, teaches them about…uh—your ways."

"I suppose she does, a little—I mean as far as it goes," shrugging; "Ondine is old. One's point of view evolves a bit. Or at least one hopes so."

"I understand." Aliette sips her beer. "It's just that you were so intent on protecting her."

"Her good name—of course. But if Ondine has done something to implicate herself…well, I can't be responsible for her actions."

"Nor her beliefs."

Flossie swishes the ice in her drink. "No."

"No, I guess you couldn't." Quaffing again; "…this is good beer."

"Dorise made it."

"Dorise has a talent."

"We think so."

"How is she?"

"Getting along…her mother died. I think she feels guilty for not going out for the funeral…"

"It's such a long way. I think if she went, she'd never come back." Flossie nods. Aliette takes another sip. Mmm! "I was out there. I went to see her just before the end. You never met Angélique?" Flossie smiles a sparkly *non*. "She drank a lot…"

"She was ninety-two. Can't do much harm at that age." Smile holding fast.

"It seemed she was very fond of this stuff she calls Maeve."

"Ah… Well, Maeve is a different story."

"So she was saying… Herméné Dupras touched on the laughter element here amongst his angels but he forgot to mention Maeve. It could have saved me a lot of time."

"Herméné has his priorities. As long as he gets there he doesn't care how. Herméné doesn't even know Maeve has a name."

"That fits. My colleague Claude Néon thought he was out on a date with Céleste."

"Poor Claude…" Flossie allows a hint of a giggle to come breathing through. "A nice man. We had some fun. Erly found him sleeping it off in the ally. I gather he wasn't quite up to it."

"Was it really fun?"

"He was laughing."

"And for you?"

"Me? Oh, all I did was sit on his face…you know?"

"Yes, I think I do… Well, there's no law against that," she muses.

"No. Perfectly legal. Fun too…if you can find the right face."

Aliette is inclined to agree. In fact the inspector has to bite her lip as she pictures it: Flossie descending, Claude's nervous eyes looking up, dancing around the way they do… "But you gave him a drug that left him practically catatonic. That's not legal at all. Why would you do that? Doesn't seem very smart, given the circumstances."

"I'm not too worried."

"He's the Commissaire."

"Exactly. He has his priorities too."

"You know your men, Flossie… But why?"

"He came snooping around, pretending to be helping you. That bothered me." Flossie swirls the ice in her drink and grins. "Look at the bright side. When your Commissaire first walked in he was thinking he wanted Louise. He might not have survived *that* at all."

"Ah…" The bright side according to Flossie. "Yes…well…" slowly tasting more of Dorise's beer; "…but things are fitting, Flossie. At long last I think I've got most everything I need."

"Good."

"Apart from Ondine, there's only one piece missing."

"What's that?"

"You. What's your story, Flossie?"

"But I told you: I was working and I can prove—"

"You misunderstand. Your *story*. Why you are the way you are. Your excuse…you know?"

"Mmm…does it matter?"

"I think so. Especially if Ondine's doesn't any more."

"I only work here, Inspector."

"No…you *live* here. Remember you told me that? Why would you throw a stone at an old man in a gold and white nightgown? Perhaps we should go back and start again there…"

Flossie's smile becomes less so. She looks down at her drink. "I would have got him. I'm a good shot…if it hadn't been for the glass bubble, I would've got him. He knew it too. Right in the head…" Meeting the inspector's eyes again: "Can you imagine what would have happened?"

"That's easy: Jail for life… They get another Pope."

"An avalanche, Aliette. Thousands of stones—flying from the hands of thousands…no—millions! of women just like me."

"Just like you. I doubt it."

Flossie Orain sits back and sighs. "So do I, now. But I was young. It's what I was thinking."

"Now it's Maeve."

"I have no qualms…"

"*Une vraie peau de vache…*" as the French say: a tough hide; quite the opposite of silk that seems to move like water.

Flossie shrugs and sips her drink. "No qualms at all… Have you heard what that same old man is telling us now, Inspector—fifteen years later?—his latest memo to the faithful? That we have to forget about conscience. Forget about trusting your heart…or—don't even think it!—your body. The rules are the rules… Experience is a myth… Well, absolutely, Your Holiness! What's a person's life worth when you put it beside *Veritatis Splendor*? The Magnificence of Truth. Don't you love it?"

"But you're not one of the faithful. So why don't you forget that old man?"

"Because I live in the world? …He tells his bishops to make war on any woman who speaks out. Any woman who knows that her body is her connection to the world. And to love. *And* to the divine. How can I forget an old man like that, with all that power and so petrified of reality? *The world will be what we want it to be;* do you remember he said that? That was why I threw my stone… Because we know who *we* is, don't we? The men who control the happy flock."

"You're very good at quotes, Flossie."

"My mother cut it out and sent it to me."

"When she was having a nervous breakdown?"

"She was always having a nervous breakdown, Inspector. Sitting in her little room all day long…her boyfriend got her into the habit of it. Breakdowns and great quotes, both…"

"Her boyfriend the priest?"

"Poor Maurice…the man just couldn't handle wanting her, much less needing her—so he brought her things to read while he kept going back and forth, trying to make up his tortured mind. Saint Paul was his favourite. Saint Paul knew exactly how screwed up a woman can get a man who's trying to love the Lord…Maurice and Maman and Saint Paul: they spent a lot of time together…they were much crazier than any *ménage à trois* I ever saw in this place… But then he chose. Because Maman lost whatever might have been left of her sparkle pretty quickly after they moved her to her little room at the sanatorium. I think Maman's breakdown kind of proved it to Maurice—that Saint Paul was right… He went off to his own little room after that. With the Benedictines. You know their motto, Aliette?" Gulping her drink and brandishing a taut finger: "*Prefer nothing whatever to Christ!* But my mother kept reading…she still does. She has all sorts of quotes apropos of the subject if you have the time to listen. I suppose my story has something to do with that. For what it's worth … Chin chin!"

Like bitterness incarnate as she waves her glass under Aliette's nose. It hits her—the sweet tinge. "Is that a Maeve?"

"*Mais oui.* So is that." Meaning: your beer, my dear.

"Ah, Flossie…" Sitting back, rubbing her goose-bumped arms, now completely aware of the thing welling inside her…throat's dryish, head slightly achy as if a fever's coming on… "Why do you have to do that?"

"She won't bite, Inspector…it's Sunday, a good day to meet Maeve."

Aliette stares across the table at Flossie's bent smile, trying to get a bead on the thing inside her system. She can feel it won't bite. But can she resist it? Or lie low…calm—let it pass over? …But no; too late; wherever she tries to hide her energy, her sense of Aliette Nouvelle, Maeve is there, gathering a face…a voice. "You have no right," she says. But where her anger should have been, the inspector feels herself becoming removed. Watching.

"She'll help you see it all very clearly."

"That's exactly what I heard on Sein."

"Voilà."

"Flossie, you have your sad story… So does everyone. You have no right to take your anger and presume to shape a person's mind with it. How can you be such a bully? It goes completely against everything she's supposed to be about."

"I think you'll like her, Aliette…"

"What about the goddess?"

"She's making up for lost time."

"Collecting bodies?"

"Gathering devotion."

"Devotion as prescribed by Florence Orain? You're too bitter to get anywhere near it, so you make others pay the price. What a shame."

"People do what they do. Some need to be pointed in the right direction."

"Do they really ask to have a knife stuck through their heart? How much do you charge for spiritual advice?"

"I only sell sex, Inspector."

"You're accountable, Flossie."

"Marilyn Monroe has to be good for more than a laugh and a few powerful men who feel the need to fuck her. If not in the real world then at least by proxy… Don't you think?"

She's trying to think but it's getting tricky…

Flossie's saying, "Maeve and I, we worked on this with Manon for a long, long time…"

The inspector's gazing at her watch…the hands are crawling in a most interesting way… Aliette, *good girl that she is!* has never experienced this sort of thing before. But encroaching hallucinations can't change the fact that it's still high noon, and in through the front door of Mari Morgan's file Claude Néon (carefully) and Cécile Botrel, with James Jamms III beside them (more carefully), with psychologist Jean-Paul Blismes for moral back-up, followed by two gendarmes escorting Christophe Giguerre, the car parts man from Lille, and Francine Léotard aka Léonie/Arletty, and then Assistant Inspector Patrice Lebeau leading the boy, René (watchful), and his rather disoriented mother in her stodgy Sunday dress. It's a parade and right on schedule and Martine, at the front desk, cannot do much to prevent it from marching into the bar.

"What is this…?" Flossie rises.

Maeve is pushing and pulling but Aliette Nouvelle still knows her job. Because people do what they do. "Sit down, Flossie. These people are here—and they will appear in a court of law to testify against you—as witnesses, accomplices and even as victims. We also have the bodies of Manon Larivière and Marcel Cyr, found in the rocks along the shore of the Ile de Sein. And a well-analyzed jar of Maeve. The charges will range from administration of a noxious substance to conspiracy to commit murder and being an accessory after the fact of murder stemming from placing the murder weapon in the hand of Herménégilde Dupras and all that that entailed…" pausing for a breath and to let the rising ringing of her own voice settle; "to desecration of a grave… And car theft. Now, it's *not* murder…" sorry, the law is less than perfect; "but it should serve to put you away for a good long while."

Flossie is riveted in her chair. Aliette turns, gaze drifting across the faces of her entourage and the faces of the Mari Morgan's girls— who are gathering, mystified, at the entrance to the bar. She's wondering if she shouldn't make a general announcement: I'm glad you've all come. The law may not fit the crime exactly, but it's a great day for justice…and…and—for conscience too! But now, since my poor mind is—how can I put it…bumping into itself, I must beg your pardon… Then she thinks, no, she won't make this speech; too much of that Girl Guide leader and no one needs to hear it, not today… And anyway, it's this bumping…becoming crashing, these thoughts that smash and give off colours: Josiane's brooch; the stripes on the American client's shirt… Aliette hears herself say, "No more lies, Flossie. Be responsible for your actions. Have the courage of your convictions. No?"

"It's Ondine… She's the one who brought all this here! She's the one who killed Manon."

"No!" Sophie's surprised at her own voice… She backs away, afraid of Flossie.

Aliette says, "Where is she?"

"I'll show you…" Flat, easy…no qualms.

"Ah, Flossie…" It's that young one. That Vivi. "You said we were supposed to—"

"I'm here." At the entrance to the bar stands Ondine, stooped and pale, Dorise the cook beside her.

"Add harbouring a fugitive," notes Cécile Botrel.

"Yes…" echoes Aliette. Yesyesyesyesyes… Really starting to wish someone else would step in and take over. Claude? No, not Claude… If not Claude… Patrice Lebeau. Come on, Patrice—my brain…

Ondine tells Flossie, "You said you'd protect me. I trusted you. Manon trusted you. And your friend Colette. And these women… Look what you've done with all that trust."

"For us!" blurts Flossie. "For *her*… You don't know anything about the world! You're just a seamstress."

"Ah, Flossie…" Louise is clearly disappointed in the one she loves.

Other voices start chiming in. "It's not right, Flossie…" "Why, Flossie?" "Flossie!"

Voices of Mari Morgan's. To an inspector they sound like a choir of angels—that is, if you want to talk results. She feels like laughing…*you mustn't!* Watching Flossie weighing the balance reflected in the eyes that watch her…yes, here it comes: Flossie twigs to it; now Flossie seems to understand the larger picture.

Flossie accuses Ondine. "You…you betrayed me! These last weeks while you were in there…"

Ondine says, "Flossie… You were never patient enough. I wish I could have done something to show you. I…" It's difficult to know what Ondine wants. Apology? Confession?…standing there, hands spread, seeming to say: Come here—I'll make it better.

Flossie takes it as a cue to stand and fling her empty glass. Aliette, eyes moving at a different speed, sees it spin through the air and strike the seamstress, the base of thick glass easily denting the parchment-tight skin of her temple. There is no blood; but Ondine falls, quick and silent. Dorise is frozen. Louise rushes to her. Flossie Orain approaches too, wary, to inspect the body of the woman she has killed.

The inspector is left to spend the rest of the day alone with Maeve.

People see a woman walking in the park on Sunday. This is a touching thing to see. It always is. A woman walking alone will strike a chord—the beauty of Sunday framed in solitude seems deeper with each step… Looking for the goddess? It takes all day, part of the night. Where is she, Flossie? Where is she, Angélique Menou? Looking…*feeling*, these relentless feelings, rehashing every instinct's clue, Maeve's voice is pure insistence, distracting, disrupting, not much help at all. How could I be more a part of this world than I am, than I know myself to be? Can you tell me that, Maeve? My own motion, my own heart's rhythm, these are the transforming elements that lead from one heart to the next and on to the one I love—one day; this is what will change the world in time. But not today… And not easy in the evening, worn out, any accomplishment bloated like a gorged meal. Sleeping? No, the soul is cramped for room. Maeve becomes humidity, nothing more; heavy, unclear, this irritated bitch expressing her discomfort, alone in the night.

Piaf keeps his distance.

That voice again, sighing, tired too: *ma pauvre.* Long day. Long investigation.

EPILOGUE

Ondine's death brings them back to the question of whether it will be an assassination charge or something less. Maeve is reduced to an exhibit. Dorise becomes a major witness, probably for both sides...she has admitted to lacing the icing on the boss's chocolate cake with a knockout quantity of opium. The people minding Louise Lebraz report she's struggling through some kind of breakdown and it's not sure where she'll settle viz. her version of events.

Georgette mourns, of course; but it's more than that. The old artist's model sinks deep into one her silences. Aliette's heart goes out to her, but... Well, it had been her impulse, hadn't it?—the older sister taking the younger sister by the hand: here, these people will help you; they're the police; that's their job. Then a cop (who also has a younger sister, don't forget) gets a bright idea and issues a challenge. What can you do? Impulses, ethics, decisions and their consequences. Anger? Can't be part of it... Welcome to my world, Georgette.

But, Aliette, it was your note that set the wheel in motion.

Perhaps, but I'm not the one on trial here.

Don't kid yourself—I've got my eye on you.

I can live with it.

Herménégilde Dupras is set free (against some people's better judgement). But with official Police Department yellow tapes over the doors to his office and bar and now his kitchen too, Mari Morgan's business operations are going to be suspended for some time to come. "I can deal with it," he tells local media people. Standing on the steps of the Palais, looking good (lost twenty kilos while incarcerated) in his cleaned-up velvet jacket, he pokes his cigar into the air as he makes his points. "I'll make a trip to America. See how our industry does things over there. This country is in love with America and there is money to be made in that! My only real concern is for the well-being of my girls."

Just so, monsieur… And without the middle ground of Mari Morgan's, Vivi Namur, a girl Herméné never met (or tried), soon drops any illusions she may have entertained concerning Mr. Jimmy Jamms. Aliette wonders what will become of her. Does Vivi have a destiny? Maybe she'll go back and find that boy…what was his name? …*Jerôme!* yes…find Jerôme and find out.

Try, Vivi. Your heart's worth saving.

The American, meanwhile, although no longer in the employ of the world's most famous mouse, must stay in France. He is being prepared to testify for Claude and Claude will testify for him. It involves a lot of coaching on Cécile's part. So much will depend on the telling, the words used to describe the thing that occurred in Flossie Orain's bed. Claude's version will be their showcase. They'll give him the benefit of the doubt—frame it as "in the line of duty." Claude will become the first cop in the history of the Republic to bring charges of this nature against a prostitute. If done right, it promises to be a big step forward for all French males, professional or otherwise—and for any Americans who might be watching. Substitute Procureur Cécile Botrel is excited.

Like one of Epona's ponies, Inspector Aliette Nouvelle is proud.

Mais oui. I in you and you in me. Vas-y! Let's go, ma belle.

~ End ~

John Brooke became fascinated by criminality and police work listening to the courtroom stories and observations of his father, a long-serving judge. Although he lives in Montreal, John makes frequent trips to France for both pleasure and research. He earns a living as a freelance writer and translator, has also worked as a film and video editor as well as directed four films on modern dance. Brooke's first novel, *The Voice of Aliette Nouvelle*, was published in 1999. His poetry and short stories have also been widely published and in 1998 his story "The Finer Points of Apples" won him the Journey Prize.

ALSO BY
JOHN BROOKE

ISBN 0-921833-65-2

In his heyday, Jacques Normand was France's Public Enemy Number One, a glamorous rogue who captured the imagination of the entire country. As he led the police on a merry chase, he also made the career of Commissaire Louis Moreau, former head of the Paris Anti-gangs unit, now the commander of a small Police Judiciaire force in a sleepy border town.

After escaping from prison, Normand fled Paris and has been neither seen nor heard from for more than ten years. And because the Normand file has lain dormant since before she joined the force, Inspector Aliette Nouvelle has naturally assumed that everyone's favourite outlaw is dead and the case closed. But one afternoon, Commissaire Moreau drops Normand's file on her desk. The Commissaire is convinced that Normand is still very much alive and in the vicinity. Find him, he commands Aliette. Bring him in. Put him away for good.

Aliette Nouvelle is a new heroine for the 90s—smart, single and intuitive, but more interested in quietly and non-violently getting the job done than in receiving front-page coverage for her sometimes unorthodox methods of crime-solving. She knows she is regarded as a rising star in the force and believes that her years of hard work are about to bear fruit. She senses, rightly, that the soon-to-retire Commissaire has chosen to pass the torch on to her. And so, although she remains skeptical, Aliette accepts his challenge. She sets out to dig up a forgotten hero.

"This book dropped into my lap and I was smitten: interesting premise, fascinating central character and good writing. In a sleepy French border town, Inspector Aliette Nouvelle is ready for more than ordering around local thugs. Then her boss drops a cold case on her, which might mean a promotion. Ten years ago, Jacques Normand excaped from a top-security prison. Now she must ferret him out. Poetic images, film stills and literary writing, none out of place."
— *The Globe and Mail*

"*The Voice of Aliette Nouvelle* is a very unusual mystery story that challenges all sorts of conventions. It's definitely not a traditional murder mystery. For one thing, no one gets murdered. It's not a spy thriller either. Instead it's a poetic and dreamlike tale told in many voices where a police inspector sets out to trail and capture an outlaw, a man who's a thief, who's labeled public enemy number one in France, where he lives." —"Art Talks," CBC Radio

"*The Voice of Aliette Nouvelle* is not just another detective story, and you don't have to wait until Chapter 10 to figure this out. When the story opens, Aliette is already a mythical figure in the police force: her voice is 'delicate but absolute, as if your *maman* were calling you for in supper'; it can make hardened criminals feel weak and stupid. She looks like a young schoolteacher but she's a hotshot police detective and her boss's favourite. He assigns her the job of finding France's 'former Public Enemy Number One,' Jacques Normand, who has not been seen or heard from for ten years. Aliette's given a temporary assistant, Claude Néon, whose sexual fantasies sometimes include Aliette but who would like nothing better than to get back to working with the boys. The two of them sometimes work with each other and sometimes work against each other…. As both Aliette and her quarry confront the myths that have been created around them, we feel as if we are right there, in France, 'in a city on the Rhine.'" — *Geist*

"*The Voice of Aliette Nouvelle* is a fascinating story of detection in which one soon begins to wonder who is tracking whom. In essence, this novel becomes a study of two characters locked in combat, with any number of possible outcomes." —*Halifax Daily News*